My Life
as a
Doormat

ISBN-13: 978-0-9914332-4-7
ISBN-10: 0-9914332-4-0

First printing, October, 2014

Cover design by Ivy Tobin and ThomasMax

Author photo by David Vance ©2014.

Published by:

 tm

ThomasMax Publishing
P.O. Box 250054
Atlanta, GA 30325
www.thomasmax.com

My Life as a Doormat

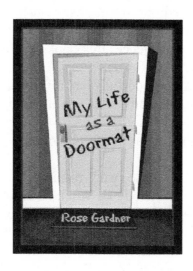

by Rose Gardner

ThomasMax

Your Publisher
For The 21st Century

Acknowledgments

I am grateful for the creative inspiration provided by my family of origin: my parents, Sam and Sara and my sister Fern.

Many thanks and much love to my husband Harry, for the countless hours spent editing my drafts. Your persistence and honesty sometimes caused arguments but you never stopped pushing me forward. Without your diligence, this book would never have come to fruition.

Much love to my wonderfully creative and ever changing child Sara. Thanks for being exactly who you are and for your help on the computer.

A very special thank-you to my photographer and long-time, dear friend David Vance.

Hugs and love to those who inspired me during my writing process. Many thanks to Melody B. Mitch P., Debbie S., and Loren L.

With gratitude and appreciation to my village of friends who are supportive and remain constant cheerleaders: Beth and Emerson A., Jill B., Christine C., Bernadette E., Vicky and Ian J., Lisa L., Mara and Barry M., Leslie and Peter N., Kyle P., Terena S., Dr. Harold S., Kerrie and Bill S., Dr. Terry S., Lisa and Eddie T., Sally, Neda and Stacy T.

In loving memory of Ron Feinberg, my writing professor at The University of Miami and David Feldman, my high school drama teacher who always said "If you knock on enough doors, one will open."

Special thanks to Lee Clevenger at ThomasMax Publishing for all your help and support making "My Life as a Doormat" a tangible reality.

A doormat would apologize for forgetting to acknowledge someone who influenced them. As the founding member of "The Society for Recovering Doormats" Facebook page, let me just say, if you feel offended, hurt or left out just know it wasn't intentional.

For all those struggling, thinking you're not good enough or deserving, I hope My Life as a Doormat *brings you hope, encouragement, insight and laughter.*

You don't have to be doormat to enjoy this book; any neurosis will do.

Praise for *My Life as a Doormat*

"Ivy Tobin, writing as Rose Gardner, has a knack for reaching in and grabbing your heart. We all have friends like Rose, or we're related to her, and in many instances, we are Rose. We all dream the same dreams of success, romance and happiness. But life doesn't always cooperate and *My Life as a Doormat* exemplifies this through the lens of the millions of people who suffer, like Rose, from low self-esteem.

"With nearly thirty years experience as a licensed psychotherapist, I can attest to the importance of this widespread issue. In its darkest expression, it results in depression, feelings of unworthiness, victimization at the hands of others and suicide. Ms. Tobin, through Rose, soulfully demonstrates the heart-breaking vulnerabilities of a doormat personality, as well as the triumphs of life as a recovering doormat. Her humor and generous spirit allow us to gently examine our own behaviors and invite healing."

—**Dr. Terry Segal**, Ph.D. in Energy Medicine, Licensed Psychotherapist Author of *The Enchanted Journey: Finding the Key that Unlocks You and Hidden Corners of My Heart.*

* * * * *

"Every woman will identify with Rose and her struggles and will be inspired by the way Rose overcomes crippling self-doubt. I want to take Rose out for coffee and thank her for showing me how to find confidence. "

—**Terena Scott**, Publisher, Medusa's Muse Press

* * * * *

"This book is filled with fascinating and intriguing characters. Especially Rose. You can't help but fall in love with her and want to take her in your arms and protect her, giving her the love and support she needs and deserves. I know when a book has truly touched me; it's when I'm coming to the end and I stop reading every few minutes just to delay the inevitable."

—**Mitch Poulos**, Actor, Director, Coach, Playwright and Survivor

Chapter 1
The Arrival

The year was 1980, a time of innocence compared with what would lay ahead. Marijuana was illegal and not available at the corner pharmacy with a doctor's note. An era when "cell" referred to miniscule components comprising organic life, or a room in a jail. Cell phones were available but expensive, and used mostly by celebrities who had an entourage to carry them. Terrorist cells w ere obscure, not on the front page of every newspaper. The horror of 9/11 was in the distant future. Yet, despite the relevant safety of the times, I was terrified.

Here I was, the elevator doors just closed behind me and I dragged my suitcases out to the eighth floor hallway of the building that would be my home. Roberta's distinct raspy voice hurling obscenities at my best friend Ce echoed throughout the empty corridor.

"I'm not your friggin bank," Ce screamed back. When Ce had suggested Roberta as a third for our New York City apartment, I was hesitant because I didn't know her very well. Apparently neither did Ce.

My stomach clenched and I heard Mom's words resound inside my head. "Come home. Rose!"

"No," I whispered as my mind raced and contemplated her suggestion. "NO!" I repeated. I took a deep breath and tried standing up straight while I pushed down my fear. My roomies screaming at each other like two rivals from a bad soap opera wasn't a sign I should go home. Or was it?

The yelling continued from behind the door of apartment 8A as my grip tightened around two dilapidated luggage handles. What had happened to make Ce and Roberta sound like they were murdering each other? Sweat beaded on my brow as I heard the elevator doors close behind me.

"It's just 'til next week until my checks clear," Roberta raged.

"That's what you said last week!" I'd never heard Ce in such a state. I felt immobilized but forced my feet to move and shuffled towards the apartment door, dragging my over-stuffed suitcases. Lingering outside the door, I waited until all was quiet.

Silence. What was going on in there? Just as I was about to ring the bell another round of Roberta's diatribe began. My finger froze in mid-air.

"Do I look like Wall Street?" Ce yelled, her shrill scream sent a shiver down my spine.

"I should've stayed in the cab," I whispered to the pale gray carpeting as my body stiffened. Returning to the lobby seemed like a safe alternative to the war zone inside my new home so I parked the two suitcases next to the door and headed back to the elevator bank. But then I froze. *What if I get the unlucky elevator?* Paralyzed with fear, my feet wouldn't move while my eyes darted back and forth from the closed elevator doors to my new residence.

Roberta's voice bounced off the hallway walls while informing Ce she didn't need the lousy apartment.

"FINE!" Ce screamed.

"FINE!" Roberta screamed back.

Five hours earlier I'd been safe and secure in my hometown of Coral Gables, Florida. But now, here I was in an unfamiliar hallway in the giant city of Manhattan, and wondered what the hell was I doing there.

Three months out of college, and much to Mom's dismay, I decided to move to the Big Apple and be an actress. "You're not going to live alone in that filthy, crime-ridden city!"

"I won't be alone. I'm going to share an apartment."

"With who?" Mom opened the oven door, and smoke billowed into the air. "Damn it, Rose, you've got me so upset that I've burnt dinner!" My mother blamed me for everything. "Blame" should've been her middle name, instead of Blanch.

"Sorry," I whispered, and then listened while she laundry listed all of the terrible things I'd done since birth. "Sorry," I repeated and accepted her accusations as absolute truth. She was my mother after all, and I was a respectful child. I stared into space while she removed the charred chicken and placed it on the kitchen counter for her regular scraping ritual.

"With *who*?" she repeated. "Rose! Answer me."

I rolled my eyes, and left Mom in the kitchen with the burnt bird and soggy vegetables. Every day since graduation we'd had the same argument. I walked into my bedroom, and closed the door. I loved my mother, but hated the worthless way she made me feel.

"Rose!" I heard Mom shriek from the kitchen. I put my hands over my ears and tried muffling the sound of her voice. Was everyone's mother like her, or just mine?

"Get out," I heard Ce scream from inside the apartment and zapped back into reality.

I'd known Ce since kindergarten. Kindergarten; even at the tender age of six, little girls were bitchy and cliquey. Snotty brats clothed in frilly dresses pulled my hair and laughed at my bleached-out overalls and nautical-themed outfits. All of them, except for Ce. It was the second week of kindergarten when she had approached me as I sulked alone in the far corner of the large playroom where daily gymnastics were held (and recess when it rained). While the other kids played checkers and patty-cake, I crouched alone on the far edge of a gym mat, coloring Wilma Flintstone red in a worn coloring book.

"Hi, I'm Chelsea!" The girl with blond pigtails dressed in a pale cornflower-blue dress that matched her eyes kneeled besides me and asked if I wanted to play Chinese Checkers

"Sure." Startled, I dropped my crayon as Chelsea led me over to a game next to the popular girls. One of them pointed and warned Chelsea she'd get my cooties as we sat Indian-style across from each other. "I don't know how to play," I blurted out. My eyes welled up while I tried blocking out the popular girls remark. Certain that Chelsea had heard her too and would go back to the clique of kids who already knew how to play games and wore pretty dresses, I felt invisible.

"That's OK. I'll teach you." Chelsea smiled, and I noticed her two front teeth were missing, just like mine. She reached across the game board and squeezed my hand. "Ill teach you." She repeated. Her smile was reassuring.

"Thanks." For the first time in my short little life I felt validated. From that moment forward we were best friends.

After kindergarten, we went to different elementary schools and my best friend vanished. It wasn't until twelve years later that our paths crossed again.

"I'm in a huge hurry," she'd said the first day of college registration. "Can I cut in front of you?"

Intimidated by the confident stranger with bright blue eyes, blond hair and killer body, I nodded.

"Thanks. I have a plane to catch, and I'm so friggin late!" She sighed then flipped her hair over her shoulder.

"No problem."

"Where ya from?" She asked while the line inched forward at a snail's pace.

"Coral Gables. And you?"

"Miami Beach. I went to Beach High. Where'd you go?"

"Gables."

"You went to Gables?" Her eyes flashed and the beautiful stranger asked if I knew this one and that one. The game of high school who's who was afoot.

Halfway to the registration table, a small flower-shaped gold ring with a tiny red ruby in the middle on her right pinkie caught my attention. "What an unusual ring."

"This?" She rested her hand on her thigh, directly beneath the hem of her micro mini skirt. She claimed it was babyish, and assured me she'd outgrown it. "But I've had it since kindergarten." She smiled. "My dad gave it to me when I was five."

Her ring looked familiar, as if I'd had that exact ring on my finger but couldn't remember when. "I've seen that ring before."

"Yeah?" She looked at her ring, and then studied my face. "My dad had it custom-designed for me," she said and assured me that I must be wrong.

"I remember trying it on," I insisted. "We've met before."

After another round of Florida geography, it was obvious that I'd made a mistake, and my face flushed.

Ce wouldn't give up the game and asked where I'd gone to kindergarten.

"Dearborn."

Ce nodded, yes, she'd gone there too.

"Miss Dundee" we said in unison.

"What's your name?" Ce removed her Foster Grants and stared through me.

"Rose. What's yours?" My shoulders hunched forward as I scanned the ground.

"Ce." She stood up tall and thrust out her chest.

I didn't recognize her name, and shook my head. Another dead-end. A moment later our eyes met and after a long silence, Ce's eyes flashed.

"Rosie Posey! Chinese Checkers! Kindergarten! I was Chelsea

back then."

"We were best friends," I said with sudden recollection.

"Yes!"

"And you let me wear *that ring*. 'Here ya go, Rosie,' you said. I remember feeling like a princess."

"Next!" Said the registrar behind the table.

After registration we walked outside, and Ce stopped short in the middle of the sidewalk. "Where the hell is it?" she said while rummaging through her purse. "I know I put it in here." A moment later she dumped the contents of her purse onto the pavement.

"What are you looking for?"

"My plane ticket." she muttered and crouched down on bare knees and dug through the large pile. I watched her flailing arms, and sweat pouring down her neck and realized my initial impression of Ce was wrong. She might've looked confident but wasn't. A confident peep wouldn't be caught dead on their knees. "Here it is!" she said a few minutes later.

She let out a sigh, but her relief didn't last long. "My flight is tonight, not this afternoon!" she whined. She crumpled the ticket then stuffed it back into her purse, along with the rest of her stuff. "I guess I read the time backwards."

"Oh." I stood beside her, smoked a cigarette and tried to hide a smile. I'd found my long lost friend and didn't want to lose her again. "It's a sign," I said, and then helped her to her feet.

"Sign?" Ce put her Foster Grants on and looked like a celebrity.

"Yeah, a sign that we should hang out and catch up." I smiled.

Ce smiled back, and we went for coffee at the Howard Johnson's across the street from campus and picked up where we'd left off twelve years prior. After countless free coffee refills it felt as if we'd never lost touch and I knew that we'd be best friends forever. No matter what.

Once more my best friend's voice echoed up and down the hallway. Had her body been invaded by an angry alien? The obscenities she railed at Roberta were uncharacteristic of her docile nature.

During college, most girls kept a cool distance from Ce because they were jealous and felt threatened. With her long, white-blond hair and big, blue eyes, she looked like Goldie Hawn's younger sister. Paper thin, (without the help of an eating disorder) every ounce of her was in the right place. Ce was the Rolls Royce of the female species.

"Here comes the Ice Queen," I'd heard whispered behind Ce's back. Perhaps because I saw her through my kindergarten eyes, I didn't understand those girls' perspective. Ce was the warmest and best natured person on the planet. Although I felt like my father's Oldsmobile next to her, I couldn't help but be her comrade–in–arms, and in reality, I had no choice.

We were the same person on the inside, but Ce was an excellent actress and faked courage. She exuded confidence while flipping her blond hair over her right shoulder and standing her ground. "Fake it 'til ya make it," she'd tell me. But when confronted with adversity, I'd panic, obsesses, and devour doughnuts.

Ce helped me overcome my fear about leaving Miami after college graduation. "Rose, you can always come back to Florida to die," she'd responded to my obsessive worries about leaving my safety net. She wanted to be a movie star. "If I can't be a movie star, then I want to marry one - or a millionaire. I have lots of contacts in New York," she assured me.

Wither in Coral Gables, or bloom in the Big Apple? Which was it going to be? With a roommate like Ce, who'd take me with her to exclusive parties and all the hot spots in Manhattan, relocating to New York City was too wonderful to pass up.

Now, three months later, I'd won my independence from my family, on my own and scared stiff.

Anxiety had squelched exuberance while I'd walked alone through the airport. I clenched my teeth, and felt more invisible than usual inside the unfamiliar terminal. My stomach was tied in a gigantic knot as the reality of being far away from my home set in. I'd lived with my family my entire life, and even with all of our disagreements and fights, I already missed them. Especially Mom. And on the long taxi ride to the apartment my mother's words had replayed in my head. "You can always come home if it doesn't work out, Rose. I won't change a thing in your room." Mom's cheeks drew inward as she inhaled on her cigarette. What confidence she had in me.

"How will you survive in that cold weather?" she had asked daily. "You have Florida blood for God's sake!"

But fall in New York was spectacular, and none of my mom's fears would keep me from opening the door to my future.

Roberta's shrieking refocused my thinking.

"No money. NO apartment. GOT IT?" I heard Ce, the

wannabe millionaire movie queen screech back at Roberta.

Roberta. She was the second roommate, and the complete opposite of Ce and me. Also a drama major at the University of Miami, Roberta was more interested in engineering spotlights than being in one. She designed light boards, built sets, wore overalls and got her hands dirty. The set crews for our college theater productions called her "Bert." She seemed pretty mellow and was the theatrical equivalent of Wonder Bread. Although Ce and I didn't know her well when she expressed an interest in moving to New York City, we decided she would bring the perfect balance to our apartment. Besides, she needed a place to live and had the finances to move to Manhattan, or so we thought. We never suspected her to be a pathological liar with unsavory motives and hidden agendas. Never.

"Oh go to hell!" Ce screamed again, louder then before.

Roberta mumbled something unintelligible, and the sound of broken glass followed. No longer immobilized, I took several more steps towards the elevator bank.

"This is just not going to work out." Ce's rebuttal to Roberta's unintelligible comments was deafening.

I stared at the thin black and gray stripes on the wallpaper in the empty hallway and fought the urge to count them. Flashbacks flooded my mind about my first visit to New York City. "I can't live here. The buildings are too tall!"

"Don't worry, Rose. They won't fall on you," Ce had joked.

I had faked a smile but had wanted to back out of our great New York adventure.

"Rose you are making a huge mistake." Mom's parting words at Miami International Airport repeated over and over. Maybe she was right after all.

I'd been living life guided by Carole King and Carly Simon songs and now, at last, the journey that would confirm or deny all the things I'd only heard about through their music had begun. I wouldn't be answering to my mother anymore, or listening to my dad's insanity. I'd stay out all night drinking French wine with interesting men in secluded bistros. We'd French kiss in the backseat of a cab while it sped up the avenue en route to their cozy apartment. But will they still love me tomorrow?

"No, I'm not going back to Coral Gables." I said out loud.

The elevator doors opened but no one got out. As I stared at the empty elevator I realized it was the lucky one, as if it had come back for me.

"I only ride on lucky elevator number one." I informed my mom when I was nine years old. She had rolled her eyes, believing that some day I'd grow out of this odd behavior. But I didn't.

I can just turn around, walk through those lucky doors, and go home. Hail a cab to the airport and go back to Coral Gables. But a stronger urge stopped me from running away. I had dreamt of this moment. Real life was about to start. Excitement replaced fear and I whispered, "Free at last. Free at last" and heard the lucky elevator's doors close.

Backing away from the elevator bank, I returned to the apartment door and stood beside my two brown suitcases, which held everything I thought I would need to make a start in this strange, exciting city. There was silence on the other side of the apartment door, so I held my breath and rang the bell.

Chapter 2
The Beginning

Ce opened the door and embraced me with a giant bear hug. "Thank God you're here," she whispered. She looked like hell! Her flowing blond hair was scrunched into a ponytail and last night's make-up was still piled on her face. Dressed in filthy white tights and a cut-up T-shirt, the outfit, combined with her unkempt appearance spoke volumes and confirmed something was wrong. Very.

"Now that she's here, I don't stand a chance!" Roberta pointed her hand at me like a gun. "It's two against one." Her voice was full of vengeance. Dressed in overalls and a plaid shirt with her short, bowl-cut hair, Roberta looked the same as always, but with an added bad attitude.

"Nobody's against anybody, Roberta," Ce continued, lowering her volume in an attempt to sound calm. "We share this place, and that includes paying for it." She let out an exaggerated sigh, and rolled her eyes while lighting a cigarette.

Roberta kicked a chair in our direction and stormed into her room. The next thing we heard was a loud crash as she punched a hole in the wall with a most powerful fist.

Ce and I looked at each other. "She's outta here," Ce said, emotionless.

I should've taken the lucky elevator back down to the lobby.

Roberta slammed her bedroom door, and for the next thirty minutes we heard sounds of drawers slamming and lots of cussing. When she emerged from her room, dragging her three suitcases behind her, Ce and I tried to hide relieved smiles. Without saying a word, Roberta opened the door, put her bags in the hallway, walked out and slammed the door behind her.

"You have no idea what a nightmare she was, Rose," Ce explained in her most dramatic voice. Over the next hour, we discussed how glad we were to be rid of the whacko. Once the elation of Roberta's departure wore off, it dawned on us that we would need another roommate to share expenses. Two jobless twenty-one-year-olds embarking on acting careers, in search of stardom, in New York City couldn't afford to lose a roommate!

"What the hell are we going to do Ce? What are we going to do?" I was flipping out while Ce stayed calm and flipped open a box of Marlboro Reds.

"I guess we need to find a new roommate."

How could she be so la de da when I was so panic-stricken?

"Let's have a cig on the matter." Ce lit our cigs as we sat on the large maroon couch, the one piece of furniture in our living room, contemplating whether we knew anyone who might need a place in Manhattan. Many of our alumni headed to Los Angeles hopeful of stardom. Others bagged the whole acting dream and continued on to grad or law school. After almost an hour, we'd come up with absolutely no one.

"I don't want to call one of those roommate services," Ce snorted.

"Neither do I. We don't need another Roberta."

I could hear my mother's I-told-you-so in my head. "I warned you it would be a mistake to include that girl, Rebecca."

"Her name is Roberta, Mom." Even in my imagination, Mom always got names wrong.

"It's a good thing it didn't work out," I imagined Dad chiming in. "She looked like a dyke, and we didn't pay all that money for you to go to college then catch lesbianism from your New York roommate."

Dad was a narrow minded racist, bordering on insanity.

He judged everyone according to religion, race and appearance. Seated in his faux leather recliner he seldom left the fortress of our den. A voracious reader, Dad hid behind books. Historical accounts about Hitler, Stalin and Mussolini were his faves. Sometimes he'd break from his light reading and spouted opinions about current affairs. Dad knew all politicians were corrupt, anyone with a tattoo was a *schleper*, and bleached blonds were all prostitutes. Including Ce.

"Just don't let her drag you into prostitution, Rose," Mom added. Weighing two hundred and fifty pounds, my mom thought anyone thinner was a whore or had whore potential. She'd been brainwashed by Dad's warped view of life and accepted his ideas as facts. I suspected my mom gave up on obtaining personal happiness. Perhaps deep down inside, she didn't feel worthy of it.

I forced myself to stop listening to my parents' imaginary comments. Hadn't I moved over two thousand miles to get away from hearing them? What did they know? But while watching Ce's ashes burn a little hole in our couch, their vague whispers continued in my brain, and for a fleeting moment I thought perhaps I'd made a mistake. Ce had the money to share this place, but I was afraid she'd burn it down before we ever got a chance to go to an audition.

"Rose, I'm hungry. I can't think on an empty stomach. I'm getting some Fritos." She pried herself off the couch, and walked into the kitchen.

Too tired to move, I stretched out feeling frustrated. The minute I got comfortable, the phone rang. "Where's the telephone?" I yelled to Ce, still in the kitchen.

"In our bedroom."

I raced into the large bedroom with two twin beds positioned at opposite ends of the room. I leapt over Ce's clothes thrown into a large pile in the middle of the floor, and followed the ringing. The phone was hidden underneath several wet towels and I hoped I wouldn't get electrocuted when I answered.

"Rose? It's Pam." Pam was a mutual friend from college and had moved to Hollywood to be a movie star. Why was she calling me now?

"Hi, Pam. How's L.A.?" Had she been discovered yet?

"I'm still in Long Island."

"Long Island?"

"Yeah. At my parents' house."

"Oh."

"Things kind of fell apart, and I don't think I'm going to California after all." She sounded depressed, an unusual state for her. During college she was upbeat and effervescent. She was one of the lucky few that had a car on campus. I'd see her getting into her red Mustang convertible and envied her charmed life. It was rumored that Pam sent her dirty clothes back to Long Island via UPS, for her mom to wash. Yep, Pam had it all.

"I couldn't find a decent place to live, and I can't afford to just trek out to Los Angeles and rent an apartment on my own."

I understood and was grateful for at least one roommate, even if she was a bit of a fire hazard. I couldn't have moved to New York City alone.

"If I had someone to share expenses, maybe it would've worked out."

My mind raced while listening to her. "Pam, come live with Ce and me. We can share expenses, and it's a lot cheaper than living alone."

"What about that girl from scene design class? I thought she moved in with you."

"Roberta turned out to be a little irresponsible and stormed out of here, so we need a third."

Ce entered the bedroom with a lit joint in one hand and a bag of Fritos in the other. "Who's on the phone?"

"It's Pam, and she needs an apartment. She could take Roberta's place," I half-asked, half-told my stoned friend.

Ce stared at me with glazed eyes and I remembered the last time she and Pam saw each other. Maybe this wasn't such a good idea. "Cool," she shrugged then turned around and left the bedroom.

"Rose, are you sure?" Pam asked. For the next ten minutes we discussed specifics; the address, diet soda preference, and the dollar amount necessary to reside in apartment 8A. Then in a cautious tone, "Are you sure it's OK with Ce?"

"Pam wants to know if it's OK for her to move into our apartment," I called out.

There was a long pause, as if Ce were thinking about it. Or maybe she was pausing because she was stoned. After the long elaborated silence she sing-songed, "Heeeeell yeeeeah," from inside the one bathroom.

Within ten minutes, we had lined up a third roommate. God works in mysterious ways. When one door slammed shut, another door flung open. Even though we were left with a hole in the wall, it was better than having a hole in our wallets.

Chapter 3
Period of Adjustment

Eight days later, Pam arrived. "I'm so excited to be here." She put down her two matching Burberry suitcases in the living room, and then the three of us sat together on the couch, drinking Tab and smoking cigarettes as we caught up on gossip.

Pam sat between Ce and me as she flicked her Bic. "What a trek! The train crawled through the tunnel," she lamented, recounting her forty-minute ride into the city. Cigarette in one hand and ashtray in the other, she took several dramatic pauses as she dragged on her smoke. "I am so exhausted" she concluded then stubbed out her butt without even looking at the ashtray. Pam was a drama queen with excellent smoking skills.

"Want the fifty-cent tour?" I asked after an hour of bull shitting.

"Sure." Pam stood up then stared at the Peter Max poster scotch-taped above the couch. It was the only artwork we had and the only color on our white walls.

"Cool print. Perfect use of colors." Pam sounded like an art critic.

Next stop: the can. The three of us crowded into the one bathroom we'd soon be sharing daily. "Whose mints are these?" Pam laughed, pointing to the toothpaste remnants in the sink.

Ce and I were nervous to show Pam our bedroom. Rumor had it in college that in addition to sending her laundry home that she was also a neat freak, and our bedroom was a disaster area. Trash covered the floor, and old Chinese takeout cartons added a three dimensional charm to Ce's bed comforter. The room looked like a small bomb had exploded. Ce's pile of clothes were now relocated onto a chair reaching half way to the ceiling. My bed, littered with old newspapers, magazines, mail and receipts, wasn't much better.

Pam hovered in the doorway. "Nice floors."

We continued the tour of our 950-square-foot apartment, concluding with her bedroom, located off the living room.

When Pam asked where the window was, Ce and I looked at each other. We'd forgotten to mention that small detail.

"There isn't one," Ce said.

Pam looked concerned then asked why.

"This room was part of the living room, and the wall was built so we could have two bedrooms," Ce answered as we exchanged nervous glances, hoping Pam wouldn't change her mind. Even though Ce wasn't thrilled about Pam as our roommate and harbored resentment about a disagreement during the last semester of our senior year, she was thrilled about having Pam's cash.

"The window went with the living room area when they put the wall up," I added, hoping she wouldn't notice Roberta's memento.

As if she were reading my mind, Pam's eyes focused on the back bedroom wall. "What's that?"

"Roberta punched her fist in there. The super is fixing that hole next week," I lied.

"Wanna smoke a joint?" Ce asked, breaking up the palatable tension.

"Sure," Pam's voice sounded uneasy. "I can unpack later."

That evening, we strolled up Third Avenue arm-in-arm-in-arm, singing show tunes.

"We have to find the perfect restaurant to celebrate!" Pam said.

"Yes, a dinner in honor of our roommate-ship," I smiled.

Ce stopped and pointed to the Greek diner on the corner of Thirty-second and Third. "Let's eat there." A moment later we entered Mikos, the Greek diner with a *"Waitress Wanted"* sign in the window. We sat down in a large booth covered in torn plastic located in the back, next to the kitchen. We gave the waitress our order, lit up our cigs, and continued our gabfest. Five minutes later our food arrived and we devoured our Greek salads with extra feta in ten minutes flat. Instead of dessert, we got three applications for the one waitress position. "I gotta use the can," Ce said, stashing the application in her purse.

My lucky pen was at home, so I tossed the application into my purse too. Pam filled out the form with lightning speed, and then gave to the manager. Ce returned, as Pam was divvying up the bill, and we gave the money to the cashier. We left Mikos the way we arrived, (except we weren't stoned anymore), arm-in-arm-in-arm, singing a show tune, ignoring the bum seated in front of our building as we went into the lobby, entered lucky elevator No. 1 and went upstairs to our home.

The next morning Pam was on the phone when Ce and I stumbled into the living room. "Yes, I have black pants," she said. "Got it, I'll be there on time. Thanks so much." Pam hung up the phone as Ce was looking for her matches. "I got that waitress gig," Pam smirked. "You snooze, you lose."

Ce and I hugged Pam, and pretended to be happy for her but we both felt a little jealous. Ce more than I because of the run-in they'd had our senior year. Although they'd cleared the air and agreed that all was forgiven, some residual resentment remained.

"Jeez, Rose, here she goes again," Ce said while Pam went into the bathroom to shower.

"Shush. She'll hear you."

"I don't care!" Ce whispered.

"It's not the same thing."

"Yes it is. Well, it sort of is. No you're right. The intern job was worse. Do you remember how she was all over that, too?"

I nodded. I'd heard this story a million times during the past months, but no matter, here she went again.

"Remember? I told her I was gonna interview for that intern spot and then she jumped on it. They didn't hire me 'cause they'd just hired a college student earlier that morning! She took the friggin job that I told her about. The one I was interviewing for," Ce's voice picked up speed and grew louder with each word.

"Shush, Ce, she's gonna hear you."

"We've already filled that spot,'" they said. Ce's face turned red.

"Oh, who cares about that?" I tried brushing it off and hoped Ce would calm down, but no such luck as she was on a rampage.

"Then she got to be the weekend weather girl! That could've been me."

"It was just one time, and it was a stupid cable show." I tried reasoning with her. "How many people do you think watch TV at two o'clock in the morning?"

"Bitch!"

"Ce, stop," I whispered.

Ce stared at me with the same big eyes I'd first seen in kindergarten. With her arms crossed and her mouth bunched into a pout, she looked like a small child who'd just lost her favorite stuffed animal. "Bitch," she whispered.

"Hey, who cares?" I said again. "We came here to be stars, not waitresses."

"She better not try to take anything else away from me." Ce's mood softened.

"She won't." I reassured her, glad she'd calmed down.

"Pam better not try to be your new best friend!"

"Never," I whispered, and then walked into the bedroom and phoned in our coffee order to the deli across the street and hoped the delivery boy wouldn't forget to bring the Sweet 'n Low.

A few minutes later, the bathroom door opened. "I'm done," Pam's too-chipper-at-this-hour-of-the-morning voice sang out. I grabbed my towel and headed into the shower while Ce sat down on the couch, cigarette in one hand and rolling papers in the other.

This (minus the drama) became our morning ritual.

Chapter 4
The Competition

Not long after Pam moved in and snagged the waitress job, I had an epiphany. Our becoming-a-star escapade was going to be harder than expected. Ce had been even more clueless than I.

"Let's go to New York City and be real actresses," she'd suggested at graduation, confident it would be simple to break into showbiz. We'd been in the city for more than a month and couldn't even get decent waitress jobs, let alone acting gigs.

Soon I was filling in for Pam at her waitress job while she went to auditions or got acting jobs. By mid October, I was working at Mikos more than her. Ce filled in for the cashier when she went on maternity leave. Mikos became a job share.

I went on auditions but hadn't landed anything. With each rejection, my quirky behavior escalated. I never stepped on sidewalk cracks or walked under ladders. I never did anything important on Friday the thirteenth, and I counted all the blocks while pounding the pavement. My wardrobe consisted of clothes that contained lucky vibes. The unlucky pieces of my wardrobe were replaced.

"Ce, can I trade you my red sweater for your red turtleneck?"

"They're identical, Rose. What's up with this? Those black pants you traded for last week are the same ones you have from the GAP."

Why did Ce choose the time when I most needed her to be the dumb blonde to turn on her brain? I didn't want to confess the truth behind the clothing exchanges, fearful she'd think the stuff was unlucky, too, and not make the trade. Although she acted like a dumb blonde, Ce wasn't stupid. She didn't have a major anxiety disorder, (like me) but Ce had plenty of quirky behaviors and issues too. Plenty.

Pam and I wore the same size, but she'd told me she wasn't interested in a clothes-share arrangement. "I'd rather not," she'd said, and stared at the coffee stain on my shirtsleeve.

The flip side, of course, was my lucky shirt, pants, bra, underwear, purse and the lucky pen with which I always wrote. If there were a penny on the street, heads up, it was mine. If it were tails, I looked away and left that unlucky coin for some other *shmuck*. The power of luck influenced and determined the results of my decisions. Ce, on the other hand, relied on another method, which rhymed with luck. Pam (unlike the two of us) was organized, disciplined, and used logic, determination, and common sense. She put stamps on the pictures she mailed out, was prompt in returning phone calls and punctual. She took *any* elevator, and the labels on her clothes were from Lord and Taylor, not Lucky's department store. The one thing Pam and I had in common was our hair colorist: Sun In.

Like Ce, Pam had two goals. Although she didn't share her intentions out loud, it was obvious that she wanted to be a star. Her second goal was foremost on her mind and over shared on a daily basis. "I don't care if he's just a dermatologist; I am going to marry a doctor." Pam was on a relentless mission to marry into the medical field; this would be apparent to Helen Keller.

It was our three-month anniversary as roommates. Ce no longer worked at Mikos. She had a real waitress job working nights. I took all of Pam's shifts at the diner 'cause she was too busy auditioning and working as an actress. I tried ignoring my jealous feelings but each day my hazel eyes grew greener. We were seldom all together in the apartment, but one bone-chilling day in November, Pam walked in with a bag of bran muffins. Ce and I were in the kitchen sharing a Steak-um, a meal Ce loved and had persuaded me to try.

"Hulloooo," Pam bellowed in a phony, baloney British accent.

"In here," I said, throwing the half-eaten, faux Philly sandwich meat in the trash.

"In here." Ce parroted and rolled her eyes.

"Guess what? " Pam asked, then handed me the bag containing the muffins. Ce and I feigned interest while Pam continued. "I've signed a contract with a talent agent. Now that I have an agent, I won't have to go to those awful open calls and wait in line like cattle."

"Like us," Ce snapped, then forced a fake laugh and gave Pam an even less genuine congratulatory hug. Over the next weeks, we were green with envy when Pam's agent sent her on tons of casting calls, and it wasn't long before she was screen-tested for a lead part in a pilot on NBC. That fell through, but two days later she was cast in a low-budget documentary. Pam's success made Ce and I feel like a couple of slackers.

All lucky streaks end, even for Pam. The day she came home at two in the afternoon with a tear-streaked face, Ce and I knew something was wrong.

"It was between this tall blond girl and me for the Macy's commercial, and... and..." she sobbed, glaring at Ce as if Ce, with her blond hair and tall stature, was guilty by association.

"Why are you looking at me like that?" Ce's tone was razor sharp.

"Like what?" Ce's directness caught Pam off-guard, and she stopped crying. "Like what?" she screeched again.

"Like I was the blond girl who got your gig. If anyone is guilty of taking something that is someone else's it's you, Pam."

"Ce, stop." The blood drained out of my face. "Let it go," I whispered.

"That stupid cable thing again? I said I was sorry," Pam shot back.

"She's way over that; she's just a little premenstrual today, that's all." I hated confrontation and tried being a peacemaker, although my bias was obvious.

Pam burst into tears again. "Well sooo am I!" she cried as Ce's eyes met mine and the visual message we sent each other about Pam was clear: *bitch*. The one time Pam's life didn't go according to plan, she was in nervous-breakdown mode. Jeez, she was making strides in show biz and now complained because of one rejection? What an ingrate. She'd transformed from a complaining waitress into a melodramatic drama queen, and her act was getting old.

By the end of November, Pam's luck returned, and she got a small part in a toothpaste commercial. She was on cloud nine and strutted around the apartment like a first-rate star, and treated Ce and me like nobodys.

Pam's second goal, to marry a doctor, was working out too. This was apparent by the string of interns parading in and out of our apartment. The entourage of men clad in green scrubs often spent a night or two on our couch. The infamous maroon couch that could populate a small country from leftover sperm samples. The DNA couch – the one real piece of furniture we had.

"She's a friggin wonder girl. How does she do it all?" Ce wondered.

"Maybe her bedroom is lucky," I suggested. It might've been magical, but I wasn't offering up my share of a room with a window to find out.

More infuriating than her career taking off was when she started dating a neurologist, who spent all his free time getting on our nerves. "It's not fair," Ce complained. "Why can't they hang out at his apartment?" When they weren't screwing their brains out, they were out on the town seeing Broadway shows, or dining in real restaurants, not in Greek diners or at McDonalds.

The people Ce and I dated were out-of-work actors and waiters. I couldn't even imagine what being treated to a real date, one that didn't end with splitting the bill, felt like. "Can't we meet some of his friends?" I asked Pam.

"Yeah, Pam, doesn't your boyfriend have any eligible intern buddies? We feel left out!" Ce said.

Pam turned a deaf ear on our requests as she continued looking out for number one. She was all about "Pam" and didn't share (except for the one waitress gig at Mikos). The sounds emanating from inside her eight-by-ten-foot bedroom was a constant reminder of how little luck I'd had with finding a boyfriend. Ever.

"I can't believe I'm going to be in a scene with Mia Farrow," Pam boasted one day in early December. She told us Woody Allen was the director. "They call him the Wood Man." She concluded as if giving Entertainment Tonight an exclusive interview.

"We'll show her," Ce said within Pam's earshot. Pam shot her a sly smile then left the room. Pam might've treated us like doormats but Ce wasn't going to lie there and take it. Unlike me, Ce stood up.

"Shush," I snapped, fearful of another confrontation.

"We'll show her." Ce whispered.

"Yeah. Whatever," I whispered back, and then went into the bedroom to take a nap. If I couldn't accomplish what I wanted in the real world, there was always the option of dreamland. Sleep — uninterrupted, delicious sleep. Ce preferred pot.

Chapter 5
Buzz Buzz

It was a freezing December day, and I was snuggled under my blanket in a deep sleep when Ce woke me from a comatose slumber. "Rose," she screamed. "I got us both our first professional acting job!"

"Are you kidding?" I forced myself awake.

"I got fired."

"Again?" I wasn't surprised. "What does that have to do with acting jobs?"

"Listen," Ce plopped on my bed. "The dyke tending bar kept hitting on me, and I told the manager 'cause it was getting on my nerves. Cynthia, the manager, is dating Dolly."

"Who's Dolly?"

"The big lesbo bartender, and then Cynthia got pissed off and fired me!" She paused for a second to light up a cigarette. "Turns out, they're lovers." She stated this as if that would make clear what the hell she was talking about.

Sharing her cigarette and barely understanding the story Ce was telling, I listened to her blab away, and hoped against all odds that this tale, unlike most of her stories, had a point to it.

"So I'm on the Third Avenue bus when I run into Mitch."

"Mitch?" Who the hell was Mitch?

"Mitch from acting class," she clarified as the ashes from her cigarette fell to the floor. "His agent needs to send six people on this promotion for a new hair salon. Two of the girls scheduled have mono, and he asked if I knew of anybody who might be interested."

"When is it?" I didn't care what kind of promotion it was or what I had to do. This perspective was risky, considering Ce was involved, but money was money.

"Saturday, and we have to go by the wardrobe department and get our costumes tomorrow."

"Costumes? What kind of costumes? What about an audition? Don't we have to meet the agent to see if we're the right type?"

"Mitch told me he'd tell his agent about us. Rose, I just told you we are wearing costumes so his agent doesn't care what we look like. I guess they're desperate."

The next day, we arrived at a converted warehouse in the meatpacking district in lower Manhattan. It didn't look anything like Coral Gables. Or even Midtown. Feeling edgy and homesick again, I asked Ce, "Are you sure this is the right place?"

"Yeah. Come on, Rose, we're half an hour late already."

We climbed the three flights of stairs in our four-inch heels and knocked on the door that read "BJ Productions."

"It's open," a voice boomed from inside. We entered a lobby reeking of stale cigarettes. The woman behind the desk looked up, and asked, "You the bees?"

"That's us." Ce stood up straight and puffed out like a proud peacock. "This is Rose, and I'm Ce."

"Max, the bees are here for their costumes," she screamed into the next office.

"Bees? We're playing bees?" I whispered. I'm allergic to bees.

"It's something, Rose. Better than slinging hash and we'll get a hundred bucks cash."

Max came out holding two yellow-and-black outfits. His lazy eye made it impossible to tell who he was looking at. "You girls here for the Bumble & Bumble promotion?" he asked with the gruff voice of a three-pack a day smoker.

"Yes, that's us," we answered like the Bobbsey Twins. We got the details while taking our costumes and assured Max we'd be on time for our first acting job.

As we headed for the door, Max ran after us, holding the top part of our Bee outfits. "Girls, I almost forgot; here are your heads." He rolled his good eye.

Heads?

Saturday morning was cold. Real cold. Friggin Antarctic cold. Really, really, really cold. We stood on the corner of Lexington and Forty-second street, wearing our bee costumes while freezing our stingers off, waiting for the "queen bee" to arrive and give us the fliers we were to distribute to passers-by.

"Some acting job!" I shivered.

"Let's put on our bee heads so we'll be ready when the queen arrives with the stuff," Ce suggested. She was serious about our NY acting début; pot made her like that. She'd had a few hits off her new bong before we left for our job. She'd received the toy from one of her dates and now replaced the thin cigarettes she hand-rolled with the new contraption.

"Yes, let's put on our bee heads so no one will recognize us." With nothing but caffeine in my system, I knew the true reality. We were two college graduates, standing on a street corner in near deadly ten-degree weather, dressed like bees.

We were about to put on the five-pound carpeted bee heads when a familiar voice boomed nearby. "Ce? Rose? Is that you?" We turned to see the queen – not the queen in charge of delivering the handouts, but the other queen – our acting teacher, Stephan. "That's Stephan with a 'ph' and not Steven with a 'v'," he'd told us the first day of class, emphatic that his name not be mispronounced or misspelled. He was a flaming queen and we loved him. Gay men magnets that we were, he loved us as well.

"I see my acting classes have paid off," Stephan teased. "What are you girls doing?" Ce bragged how she'd gotten us this gig, just as the queen bee arrived.

"Are you girls Max's bees?" A large woman approached us with a stack of papers in hand. I thought Ce was going to faint. It was Dolly, the drone from the restaurant, day-lighting as a queen bee.

"Dolly?" our acting coached smirked.

"Hi, Stephan," she said. She gave Ce an icy look and continued. "Sorry ya got fired." She sounded most insincere.

As Stephan explained that Dolly was a former student of his, I saw a strange correlation between studying the craft of acting with Stephan and being destined for "beedom," as in a future life metaphor for mindless, meaningless employment.

Dolly made it clear that Ce and I couldn't work on the same corner, so after she and Stephan left, Ce crossed the street.

"At least this will keep my face warm." I put the five-pound, carpeted piece of shit over my head. The bee head shielded the wind from my face, but I felt unsteady and ready to topple over. Feeling more like a character at Disney World than a recent college grad with a star-filled future, I laundry-listed my doubts: Had I picked the right acting coach? Was a drama coach even necessary? Should I go back to Miami and go to law school instead? Was I the loser my mother always told me I was? Even though the snowflakes started falling and stuck to my stinger, I was sweating inside my costume. I felt panicked and claustrophobic so I flung off the bee head. I watched as if in an altered state as it slipped out of my hands and, in slow motion, rolled down the sidewalk toward the street. I chased after it, and my ankle twisted as I fell onto the pavement. "Ouch!" I cried, lying on the ground staring at a sidewalk crack. I tried to stand up but it was too painful. After three more attempts I gave up and inched across the pavement on my belly and watched the bee head submerge into the gutter. Unfortunately, I didn't notice the bugs when I retrieved it a few minutes later. "Shiiiiiit! What the..." One of the buggers bit me. I cringed and observed my hand as it swelled up like a balloon. Five minutes later, thankful I hadn't died from a poisonous bite, I tucked in my knees underneath my body and stood up. I left the bee head, along with my pride, in the gutter. "Ce!" I screamed at her back, but she didn't turn around. Maybe she didn't hear me. "Ceeeeee!" I shouted again while she walked in the opposite direction. Some tall guy (who would probably end up on our couch that night) had grabbed her attention, and she was oblivious to my cries.

"Ouch!" I cried while sharp shooting pains traveled up my leg as my left ankle began throbbing. "Oh my God, what if my ankle is broken!" I limped to a trashcan to toss the remaining fliers, and then began limping home. *"What next?"* resounded inside my head, blinding me to the beauty of the snow. *"What next? What next?"* I said out loud feeling traumatized, trampled and defeated on the long limp home. "What next?" would soon become my mantra in the months that followed.

Chapter 6
Moving On

Four months from the day she moved in, Pam told us she was moving out. "I got a call from my cousin in California, and her best friend is a casting director who can get me a major part in a new film with Tom Hanks." Pam's voice quivered as she continued with her news. "The filming will last at least a year, and so I'm moving to L.A.!"

Her news wasn't a surprise. I'd spent the week stretched out on the DNA couch, recovering from my bee injury, and even though Pam was around more than usual, she seemed to be avoiding me. Ce noticed Pam's standoffish behavior too. Sequestering herself in her windowless bedroom with the door shut was the first red flag.

"What are you doing?" I whispered, when I saw Ce with her ear pushed against Pam's bedroom wall.

"Quiet," Ce whispered. "Pam's on the phone. I wanna hear what she's saying." The secret phone calls and Pam's sudden indifference to all the filth and mess in the apartment was another clue. And Pam not mentioning the roaches that played in the sink full of dirty dishes was a full-blown alert.

Ce leapt away from the wall and a moment later Pam opened her door and walked into the living room.

"We need to talk." Pam looked serious as Ce stopped pretending to clean off the dining room table. The three of us sat down on the maroon couch, covered in stains and burn holes. Ce's eyes were giant saucers, and I leaned into Pam paying close attention to what sounded like a well-rehearsed, scripted speech. We sat in silence after she told us her news.

"When?" I blurted out.

Tears filled her eyes, and even though Pam had excellent acting skills, her tears seemed genuine. "I'm taking the red eye to L.A. on Saturday."

I was dumbfounded. I'd never seen this coming, and since a heartless cardiologist had recently dumped Pam, part of me thought she was going to tell us she wasn't going to date doctors anymore. Or date.

Period. I never suspected she was going to leave Manhattan.

Ce didn't seem surprised. "I guess you've had enough of living life in the dirt zone anyway," she snickered. My pretend, dumb-blond friend had a point. The rumor from college was true: Pam was a neat freak, and she probably welcomed any opportunity to leave our world of overflowing ashtrays, towels and sheets stained with God-knows-what, and a refrigerator filled with plants growing out of three-month-old Chinese food containers. But as I watched heartfelt tears stream down her face I knew that she was sad to leave us and felt my eyes well up, too.

Pam got off the couch to get some tissues and her wallet. "Here's money for next month's rent." She sobbed as she handed me some cash. Crying, I left the comfort of the couch and hugged her. Ce joined in the cry fest, and the three of us stood in the middle of the living room, with our arms wrapped around one another. Then Ce began singing "The Sun Will Come Out Tomorrow." Although she didn't feel warm and fuzzy about Pam, Ce never missed an opportunity to belt out a good show tune.

Pam and I joined in, laughing as we cried. We stayed wrapped in one another's arms until we sang the last verse.

Four days later, we enacted a farewell that was Academy Award worthy. It was an emotional good-bye with more hugs, kisses, and promises to stay in touch. Granted, Ce and I were slobs, and the ongoing jealousy had been irritating, but we were still friends. After all, we'd experienced so many disappointments and gone through the depths of despair together. We were twenty-something drama queens and our shared moments were the bonds that glued us together.

"I'll miss you," we said in unison, as Pam picked up her two Burberry suitcases and left apartment 8A. Forever.

Once again, Ce and I had our special room for rent: the phone booth bedroom with a revolving door but without a window or air conditioning.

"Now what?"

"Let's not worry about finding a new roommate today," Ce advised and counted Pam's cash like a bank teller. "She gave us a little bit extra."

"Wow." I breathed a sigh of relief, but the feeling didn't last long.

"We have plenty of time before we have to think about some new person living here," Ce reassured me the same way she'd convinced me that it would be a snap to break into showbiz.

The weekend after Pam left, Ce seemed different.

"I'm spending the night at Ashley's."

"Who?" I asked.

"From the restaurant. You know… Ashley."

"Oh… what about our movie night?" Friday nights we'd have pizza, and then see a movie. It had become our tradition since moving into the City.

"We can go next week. I promise."

But we never did.

Movie night, like Pam, was history. With each passing day, Ce grew more distant and preoccupied with her new friends from the restaurant. Ashley and the two other girls who waited tables at night to supplement their day jobs as shoe models. They were her new best friends, and I was, evidently, chopped liver.

"Ashley says I've got the perfect size feet for shoe modeling." Ce sat on the far end of the couch and snipped her big toenail with a small silver clipper, then flipped the clipping into the ashtray.

I was grossed out and moved the ashtray away from the middle of the couch and closer to her. "Maybe I could shoe model, too?"

"What?" She clipped the rest of her left foot in rapid succession while I looked the other way.

"What size feet do you need?"

"Six." She continued her pedicure, and I looked down at my feet and spotted a dead roach. I hated roaches and averted my eyes to the ceiling. "Too bad," I said. "I wear size eight."

"Yeah, too bad," she mumbled then wiggled her toes in the air. "Ashley said she'd talk to the guy that gets her shoe gigs and see if they need any more models. Ashley said shoe modeling is a blast!" Ce clipped the rest of her toes while I sat on the other end of the couch and wondered how to dispose of the roach. Picking it up (even with a paper towel) wasn't an option.

"That's nice," I said. Ashley this and Ashley that. I lit up a Marlboro and sighed. Yep, it was clear Ashley and the sweet smell of leather had replaced me. I wasn't Pam's doormat anymore; now I was Ce's. I took the ashtray off the couch, then walked around the roach and dumped her toenail clippings into the garbage.

"Oh Rose, you have to meet the girls." Ce bolted off the couch like she'd just had an electric shock. "You're gonna love them." She trotted out of the living room into the bathroom and closed the door. My stomach turned somersaults while reality hit me: I'd been replaced.

"OK." I whispered to the floor. In spite of my jealousy, I was curious about her new friends.

Two nights later, I got my chance to find out. I showered, and then pulled my lucky red sweater over a white T-shirt. My brown corduroys felt a little snug, but I put them on anyway. A little mascara here, some blush there, and I was ready to meet the girls.

"You can't meet them looking like that." Ce shook her head while appraising my outfit.

"What's wrong with it?" Her harsh criticism made me feel self-conscious.

She didn't answer. Instead, she pulled a designer skirt and chenille sweater from underneath a pile of clothing on the bedroom floor. "Here, put this on." She was insistent on a re-dress, and true to the obedient mother's child I was, I agreed. Ten minutes later, she smiled and nodded her head. "Much better."

It was six-thirty when we arrived at the trendy hot spot on the Upper West Side. "You are going to love them," Ce assured me again while we walked through the ritzy entrance of Café de Artist.

The elaborate décor in the lounge screamed out expensive. "I can't afford this place," I whispered to Ce as we walked toward the bar.

"Don't worry, Rose. It's just one drink, and I'll pay for you."

"Over here, Ce!" A high-pitched voice beckoned from the far end of the bar where three girls congregated.

"Ashlee!" Ce waved, and then ran over while I trailed behind her. Feeling like a prisoner on death row walking to my execution, I dragged my feet. Their faces blended, and they looked like triplets instead of friends.

Ashley and two other skinny bitches with long blond hair and blue eyes sized me up. Between the three of them they wore a size six. "Hi," they said.

"Hi. I've heard so much about you." I forced an awkward smile.

"Girls, this is Rose." After Ce introduced me, she slung her arm over Ashley's shoulder. I realized that although I felt out of place, Ce fit right in.

"Cheers." Her new friends tilted their cocktail glasses in my direction. Their manicured hands wrapped around the stems of tinted martini glasses while I shoved my nail-bitten, torn-cuticle fingers inside my coat pockets.

"Nice to meet you," they said in accord.

I spied their snow-white teeth through their practiced smiles and felt like puking. "Yes," was all I could muster. I was way out of my league, and dug my hands deeper inside my coat pockets and had even more reasons to despise them.

"Don't you just love Jimmy Choo?" Ashley asked, after Ce ordered us a drink.

"Uh," my eyes darted at Ce then back to Ashley. "Yes, I do." Another fake smile crossed my face. "Their eggrolls are so crunchy."

"Egg rolls?" One of the three skeletons repeated.

"Yes. I could eat ten at a time."

Ce cringed with embarrassment while her anorexic friends stared at me like I was an alien.

"She's kidding," Ce said, and then rolled her eyes at me while her new best friends snickered. "Rose knows Choos are shoes, not a restaurant." An outburst of laughter ensued.

Ce handed me a glass of white wine. I pretended to sip it and felt like a fish out of water with three land sharks ready to devour me. My stomach tied up in a giant knot and ten minutes later I set my drink on the bar. "I don't feel so good. I'm going home," I whispered to Ce.

"Oh, Rose, don't go." Ce's eyes opened wide, and she pretended to be upset. "Do you need cab fare?" she asked a second later, and handed me a five-dollar bill that she'd pulled from her bra. "See ya later," she said.

"Thanks." I wadded up the bill inside my hand. Ce turned on her heels and made a quick bee line over to her friends. "Ice princess," I whispered to her back, then walked outside to find a cab.

After that one-time meeting, I wasn't invited out with Ce and her new BFs again. Thank God.

Ce's infatuation with her new friends continued and it wasn't long before she felt like a stranger. Instead of confronting her I put my head in the sand and pretended to ignore the obvious distance that had grown between us.

January arrived, and Ce wasn't motivated to go to auditions anymore, but I dragged her along anyway.

"They need a hundred extras."

"Open calls are a friggin waste of time," she complained.

"Isn't this why we moved to New York?" I asked her as we stood in a line that stretched around the block in the fifteen-degree weather.

"To freeze to death?"

"To be actresses!" I pulled my white wool cap over my ears and kept my double-gloved hands in my coat pockets.

"Oh, whatever." She sighed like a drama queen. "Rose, I'm so bored. I don't know how much longer I can stand here, and look, the line's not even moving!"

"If we would've gotten here earlier like I suggested, we wouldn't have six hundred people in front of us!" My teeth were chattering.

"Six a.m. isn't an option, Rose, not for friggin extra work." Ce lit a cigarette.

"Neither is noon!" I said, trying to match the nasty tone in her voice, as my legs started shaking.

"Fine," Ce snorted like a spoiled brat and turned her back on me.

"Fine!" A few minutes passed, and I felt awful that we'd fought. "Ce." I called at her back, but she stood frozen in front of me. "Ce?" I said a little louder. She didn't budge, pretending not to hear me.

After fifteen minutes of silence, Ce shouted, "This is friggin ridiculous" over her shoulder, and then left me alone in the line.

"Ice friggin Queen," I said out loud, and watched her trot off. Now I completely understood her college nickname. "Ice Queen," I whispered and noticed frost billowing out of my mouth like smoke. Sure, Ce had had confrontations and fights with others, but not with me. I'd never been on the receiving end of her deep freeze. Ever. But now, the word "bitch" repeated inside my head. A cold chill traveled down my spine, and a minute later I began backpedaling. "No, no, she's not a bitch," I tried to sell myself. "She's just in a bad mood," I justified as I stuffed my true feelings down into the pit of my stomach. "She's just in a bad mood," I repeated but felt layers of our friendship melt away.

A half-hour later, my toes felt numb. The line was at a dead halt. Feeling defeated, I left the audition line with my picture still in hand, and headed for the subway.

Ce was on the phone when I got home. She told me in an excited voice that she was talking to Pam.

"How is she?" We hadn't heard from her since she'd moved to L.A.. I smiled, forgetting how pissed and hurt I'd felt just moments before. "Is she famous yet?"

Ce smirked, then shook her head, and mouthed "no." I was glad that Ce was back to her happy-go-brainless self and seemed to have forgotten the fight we'd had. Or maybe she was just stoned. Ce handed the phone to me then headed into the bathroom.

"Pam, how's the movie going?"

"Oh." There was a long pause. "There's a delay on the start date, and they aren't even auditioning people until February. That's Hollywood." Pam faked a laugh.

"Bummer," I said, but part of me smiled inside.

"Yep, big bummer. Oh well, that's showbiz." Pam faked another laugh and changed the subject. "L.A. is so beautiful, and I met this great guy on the flight here."

"Is he a doctor?" I asked, even though I already knew the answer.

"Third-year medical student, and he's the one. I just know it!" Since Pam thought she'd marry every medicine man she dated, I took the comment in stride. But, what she said next grabbed my attention.

"Marty, my new boyfriend, has a friend transferring to New York Hospital, and he needs an apartment. Is my old room still for rent?"

"Yes." My palms started to sweat.

"His name is Ethan, and he's such a doll." (Another adjective she always used describing anyone dressed in scrubs.) "He needs a place to live starting February."

"Sounds great, but it would be kind of weird 'cause he's a strange guy, and…"

"He's a great guy, and he's a doctor." Pam sounded defensive. "Maybe he could introduce you to some interns at New York Hospital." Yeah, just the way you did, I thought. Pam's hard sell of Ethan made me wonder what was in it for her? I felt anxious and knew I couldn't decide anything right then. Besides, I had to talk to Ce about it.

"I'll call you over the weekend," I promised and hung up.

Ce bounced out of the bathroom. "BF, let's smoke a joint and order in pizza." This was her way of making up. For a few brief moments our closeness returned. But it was only when she was in an altered state of mind. She'd never apologize; 'sorry' wasn't in her vocabulary. Ce offered mind-altering drugs and a treat for dinner to show she cared.

Fifteen minutes later our pizza arrived.

Ce passed me the joint and opened the pizza box. "Yuuuuuum!"

She handed me a slice.

"Great news!" Ce cheered, after I'd told her about Ethan. She toked on the joint and scarfed down pizza. The less she had to make real-life decisions, the more she liked it.

"Great" I agreed. By the time we'd finished the pizza, all the bad feelings I'd had earlier were gone and replaced by guilt. How could I ever have thought that my best friend was an "Ice Queen," even for a second?

On Sunday afternoon, I called Pam and gave her the thumbs-up on Ethan. Then it was time for the Sunday phone call with my mom. She took full advantage of the cheap weekend rate and talked at me nonstop for an hour. Ready to cut my wrists, I knew the news about our new roommate would shut her the hell up, and so I played my ace-in-the-hole.

"A strange man is moving into your apartment?" she said after a long pause.

"He's not a man, Mom; he's a kid, twenty-something," I answered, realizing how much I loved living in Manhattan, eighteen hundred miles away from my family.

"You don't know the first thing about him. What if he's a rapist?"

I should be so lucky.

My younger sister was whining in the background about how unfair it was for Mom to let me live with a boy. Heather, my sixteen-year-old sister, wasn't allowed to date yet. "Rose is such a slut." She screeched.

Heather was "sister dearest." Her biggest gripe was being born *after* me. She was the baby in our family, and that didn't make her happy. "*I* should've been born first," she'd complained. She equated being the second child to being second best. It was an absurd logic because birth order is something that no one has any control over. But, nonetheless, she blamed me for her birth status and for all that made her miserable. As kids, we fought like cats and dogs, a constant struggle of sibling rivalry. It was the "Mom always loved you best" syndrome that never went away. I heard the slamming of a door and knew Heather had barricaded herself inside her bedroom.

"He's a good friend of Pam's boyfriend," I continued, pretending I hadn't heard my sister's tirade. "And he's in medical school." I played the doctor card. I heard Mom suck deeply from her Pall Mall before she asked the standard questions regarding race, then religion.

"Yes Mom, and Jewish." That answer justified everything, but a sudden sharp pain in my neck reminded me that no answer would ever stop her questions. Ever. There would be endless interrogations until one of us dropped dead. But for now our talk about the strange man/boy was over.

Guilt prevented me from speaking my mind. "Leave me alone. I'm an adult!" I'd wanted to scream during these irritating conversations, but I remained silent. It was easier to first agonize through her well meaning advice and then suffer through the inevitable anxiety attack than to feel remorse from being disrespectful to the woman who gave me life, and never let me forget it.

Chapter 7
Ethan Schwartz

On February first, Ethan Schwartz moved into our apartment. We'd spoken a few times on the phone, and he sounded normal. A check covering six months' rent, arriving before he did, sealed the deal. It was an exciting moment as Ce and I raced to open the door to meet our mystery roommate. An average boy/man who didn't look old enough to shave stood in the hallway with two army-style duffle bags and an animal carrier. There was an awkward moment of sizing each other up before Ce broke the silence.

"Oh my God, you have a kitty! I love cats." Ce took the traveling cat case inside as Ethan dragged his two large duffle bags into the living room. Ce sat on the couch and petted the small gray cat that cowered in her lap.

"I'm glad you like cats." Ethan sounded as nervous as his cat looked. "I guess I should've mentioned Pirate. I forgot." The cat had one functioning eye, while the other was sealed shut. The name "Pirate" suited him.

"That's OK," purred Ce. "I love Pirate Kitty."

"It's a *great* surprise," I reassured him. I loved cats and welcomed the new addition, but I wondered what *else* this strange boy/man who "could be a rapist," forgot to tell us. I dismissed my mother's thoughts and smiled as I observed the new dynamics of our apartment. Welcome to "Three's Company."

The more things changed, the more they stayed the same. A week after Ethan moved in I watched him extinguish his cigarette in the one potted plant in our living room and knew we had another slob mate. Within a month, Pirate Kitty had decimated the plant, and the empty planter overflowed with Ethan's cigarette butts. I wondered whether I was the sole person in Manhattan still using an ashtray. I was still slinging hash, dating waiters, and waiting in long audition lines at casting calls. Same shit; new living arrangement. Ce picked up more shifts at her restaurant, the adults-only ritzy glitzy joint on the Upper East Side. She worked long hours and no longer auditioned but still went to acting class. It was the one thing we still did together.

The DNA couch now had cat vomit and hairballs added to its

layers of grime, and our bathroom smelled like a Port Authority bus terminal at three o'clock in the morning.

"It's a good thing Pam moved to L.A.. She never would've been able to stand living here now," Ce said.

"If Pam hadn't moved to L.A., Ethan wouldn't be here, and this place wouldn't be so disgusting," I reminded her.

"You've got a point." Ce nodded her head while rolling a joint.

Our neat-freak former roommate, now living the clean life in California, was no longer around to enforce sanitation laws and pick up after us. Without her diligence, our place turned into the Bowery the night before garbage pick-up. The bathroom was a health hazard. When I considered buying a HAZMAT suit before using the toilet I knew it was time to clear the air with something more than Glade.

"Let's have a big spring clean," I suggested to my slob-mates on a snowy morning the first Saturday in March.

"It's not spring yet!" Ce protested.

Ethan spent most of his time at the hospital, and objected, too.

"Your cat is here twenty-four, seven, and the litter box stinks." Then, after a half-hour of debating with me, Ethan backed down and although he wasn't a happy camper, agreed to clean the bathroom.

Seven hours later, you could eat off our floors. Well, that's an exaggeration, but you could eat something that fell on the floor and not need hospitalization. The three of us sat on the couch, tired but proud of our major accomplishment. It was a cathartic experience tossing all the junk that had piled up and scraping off the accumulated filth in the sinks and bathtub. Pam would've been proud.

Three days later the apartment smelled like cat shit again and the dishes piled high in the sink. Living the clean life was a novelty and the big clean was just a one-shot deal.

The following week I came home from an audition, and Ce was in our bedroom with Pirate Kitty. Ce's maternal instinct was equivalent to Joan Crawford's in "Mommie Dearest," but she had this special bond with Ethan's one-eyed, cat.

"Come back here," I heard Ce yell from the bedroom as the feline scurried past me into the kitchen.

"What's the matter, baby? Come to momma," Ce appeared and scooped up Pirate, snuggling the cat next to her face. After a quick, "Hi, Rose," she scanned the living room, then picked up the *People* magazine off the floor and walked back into the bedroom, cuddling Pirate Kitty in her arms.

Ce remained in the bedroom with Pirate enjoying her two favorite pastimes: smoking pot and looking at herself in the mirror. Ethan came home a little while later and planted himself on the couch.

"No rounds?" I asked, realizing it was odd having him home at night.

"Nope. I'm takin' the evening off." He started reading some medical journal. It occurred to me how little I knew about Ethan. He smoked, was a slob, hated to clean, liked cats and was an intern at the hospital. That was all I discerned, and it seemed wrong that we shared an apartment but remained strangers.

"Wanna play Scrabble?" I asked. You could tell a lot about someone by the way they Scrabbled.

"Sure." Ethan tossed his medical book onto the floor, and then sat down at the dining room table.

I remembered stashing the one board game I owned underneath a pile of unlucky clothing on a shelf in my bedroom closet. Ce had fallen asleep and looked peaceful with Pirate sleeping on top of her head. I tiptoed, careful not to disturb her, and thought I heard Pirate hiss as I left the room.

I joined Ethan at the table and handed him the box. Within two minutes he had the game set up and picked seven letters out of the gray pouch.

"I'll keep score," he said.

"We're keeping score? I thought we'd play for fun."

Ethan looked at me like I had four heads. "What fun would it be if we didn't keep score? No one would win."

"It doesn't matter who wins. It's just fun to play."

Ethan smiled and told me it was all about winning. His attitude made me think he should be in law instead of medicine.

Ten minutes into the game, I knew I was right. He challenged the words I put on the board and gloated when he used all his letters during several plays. He was methodical and strategic and placed his words on all the double and triple-point spaces. My two-and three-letter words weren't cutting it. The score was 262 to 98. I laid down the I M B O under the L, and the game was over.

"Great job," he cheered.

"Yippee. A five-letter word." LIMBO. The word didn't just end the game, but also summed up my life. "You won. Happy?"

"It's not about who wins, Rose. Didn't you tell me that?" His sarcasm was diffused a bit by the sparkle in his slate gray eyes. Up until this evening, Ethan had been just some random person, but now I felt a connection to him in a friendly, not romantic way. "It's not about the winning," he repeated while his alluring eyes searched my face.

"Right." I murmured and noticed his dimples when he smiled.

"Isn't that what you told me, Rose?" He smirked.

"Yep." I whispered as a lock of his jet-black hair fell on his face. Yes, Ethan was cute, but I wasn't the least bit attracted to him. Doctors weren't my thing. That was Pam's territory. Besides, getting involved with a roommate was a recipe for disaster. When the romance soured, I'd be out what I needed most: Ethan's third of the rent. It was a good thing I wasn't attracted to him because I was feeling sad and lonesome over the past month. "Right, it's just a game," I said and felt his eyes bore through me like laser beams.

He nodded, and a moment later asked why I was upset and looked so sad.

"I'm not upset about the game," I told him, surprised that my feelings were so visible. "I'm just..." What was I?

"Adorable!" He grinned.

Charming was now added to my list of adjectives describing Ethan Schwartz. Our eyes locked, and for no rational reason, I burst into tears.

"Oh, Rose. Tears? Over a dumb-ass game? I'll let you win next time." He kept a poker face watching me cry.

My legs felt weak. My face burned hot, flushed with embarrassment. "It's not the gaaame." There I was, standing in the middle of the living room, having a cry-fest.

"What is it, then?" Ethan sounded confused as he inched toward me.

"Oh it's just everything." Vulnerability poured through my veins and saturated the wood floors as Ethan wrapped his arms around me.

"It'll be alright, Rose. We never have to play Scrabble again." When the gentle hug evolved into a warm embrace, and Ethan started smoothing my hair and wiping away my tears, the embarrassment vanished, and desire appeared. He held me, and it felt good to be comforted. To be touched. Soon, another feeling replaced desire: fear.

The rush of feelings I experienced in his arms terrified me.

"Thanks, Ethan," I said and felt awkward. We were standing in the middle of the living room, arms around each other, and my vulnerability was palatable. If he had initiated a kiss, I would've responded, forgetting all the reasons I had for making this behavior taboo. Sensing the vibes between us, he ended the embrace and went into the bathroom to get me tissues.

"Here," he said handing them to me. "I'm going to bed, Rose. I have an early call tomorrow. Feel better."

"Good night, Ethan," I said, and went into my bedroom, feeling something I hadn't felt in a long time - alive.

Chapter 8
That's Shoe-Biz

Between waitress shifts, I'd pull my lucky red wool cap over my head and dash from one audition to another. The bone-chilling weather was challenging for this Florida girl, but I loved living in the city. The streets were teeming with tourists, tri-state commuters and fellow Manhattan-ites (the people who felt they owned the streets.) My new home was magical, but regardless of my love for New York with its cast of millions, I still felt isolated and overwhelmed.

Ce never noticed my detachment because she was consumed with her new friends and living in "Ce Land."

"She doesn't have a mean bone in her body!" I had defended her in college. But now I knew that my defense was incorrect. Ce didn't have a mean bone in her body; she had several. "It's those stupid friends of hers. The shoe models." I told Pirate Kitty as I stroked his soft fur, and felt better for a moment. Most times I was successful rationalizing away Ce's cold self-centered behavior. I'd become a pro at living in denial.

"The only time she's nice to you is when she needs a favor." Heather's voice mocked inside my head.

"You're wrong!" I answered into thin air. "You're just too young to understand." But one night Heather's words smacked me in the face and stung like a bee. It was a Thursday after I'd come home from my double-shift at Mikos. The apartment door was unlocked, and Cat Stevens' "Moon Shadow" blasted from inside. "Ce?" I called out, and dumped my purse on the dining table.

"In here," she yelled from our bedroom.

I walked through the narrow hallway and stopped short in the doorframe.

"Hey, Rose." Ce, clad in her bra and bikini undies, stood on a black velvet square in the middle of the room. "I'm so glad you're home." She held a Polaroid camera in her left hand while bending over her bare feet. "I need you to be my photographer." Then, she lifted up her head, and looked at me after the camera's flash went off.

"What are you doing?" I tripped over a pair of her boots, and then spied a dozen more pairs of shoes strewn across the floor.

Ce slipped on a pair of black stilettos. "Rose, take a picture of my feet in these." She shoved the camera into my hands.

"OK."

A moment later, she was positioned on the black velvet square, and I snapped the camera. "Rose! I wasn't ready. Take it again."

I aimed the Polaroid. "What are these for?" The camera flashed.

"Shoe modeling." Ce raced over and picked up a pair of gold sandals. "I told you! Don't you remember? Ashley?"

Ashley. How could I forget her? I clicked the camera again and recalled that fancy restaurant where I'd met Ce's new friends. I'd felt isolated and left out, but had coped with my feelings the only way I knew how. I ignored them.

"I told you all about it," Ce snipped. "Don't you remember, Rose?" She rolled her eyes and changed shoes again. "Ashley is getting me into shoe modeling."

Ashley, the ringleader bitch. "Oh yeah, I remember." I feigned a vague recollection, although my memory was crystal clear. How could I take that milestone moment in stride? Ce had found a clique of girls who weren't intimated by her and put Ce up on a pedestal. Now that the "Ice Queen" had met some "Ice Princesses," Ce didn't need me. Now Ce was just like the popular girls in kindergarten. Her quest for becoming a famous actress was also nixed. It hadn't been an overnight occurrence. Ever since Pam had moved out, Ce had been transforming. Perhaps Pam was the competitive edge Ce needed to be motivated.

"Rose! I've been standing here for five friggin minutes. Would ya just snap the damn camera already?"

"Oh, right." I clicked the camera again. Although I knew her priorities had changed, I still had stars in my eyes. She might've given showbiz the boot, but giving up my dream of becoming a working actress hadn't crossed my mind. Ever. Why else would I stay in New York? I could waitress anywhere.

The weeks passed, and Ce's metamorphosis continued. By the middle of April her transformation was complete as she packed her valise and said: "I'm going out to the Hamptons."

"You're not going to class tonight?" I already knew the answer.

"No. I'm done." Ce rolled her eyes.

She was done with me, too, and although I didn't like it, I'd accepted it.

"With who?"

"Matthew." She put on a fresh coat of lipstick, and then smacked her lips. "I told you last week that I'm not going back to class." She capped her red lipstick, threw it in her oversized handbag, and then slammed her small suitcase shut.

Matthew was no surprise. I knew it was a matter of time before Ce hooked up with some rich business tycoon who fit in with her new clique.

Now that Matthew was in the picture, I didn't stand a chance at reclaiming our friendship. It was evident that Ce had aborted Plan A (stardom), and now Plan B (marry a millionaire) was set into full operation, and that plan didn't include me.

Unlike the Chelsea I'd met in kindergarten, Ce now chose the popular kids over me, the picture-perfect girls who had rich boyfriends with houses in West Hampton. How could getting pizza and seeing a stupid movie compete with that? "I'll miss you in class tonight."

"Well, I won't miss being there. I'm way over 'Stephan with a ph' and his blue-and-white-checkered shirts. I'm over the whole acting thing," Ce's tone was curt, and confirmed what I already knew. She was on a mission to marry a millionaire and held onto Plan B like a pit bull holds onto a steak bone.

"I know," I mumbled and mustered a smile. "Have fun with Matthew." And with your new best friends.

She spritzed herself with Bal a Versailles, a heavy-scented perfume that her mom gave her. Then, with a quick "thanks," Ce hurried out of the apartment. I shut the door behind her as my eyes filled with tears. My heart sank, and my last shred of hope was gone. I was old news and felt like a worn-out shoe that had been dumped in the trash. Captivated by her new life, Ce had moved on, and I knew it was the end of an era not having her as my ally anymore. Our days of beedom were over, as well as our moments of sitting on the couch and getting stoned together. It was time for me to stand up and stand-alone, and as much as I hated change I had no other choice. My face felt flushed, and the room started spinning as the walls felt like they were closing in. I baby-stepped my way to the couch and sat down. Knowing I was on my own, alone, frightened the hell out of me.

What next? I felt abandoned but forced myself off the couch and put on my shoes. Ce might've trashed Stephan's class; nevertheless, it was my salvation.

"One man's trash is another man's treasure," I heard Mom's voice in my head.

"Oh shut the hell up already!" Five minutes later, I headed out the door to catch the Second Avenue bus.

I'll move to L.A. and room with Pam, I consoled myself as I waited at the empty bus stop. Maybe I could. And just when I thought I'd solved my dilemma, a car whizzed too close to the curb and plowed through a mud puddle. Maybe not. My brand-new jeans, soaked by filthy water; a sign that moving to L.A. was a bad idea. Damn it! Drenched to the bone, I turned around and walked home. No acting class tonight. Now my pants were unlucky, unwearable and destined for the back of my closet next to my other unlucky clothing.

Four days later, Ce walked through the door with big news. "Oh, Rose, I'm so glad you're home." Her face glowed.

For an instant I thought that the old Ce had returned.

"I'm going to Japan!" she blurted out.

"Japan? Like the country?"

"Yes, on Matthew's private jet." She rushed over to the hall closet and dislodged a large suitcase off the top shelf. "Gotta pack." I trailed behind her like a cocker spaniel while she lugged the jumbo case into our bedroom.

"Japan," she repeated. "On Matthew's private jet." She pulled the few clothes in her closet off their hangers and piled them willy-nilly into her suitcase.

I crossed the room, sat down on the edge of my bed and watched.

She crouched down and picked up a huge pile of shirts, skirts and jeans from the floor and sniffed the lot. "I wonder if this is clean?" She took a second whiff then declared they were clean enough and threw them into the suitcase.

"Where in Japan?"

"Where? I'm not sure," she said as a blank stare crossed her face. "Oh, here, take this before I forget." She handed me a wad of bills. "It's money for May's rent, and for the summer, too." She closed the suitcase then pulled it into the living room while I followed.

"When are you coming back?" I stared at the wadded up bills in my sweaty hand.

"I don't know. I'll call you." We hugged good-bye and I held open the door as Ce schlepped the suitcase out into the hallway then over to the elevator bank.

"I'll call you," she repeated as she got into elevator No. 3, then disappeared off on another escapade.

"Right."

I closed the door and heard Pirate meow, as if asking, "Where's Ce? Where's Ce?"

"Ce's gone, little Pirate kitty," I told him while he nuzzled my feet with his head. "Completely."

Chapter 9
Pandora's Box

I was panic-stricken after Ce's departure and if it hadn't been spring I would've lost all hope. Thank goodness for this wonderful season of rebirth, renewal and change. Thoughts of Ethan danced through my head, distracting me from the fact that my best friend had dumped me. She'd reset the stage; moved all the furniture and pulled the rug out from under me. Her exit wasn't a surprise, but it was still unnerving.

Whatever. I stuffed down my feelings of isolation with a large candy bar. A gentle breeze blew through the window, and I placed some white and yellow tulips on the card table denoting our dining room. With Ce gone, Ethan and I spent a lot of time alone together in the apartment. Wednesday was his short day at the hospital, and of course Wednesday became my lucky day of the week. Of course. Ever since that night (a Wednesday) after our Scrabble game, there was strong sexual tension in the air. We didn't discuss it, and despite my attempt to dismiss its presence, the feeling was there, like a white elephant in the middle of a room.

"Let's order in Chinks and Scrab," Ethan suggested the night after Ce left for Japan. Did I forget to mention that Ethan was a bit racist?

"Sure. It's a great night for Chinese food and a Scrabble game," I emphasized dashing off to retrieve the Scrabble game. I handed the game to him and watched while he set up the board and remembered the peppermint scent of his breath as he held me after the last game. I felt an adrenalin rush and wondered whether there'd be an encore performance this evening with an additional scene or two added.

"What about the food?" Ethan asked.

"Huh?" So distracted thinking about the possibilities the night held, I'd forgotten to order dinner. He smiled, and I grabbed the phone to cover my nervousness.

"One large order of pork fried rice, one cashew chicken, one Hunan beef with two egg rolls," I told the girl on the other end of the line.

She recognized my voice and the food order. "Twenty minutes, Miss Rose," she said, not needing the address.

"Let's play for something," Ethan suggested as I sat down across from him.

"Like what?"

Ethan thought for a minute. "Dinner. Loser pays."

"Dinner?" I hesitated, knowing that I'd lose and didn't have enough cash to cover all the food.

Seeing my reaction, he pondered a moment then suggested an alternative. "Slave time," he smirked as his slate gray eyes pierced through me. Yes, Ethan was a racist.

"Slave time?"

"Yeah, if you lose, you're my slave for an hour, and if I lose then I'm your slave." Sensing I needed more info, he continued. "You could clean the kitty litter, do the dishes, pick up my dry-cleaning; stuff like that." I understood the activities he mentioned but knew it was *'the stuff like that'*, that could bring us closer to the line — the line that wasn't visible but mentally drawn. With little hesitation, I nodded my head and was oddly aroused by the potential of becoming his sex slave.

"To make things fair, I won't use any spaces that are double or triple-word scores." Ethan the Gentleman. The first word he put on the board was "excited."

By the time the Chinese food arrived, I knew I was in trouble. Ethan the Gentleman was 78 points ahead. Once again, my three-letter words, even when placed on big-ticket spaces, weren't racking up the necessary points to be a slave owner.

The last word of the night was "bedtime," another seven-letter word Ethan played, which won the game.

"I win!" He sounded ecstatic.

"No shit."

"I'll leave a list for you on the table tomorrow." He gloated as he got out of his chair and walked behind mine. Placing his hands on my shoulders, he gave them a gentle squeeze. "Nice game, Rose." He bent down and kissed the top of my head, then went into his room and shut the door.

What was that? Before cleaning up the game, I looked at the words he'd played: excitement, tease, sexual, entice, bedtime. Were these messages? Was I too naive or scared to realize Ethan was inching his way toward the line? Or had I read too many Jackie Collins novels?

As the weeks passed the Scrabble games and the slave-time

redemptions continued. So did kissing good night (on the cheek at first, and then advancing to little pecks between our lips.) One of us was bound to cave, and Ethan, a true competitor, was determined not to be the one. Any indiscretion would leave him responsible for the repercussions. It was up to me to open Pandora's box, and I was petrified.

Then one night in mid-June, during our scrabble-thon, I caught myself staring at Ethan and began sweating. We were millimeters away from "the line," and Ethan must've sensed that things were heating up because he threw me a curve that I wasn't expecting and didn't like.

"Rose, I have this friend, and he's such a great guy. I think the two of you would hit it off."

For the first time since we'd met, I had nothing to say. I pretended to concentrate on my word while Ethan pressed on. "Rose? What do ya think? He's from Florida, too!"

"What's his name?" I asked while taking my turn.

Ethan told me his friend's name was Charles, but he went by his nickname Charlie.

I felt confused and deflated. Why was he trying to pawn me off on his friend? Was it possible I'd been imagining all his flirtatious behavior?

"Sure, why not." I placed the word "coward" on the board and faked a yawn.

The next day while drinking five cups of coffee, I obsessed about the previous evening. Ethan didn't want a serious relationship. But at twenty-four, what did Ethan Schwartz know about what he wanted? If he were playing me, then I'd play along and wear him down until I won.

A few days later he mentioned his friend again.

"You will love Charles." Ethan sounded confident. "He's so nice and has a great sense of humor."

Great sense of humor? Who didn't know that was code for ugly, fat, or having uncontrollable gas?

Calling Ethan's bluff, I agreed to go out with his friend, Charles, the pulmonary intern.

I wasn't expecting much when I met him at 'Mumbles and Mumbles' for a drink. I spotted a guy dressed in jeans and a filthy white sweater, and prayed he wasn't Charles. I hoped it was some other Rose he was looking for when the fashion disaster approached me.

"Yes, I'm Ethan's roommate," I confessed.

"Let's have a seat at the bar," Charles suggested.

"I like standing." I needed to make my get-away as quickly as possible and knew that sitting would only delay me. Charles ordered two glasses of white wine from the bartender and a few moments later our drinks arrived.

"Cheers!" Charles' glass clanged mine. I chugged the wine, thinking of the laundry detergent by same name. My eyes fixated on the dark brown stain on his sweater and wondered if it had ever been washed. The drink went straight to my head and I was buzzed.

"Another?" Charles asked as I put my empty glass on the bar.

Or we could switch to Tequila shots?" His eyes opened wide and for a moment he looked like a Cocker Spaniel in an animal shelter.

Maybe switching to hard liquor would help get through this blind date with Pig Pen. "Why not?"

Charles smiled then asked, "Is it warm in here, or is it me?" Not waiting for my answer he pulled the filth-infested sweater over his head. Before tying it around his waist he shook it, and I half-expected moths to fly out. The sweater disappeared from view while I fixated on the two small hills protruding from underneath his knit jersey shirt.

"Tequila, then?" He waited for my reply but I was too distracted by his man boobs to answer. "Or another wine, Rose?"

I heard my name and snapped to. "Well the truth is*," now that I've seen your breasts, your filthy sweater isn't so bad.* "I just remembered, I have an audition on the Upper West Side in half an hour and gotta get going."

"Oh." The man who needed a bra more than I did hung his head, dejected.

"Sorry, I forgot." The sweater could be washed, but those breasts were a deal breaker. There wasn't enough alcohol on the planet to get past those puppies.

"Another time?" Charles asked.

"Absolutely," I lied again, thanked him for the wine, then left the bar and headed home.

"Charles was gross," I told Ethan as I walked into the apartment still lightheaded and buzzed from the wine.

"You were gone for less than an hour. You didn't even give him a chance." Ethan sounded like my Mom.

"It took me five seconds to be turned off by his filthy clothes."
This was the truth, but the real reason I wasn't interested in any of the
men I met was because they weren't Ethan. I was falling in love with
him and Ethan knew it. The cockier he acted, the more I trailed him
like a puppy.

We locked eyes, and my face felt flush. Perhaps it was the wine
making my legs wobble as I walked away from him and sat down on
the couch. Ethan sat down next to me and rubbed the nape of my neck.

"I'm sorry, Rose. I was hoping you'd like him."

"Well, I didn't." I turned to face him, and the tips of our noses
touched. I was so nervous and felt the same way I did the first time I
jumped off the high-dive board. I knew I was going to do it, and felt my
heart race until the moment I summoned the courage and leapt. As
Ethan's lips touched mine it was unclear who initiated the passionate
kissing, but twenty minutes later it was crystal clear who ended it.

"I hate this thing," Ethan said looking at the phone number on his
beeper. "It's the hospital, and I have to take this Rose. I'm on call."

I felt dazed, sitting on the couch, watching him walk to the phone.
The past half-hour felt like a dream, and I didn't want to wake up. But
the dream was now over, for today anyway, as Ethan got his keys and,
with a simple "Later Rose," left for the hospital.

Chapter 10
Cue The Girl

The next day, I waited all afternoon for Ethan's return from the hospital. Poised on the couch, dressed in my tightest jeans and a low-cut white silk blouse (borrowed from Ce's closet), the minutes dragged on like hours. Finally, around four o'clock, I heard his key in the front door while I pretended to flip through a *Cosmo* magazine and tried to be nonchalant. A moment later, the sound of the door opening sent a shiver up my spine. My face felt flushed, and my heart raced with heated anticipation. I buried my face in the magazine after the door shut, and I heard Ethan's footsteps as he walked into the living room. "Hi." My voice squeaked while I tried to act cool as Ethan breezed by.

"Hey," he said, keeping his eyes glued to the floor while he headed to his bedroom then shut the door.

My heart sank. "I'm such a fool!" I whispered, realizing that a reprise of yesterday's make-out session wasn't on Ethan's agenda. He remained sequestered inside his room while I lingered on the couch and hoped for at least an acknowledgement of what had transpired the previous day.

Forty minutes later, Ethan re-emerged. "I'm off to the library." He walked past me and hid his face behind a tall stack of books he carried between his outstretched arms.

"Oh." All hopes of a love connection disintegrated and I was crushed.

"Rose?" Ethan said after he'd crossed the living room.

"Yes?" I bolted upright. Perhaps I'd given up hope a little too soon. Maybe, he was just taking his time. Or maybe…

"Would ya grab the door for me?"

"Sure." I dragged my feet across the living room floor and opened the door.

"Later, Rose."

Ethan left without a backwards glance. I watched him get into elevator number 2 and heard the faint sounds of the doors closing. "Later Ethan," I said to the empty hallway then slammed the door.

After that afternoon, he was never around. He'd become the

invisible roommate, and any hopes of a romance with Ethan Schwartz faded.

By the end of the month, I was done with men (especially Ethan, and any men referred by him) and focused on my lack of a career. I went to hundreds of casting calls listed in the trade papers (along with thousands of other actors.) Off Broadway didn't want me, so I tried Off Off Broadway productions and never got cast in those, either. (Occasionally, I'd get callbacks for plays located so far off Broadway they were in Staten Island. Or Queens.) Through wind, rain, sleet and hail, I schlepped to auditions feeling empathy for postal workers. At least they were paid for braving the elements. With the subway fares, acting classes, headshots, and missed waitress shifts, pursuing my acting career was costing me a shitload of cash.

The open calls for extra work in films, unlike the try-outs for stage, didn't require an audition, only hours of waiting in line to hand in my headshot.

"Here you go," I'd say to a production assistant while handing her my slightly retouched 8-by-10 photo, which she would throw on top of hundreds of others. Sometimes I'd get lucky. Many films, especially those directed by Woody Alan, used Manhattan and me as a backdrop. I had stepped up from unemployed actor to "extra," working in the background on one film after another.

The first time I earned a part in a film, I was ecstatic and couldn't wait to call Pam.

"I got some work on a Woody Allen film," I told her.

"That's nice." Her voice was low, and she sounded like she had a horrible cold. Or was crying. "Just make sure ya don't talk to Woody Allen unless he talks to you; otherwise you'll get fired." She sniffed.

"Whaddya mean?"

"He's a weirdo. Trust me on this, Rose. I'll call you later, 'cause I'm kinda busy right now." She explained that she was in the middle of a fight with her boyfriend, a podiatrist, and then hung up the phone.

"That's nice?" Pam's response was a letdown. I needed to share my fantastic news with someone who'd be as ecstatic as I was, so I called my mom.

Heather answered the phone. "Mom's not here." She barked.

"Heather, I got a part in a movie!" I should've known better, but the words just slipped out.

"How many lines do ya have?" she snipped, sounding annoyed.

"Uh, well… none… I'm just an extra, and Woody Allen is directing!"

"Who's Woody Allen? How much money are ya gonna make?"

"Not much, but that's not the point."

"You're never gonna be a real actress. Ever. Why don't you give up and just get a real job like everybody else?"

I couldn't answer as my tears welled up and stung my eyes.

"I'll tell Mom you called." I envisioned her smirking on the other end of the phone line and felt a hot tear on my cheek. "Gotta go."

After my tenth extra job, Heather's blasé reaction (minus the bitchiness) became my own. Granted, I was on a roll with getting film gigs. But the roll I was on wasn't soft or delicious like a plump Kaiser available from any Lower East Side deli. My roll was more like a piece of three-day-old stale bread from Mikos. Working as an extra wasn't consistent with my visions of a thriving acting career, let alone stardom.

"Cue the girl," I'd hear the production assistant say while he motioned for me to walk from point A to point B as someone yelled "picture up" followed by "rolling." What next? Maybe I'd be asked to skip, hop or even limp. Nope. Walk. I bet if I had bigger boobs someone would ask me to skip. If I had really, really big boobs, perhaps someone would put me in an aerial harness and fly me across the friggin' bloody set. Director after director appeared oblivious to my immense talent and capabilities. Couldn't they see that sticking me in the background while the stars recited their lines was a complete waste of my dramatic aptitude?

July arrived, and at last I was a member of The Screen Actors Guild.

"That is so great!" Ethan sounded warm and genuine. "I'm happy for you" he said and handed me July's rent check. "Now you're a professional extra."

"Background artist," I said, trying to impress him, even though I knew I was like mobile furniture on the set. Ethan's word "extra" made me feel invisible and insignificant. Ethan having a steady girlfriend added salt to the wound. She was a nurse at the hospital who he'd been dating casually, but then it got serious right after our make-out session. Her name was Judith and she was the reason Ethan was my invisible roommate. Even though I'd never met Nurse Judy, I hated her. Ethan slept at her place every night and never hung out at our apartment anymore. He used his room as a storage unit or a refuge for when they'd fight. That was fine. The less I saw of him, the better, I tried convincing myself. I came to New York City to be an actress and had no time for love.

Fed up with feeling like a robotic piece of meat, I decided to decline all parts without dialogue. I'd been in Manhattan almost a year, and I was through being a professional extra. Absolutely, completely done without exception — until the next call came.

"You'll be playing a secretary," the casting director said. "So whatever you do, Rose, don't wear jeans."

My ears perked up. Playing? "Is it a speaking role?"

"Not this time, but I promise to keep you in mind for anything I think you'd be right for."

We both knew she was lying. But I was broke and jobless 'cause the department of health shut down Mikos after their kitchen failed inspection. My vow to refuse extra work was about to be broken. "Thank you." I took a big bite of my stale pride sandwich and accepted the gig.

Half asleep and chugging coffee, I rode the subway at five-thirty in the morning to the location site. Carole King's lyrics to "Beautiful" resounded in my head as I noticed the other passengers. The crowd on this subway car had never heard that song. There wasn't a smile to be seen anywhere. Would I ever be traveling to a film location via limo instead of on the smelly No. 6 train? Carole's words continued to haunt me. Were people ever going to treat me better? Would I ever feel beautiful?

Yeah, right.

Twenty minutes later, with just one small coffee spill on my shirtsleeve, I checked in with the production assistant.

"Hi, Rose," said the girl, who at first glance looked like a guy. She seemed familiar, and then her flannel plaid shirt jogged my memory.

"Roberta?"

"How ya been?" She glanced up from the piece of paper containing a list of names. The same nondescript hairstyle and expressionless brown eyes confirmed it was she.

"Great," I lied, remembering the hole she'd left in the wall of my apartment, the hole that had never been repaired.

"How's Ce?" Roberta asked.

"Ce? Oh, she's great. She's a shoe model now. And in Japan for the summer."

"Figures," Roberta said in a monotone voice. She gave me a number then directed me to a room full of other women all dressed up for a day of playing secretary at the office.

I filled out the paperwork. Line two: Dependents. Dependents? I couldn't remember what to fill in there, so I just put down my lucky number: 10. I took a few seconds to study my role, which was labeled No. 45.

Familiar with the hurry-up-and-wait routine of the background artist business, I pretended to read a book while checking out the crowd. All types of people were here, and I knew the production company was adhering to the casting rules regarding minorities. We were all represented, the young, the old, the Asian, African-American, Native American Indian, Spanish and a few Jews among the WASPs. We were a big blended family sitting together in a large room with a funny smell. What if there's a gas leak? Or something worse.

"Big deal." Heather's mocking voice drummed inside my head. "Isn't being poisoned just a small price to pay for a second or two of fame?"

I ignored her imaginary comments, and the smell, while my eyes focused on a group of women in their forties instead. "That's never gonna be me," I whispered while I eavesdropped on their game of one-up-man-ship

I heard the overweight, bleached-blond actress pushing fifty claim it was between her and Goldie Hawn for the part in 'Private Benjamin.'

"It was between me and Mary Tyler Moore for the lead in 'Whose Life is it Anyway?'" another wannabe chimed in.

Another nobody touted how she declined a part in "The Shining" because the script was too scary. If these celebrities in their own minds were on the verge of stardom, then what the hell were they doing here? It was moments like these when I missed Ce the most and wondered what time it was in Japan. If she'd been with me, we would've laughed together while trashing these women to bits.

"I'll only accept background work until I'm thirty, and if I'm not a star by then." I'd say.

..."I'll consider leaving New York and going to law school," Ce would've finished my sentence. Now all I had to listen to was the irritating voices of all these wannabes and the memory of my mother's last phone call.

"Rose, you can always come home if New York isn't working out. No one will think you're a failure," Mom said, showing deep confidence in my talents. "If you went to law school, then you could get a real job, with health benefits. Isn't being a lawyer just like acting? You might even meet someone and get married." A husband for me and a son-in-law for her was what she wanted, not a daughter waiting tables and checking coats while chasing a dream. "I deserve some happiness," she'd say, and then remind me that all of her friends' daughters were married. All her friends had well-off sons-in-law and bragged about their grandchildren. "I'll send you Elaine Feldman's wedding announcement, a full-pager in the Sunday Miami Herald."

"Please don't." Elaine and I hadn't spoken in years. And besides, who friggin cared!

"Well, just give law school a thought," Mom persisted; thinking maternal hocking could be effective.

"I'll think about it," was my standard less-than-true closing remark each time I'd hang up the phone, doubt my choices and wonder what was to become of me.

"I need numbers twenty-eight, twenty-nine, and forty-five," Roberta boomed in a loud voice, bringing me back to reality. "Let's go, people, they're ready to shoot the scene." I followed my ex-roommate to an elevator bank.

"Bye, Rose," Roberta said, leaving us all to pile into the middle elevator. I was disappointed that lucky No. 1 hadn't shown up, but settled for the neutrality of No. 2. "Bye Roberta," I yelled back as the elevator doors closed.

We rode up to the fifteenth floor in silence. The short African-American girl in her twenties (No. 28) stared straight ahead while No. 29 (a beautiful Asian woman pushing forty) dug around in her purse. I held my breath then breathed a sigh of relief when the elevator doors opened.

A man holding a walkie-talkie escorted us to the set, which was an office containing three desks. He sprinted out and now the assistant director was in charge. He told the Asian woman to sit behind the first desk and instructed her to type. The African-American girl was picked next and placed behind the third desk.

"Thumb through some papers and look busy," the assistant director told her. "Number forty-five, go sit at the desk in the middle."

I raced over and sat down behind the desk. "What do you want me to do?"

The assistant director thought for a moment. "Say 'Good morning' as Michael passes by your desk."

"You want me to speak?" I asked dumbfounded that fate had at long last twisted its head in my direction.

"Yeah, do ya have a problem with that?" the assistant director asked, then walked away.

Did I have a problem with that? Was he kidding? I was on cloud nine and wished I could call Ethan and tell him the news. Perhaps he'd be so impressed he'd dump the nurse and realize he wanted to be with an aspiring star instead. Now that I had a speaking part on camera, I felt confident my career was on the upswing. A few moments later, still stunned, I rehearsed my line with the assistant director as the other two background artists shot green daggers at me out of their eyes. Their evil glare didn't faze me; it enhanced my performance.

"Good morning," I said, over and over again tilting my head this way and that. Yes, I was ready for my close-up, Mr. De Mille, and had been for years. This was long overdue, and if anyone thought they were going to rain on my parade, they could just forget it! Especially the two ethnically diverse clones sitting behind me.

Ten minutes later, the star of the movie sauntered in. He'd been working out in his Winnebago with his trainer from "Body by Jake." He stubbed out his cigarette as the assistant director told him we'd rehearse once and then yelled "roll tape."

"Scene eighteen, take one and action," I heard as the young star dressed in a suit walked in front of the three desks and stopped for a moment to be greeted by my "Good morning" monologue. The whole experience was surreal, yet it was happening. I was speaking after working in all those films where my acting parts were as silent as Greta Garbo's earliest on-screen appearances. We rehearsed and shot the scene. And then the party was over.

There was a flurry of activity as the director of the movie rushed in. "Sorry I'm late. I had to take a call from the coast," he said in a loud, Brooklyn accent.

"No problem." The assistant director told him. I overheard the AD assure Mr. Director that we'd rehearsed and already had one take in the can. The director looked over in my direction, checking our secretarial pool of three. The star in the suit stepped out for another smoke.

"Who's the girl in the middle? The one wearing the purple jacket?" I thought I was going to faint as Mr. Director pointed at me. Was I being discovered? Was it this easy? I felt my heart pounding, ready to leap out of my chest. I held my breath and eavesdropped some more on the conversation held less than six feet away from my desk.

"She's the secretary who greets Michael when he makes his entrance," answered the assistant director.

I felt the director's eyes staring through me as he said, "Well, she doesn't fit in with the other girls, so replace her, but keep the jacket so we can match the shot."

What happened? I was now starring in a horror film playing inside my head. Doesn't fit in? What did that mean? I sat frozen behind the desk, and pretended as if I hadn't heard the conversation that was audible to everyone on the set. The two other secretaries, with whom I didn't "fit in," wore vicious grins as the assistant director came over and told me there'd been a change in the scene and my acting talents were no longer needed. I was being replaced.

Bewildered and afraid that if I got up out of the chair I'd break just like a piece of fragile glass, I felt tears begin to well up. Somehow I managed to disappear off the set, find the closest bathroom and throw up. Between the tears and the vomit, I wasn't a pretty sight. Maybe law school wasn't such a bad idea after all.

The words to "Beautiful" started playing in my head again. This time I tuned them out and told them to screw off. It took half an hour to gain enough composure to exit the ladies room. Waiting by the bathroom door was the assistant director. Was he waiting for me? Had they changed their minds? Was I being reinstated? I looked like hell, but I could apply fresh make-up and be ready to go back on the set in ten minutes. After all, I was a trooper. My fantasy was abruptly interrupted.

"Uh," the assistant director looked a bit uncomfortable as he asked, "Could we borrow your purple jacket? The director liked the color."

Trance-like, I handed him my jacket so my replacement could wear it — my replacement, who would be saying my line while wearing my jacket. I felt pleasure knowing I'd used the inside of my coat as a large handkerchief to wipe away the tears and clean the vomit that had adorned my face just minutes before. If I was being robbed of my one second of fame, and the thieves wanted to use my jacket, my replacement would just have to deal with it. Of course, I made no mention of this information. To this day, I hate the color purple.

Chapter 11
Back from the Dead Zone

A full week passed before I could pry myself off the couch and return to acting class. Fellow actors told me their own horrific, born to lose showbiz stories, and hearing those tales made me feel a little better.

"I thought they were flying me out to L.A. to go over my contract, not terminate it!" lamented a girl brand new to the class.

"My twin is always cast in commercials, but not me. But, when a casting director needs twins, we never get the job," said Mitch, the guy who'd set up Ce and me on our "Bee" gig.

Mitch was a doll, with well-meaning intentions, but anytime I saw him after that catastrophic experience, I cringed. I was like one of Pavlov's puppies. It took a while before that devastating blip in my acting career faded, but once it did Mitch and I became good friends.

Ce was still in another country (or on another planet) when Mitch and I bonded. I'd called him right after the incident on "A Whisper of Opportunity," and he'd endured my crying marathon. "Those bastards! Replacing you, then using your jacket! Bastards! Don't worry, Rose, they will all rot in hell," he had assured me. "Karma never loses an address."

"Thanks, Mitch," I'd sniffled on the other end of the phone. Mitch was my rock and our friendship inevitable. I was a gay man magnet, after all. I slumped into my chair in the back row of class, which was the designated smoking section, and inhaled deeply from my Marlboro Light 100. In 1981, laws against smoking indoors didn't exist, but we did have designated smoking sections. I listened to my acting guru, Stephan, talk about some book he'd just read, wearing the same blue-and-white-checkered shirt and baggy denim jeans he wore every Tuesday evening. I wondered whether he had a closet full of identical clothing.

I zoned out, not listening to him, until the tone of his voice changed. "Well, look what the rickshaw drove in," he said to someone trying to make an unnoticed, late entrance. All heads turned and stared at Ce, who'd just walked through the door.

"Stephan, you ruined the surprise." She laughed. Our eyes met as she forced a huge smile and stretched out her arms. "Surprise, Rose! I'm back." She'd piled-on the make-up, but I could see the dark circles under her eyes, and her face was gaunt. Even though she sounded full of energy, she looked exhausted.

"Oh my God." Stunned, I squeezed past classmates and ran to hug her. "You're back! When did you...?"

"Five hours ago, and I lost my key to the apartment, so...."

"Do you two wanna get a room?" Stephan's voice dripped with sarcasm. "I so hate interrupting your reunion, but can't this wait till after class?" Just like Ce, he could be prissy at times.

"Sorry, Stephan," Ce apologized and sat down next to me.

Yep, Stephan could be a mean queen.

"You look tired," I whispered. She rolled her eyes and nodded while Stephan shot me a look that spoke volumes. Knowing how pissed off Stephan the Drama Queen of Bank Street got when he was being up staged, I rolled my eyes back at Ce and mouthed, "We'll talk."

A half-hour and one terrible scene later, Stephan announced the class break. Our classmates scrambled around the room while Ce and I remained seated, staring at each other.

"BF," Ce said, wrapping her arms around me. "I missed you so much."

"I missed you, too."

"So did I." Mitch was standing next to us and joined our hug-fest. "Did ya bring me back a kimono?" he joked.

"I couldn't even afford a pair of chopsticks. Japan is so expensive. And Matthew turned out to be such a cheapskate. What a scrooge!"

"Wait, Ce, I've had to pee since the middle of that last scene. I'll be right back. Don't start the story without me." Mitch headed to the bathroom, and without missing a beat, Ce continued.

"How could I have ever thought Matthew was so wonderful? He was so mean to me, Rose! Selfish and cheap." Ce's mouth went into a tight pout as her eyes filled with tears.

"What happened?"

"Can you imagine someone with his kind of money not letting me order room service? And his friends. What a bunch of creeps! I tell you, I'm way over rich men." She took a drag from my cigarette. "And if I see another bowl of rice or raw fish, I think I'll vomit."

Class ended, and we walked to Fourteenth Street to catch the bus.

"He was like friggin' Godzilla! 'You're such a slob,' he told me. Can you believe that? Didn't he know cleaning the hotel room was housekeeping's job? Duh! He was treating me like some geisha! That cheap bastard!" Ce was on a rant and continued venting while we boarded the cross-town bus home. "Can you believe that, Rose?" She dumped some change into the fare box. "Can you?" She repeated while we sat down. I wasn't sure of the correct answer to her rhetorical question, so I did what any good friend would do, I kept quiet, and listened, nodding now and then to show my sympathy.

The bus ride seemed endless as Ce continued her story. "He wouldn't get me an interpreter. 'How will you learn anything if you don't try to figure things out on your own?' that cheap son-of-a-bitch told me. Learn anything? I felt like I was in the twilight zone." With all the people on the bus tuning in as Ce flailed her arms and talked way too loud, I felt like I was in the twilight zone, too. We were like the accident that you just couldn't look away from.

"He wanted everything his way, and he expected me to bow down to him. He wanted to have a three-way with some geisha hostess he'd met at a club. OK, we were wasted on sake, but still, ew, gross!" Ce looked at me with the vulnerability of a five-year-old as her big, blue eyes filled with tears.

"What an asshole." I said.

"Ah soo," said Ce, squinting her eyes, pretending to look Japanese. I laughed out loud. Good old Ce, she'd had a traumatic adventure but hadn't lost her sense of humor. She scrunched her face into a ball as tears poured down her cheeks until her face was drenched.

"Oh, Ce, don't cry." I hunted for a tissue in my purse. Finding nothing except empty cigarette boxes and a pack of gum, I handed her my sweater.

"Thanks, Rose." Ce wiped her tears, and I felt a little guilty about feeling overjoyed that the Far East hadn't been as far out as she'd expected because now the old Ce was back and I was so happy to see her.

As the days passed, the Ce who had chased millionaires and hung out with shoe models while traveling via private jets to Japan was gone. The old Ce had returned, confirmed by the pile of clothes on our floor and the new cigarette burns in the couch.

"I got my old waitress job back," she said a few days later, jumping up and down like she'd just won an Oscar. She'd been home for less than a week, and her experience with Matthew in Japan was already a distant nightmare that she was desperate to forget.

Saturday night we ordered in Chinese and smoked pot. It was just like old times. "Where's Ethan?" she asked in between bites of fried rice.

Ethan. I'd almost managed to obliterate him from my memory, but Ce's question caught me off-guard while buried feelings resurfaced. "He's around." I replied.

"Where? I haven't seen him."

"He's got a girlfriend now. Juuuudith." I tried sounding casual, but Ce picked up on the tone.

"Don't you like her?" Ce chomped off part of an egg roll, then handed it to me.

"I've never met her."

"The way you said her name, it sounds like you hate her."

"That's ridiculous. Why would I hate someone I've never even met?"

"You hated Ashley before you met her."

"That's not true." Of course it was, (and still was) but I jumped to my defense. "I hated her influence on you."

"Oh." Ce took a moment to digest her food and this information. "But you said 'Juuuuuuuudith' the same way you'd say 'Asssssssshlee'."

"I said her name normal. You're just stoned." I closed my eyes and honed my acting skills. "Judith. There." I tried my best to sound neutral but failed.

"There's that tone again." Then after a moment of silence, "Did something happen between you and Ethan?"

"No!" Answering too fast was always a sign of lying, but I couldn't help it.

"Rose?" Ce smirked and raised her left eyebrow.

Was she psychic?

"Yes! Yes, something did happen!" Her mouth bunched up, and her eyes squinted. "Oh, Rose, you slept with him."

"No. I didn't. I swear."

"But *something* happened. It's written all over your face."

My face felt flushed, and I knew I was cornered. "OK, we kissed, a little, but that's it."

"Eeeewwww… you kissed our roommate? His teeth are so gross."

Humiliated, I didn't tell Ce the whole backstory and explained my Ethan encounter with terms she could understand. "We were really stoned."

She nodded and believed my bogus answer, and the subject of Ethan Schwartz was dropped (at least in her mind).

I had Ce to myself for two weeks before I lost her to Walter. She was working on a scene for acting class from "A Streetcar Named Desire," and her scene partner was sexy, adorable and poor. Walter looked like a clean-cut, tall version of Al Pacino, with full lips. Ce spent hours rehearsing with him at our apartment because he didn't have one. He did maintenance work at the Thirteenth Street Theater and in exchange for his services, the owner let him sleep on a cot in the theater lobby. Walter kept his belongings in a cardboard box next to his "bed."

"I've always counted on the kindness of strangers," Ce said, bringing Blanche DuBois to life in our living room. I watched them rehearse and realized that line, written decades ago by Tennessee Williams, applied to both of them. Their artistic connection was electrifying. I never realized, until then, how talented Ce was.

"Stella!" I heard Walter yell night after night. Then one night I heard them both giggling long after they'd finished rehearsing and suspected that they'd become more than just two actors working on a scene for class. The sounds coming from the maroon couch at two in the morning confirmed my suspicion. Character research? Even I wasn't that naïve. Although Stanislavski would've been proud, I knew better.

Two weeks later, Ce and Walter performed their scene in class, and received a standing ovation followed by a rave review from Stephan. The scene was a wrap, and I figured Walter would be history. Once the triumph of success wore off, Ce would realize Walter was poor and homeless, and she'd dump him. Right? However, two weeks later he was still around.

"Is Walter living with us?" I asked Ce after arriving home late one evening from Mikos. Yes, the restaurant had passed the health inspection, was up to code and back in business. After being traumatized by my "Whisper of Opportunity" experience, I was happy to tie my apron around my waist and hide from the movie biz. "Is he living here or not?" I asked again, sounding too much like my mother.

"Sort of," Ce half-smiled.

Walter hanging out in our apartment all the time seemed normal. Until now, it hadn't crossed my mind that perhaps he was there to stay. "Sort of?"

Ce told me Walter was sweetest man she'd ever met. "You know he cries when we make love?"

"Yes, I can hear him."

"I think this is the one, Rose. I think I'm in love." She'd done a complete one-eighty going from riches to rags. Walter didn't have any money or a job. He strummed his guitar at the Fourteenth Street subway station for coins thrown into his open guitar case.

"How can he afford Stephan's class?" I asked.

"He's the class monitor and gets free classes in exchange for taking attendance and cleaning up afterward."

Glancing at the trash strewn around the living room, I suggested that he do that at our place. The apartment was filthy, and another big clean was in order. I'd been hesitant to mention this to Ce, knowing how traumatized she'd been by Japan, but she seemed recovered now.

By the third week of September, Walter had relocated his cardboard box from besides the cot at the theater, next to our living room couch. Ce had a live-in boyfriend, and I had a full-time maid.

Chapter 12
The Aftermath

By September's end, I was no longer happy scraping dried scrambled eggs off my waitress apron. Too many shifts, temperamental cooks and the grim reality of schlepping food sucked. My moments as a film actress had long passed, and the trauma of "A Whisper of Opportunity" had faded. After my brief hiatus, I was more than ready to get back into the acting game.

"I didn't come to New York City to be a waitress!" I walked down Third Avenue after my shift ended and stuffed my apron into my purse. "I'm ready for my close-up," I told the fire hydrant in front of my apartment building, then hurried through the revolving glass doors.

"Hello, Miss Rose," Oscar said as I sped by his concierge desk.

Eager to get home and take a hot shower, I ignored him.

"I'll cut down on my shifts, and go to more auditions," I whispered to the empty lucky elevator No. 1 as the doors closed. "My days of slinging hash are numbered!"

The elevator stopped, and the doors opened. I felt long overdue for a lucky break as Mom's voice sang in my head, "When you least expect it."

I smiled and then opened my front door. The angst of the last half-hour vanished when I saw the new angst seated on the couch: Ethan.

"Hey, Rose," he said.

"Ethan... Hi."

With the exception of a few short pop-in visits, he'd been away all summer. "What are you doing here?" I blurted, plopping my purse on the dining table.

"I live here. Remember?"

"Of course I remember." (Duh) "I'm just surprised to see you."

"Whose box is this?" Ethan asked.

"Walter's." I walked over and sat on the opposite side of the couch and rubbed some ketchup off my hand on the paisley sheet that covered it.

"Walter?" Ethan raised his left eyebrow.

"Ce's boyfriend."

"I thought his name was Matthew."

"Matthew?" I'd almost forgotten him. "Oh, no. He's old news. That was over two months ago," which is ancient history in twenty something years.

"Walter's box has some interesting stuff in it," Ethan smirked. "Funny that I've never met him."

"Well, he's been here and you haven't."

Ever since our make-out session, followed by his instantaneous hookup with Judith, Ethan sightings were few and far between. He looked tired and his hair was longer, but he was still the same old Ethan. The only thing different was how I felt about him. The butterflies that once fluttered in my stomach when he was around were dead.

Ethan lifted the cardboard container, placed it on his lap and pulled out a handful of condoms. He smirked, and then reached back inside. "Handcuffs? Is he a detective?"

"Walter's an actor." I got off the couch and went into the kitchen to grab a can of chocolate Slim Fast.

"Figures." Ethan continued sifting through the box, taking inventory and laundry listing the rest of Walter's worldly possessions. "Aftershave, hairspray, shaving cream, toothpaste, x-lax, a pair of jeans, eight pairs of bikini underwear?" He paused for a second while glancing at Walter's life spread out on our couch. "Is this guy living here or something?"

I returned from the kitchen and stared at the pile of crap strewn about. "Sorta, yeah, I guess he is. He's our maid, too."

"Maid?"

"He's a true artist and doesn't have any money." I explained that, in lieu of his paying rent, Walter cleaned the apartment. Since he'd relocated his belongings and spent all his time here, it seemed a fair arrangement.

"Is that his bird?" Ethan sprang up and strolled over to the birdcage resting on the floor in the corner of the living room.

"Yes."

Ethan crouched down and stared at the bottom of the parakeet's cage. "Who are those pictures of?"

"Ce's ex."

"Marty?"

"*Matthew*.

"Saves on newspaper. Jeez that's one filthy cage." Ethan shook his head, and then stood up. "You should tell your maid to clean it!" Ethan looked around the living room and looked panicked. "Where's Pirate?"

His sudden concern about the feline he'd abandoned for Nurse Judy was comical. "Under the bed. He's afraid of the bird."

The sound of the first of four locks opening on our front door startled us.

"Ethan, come here and help me put this shit back," I whispered.

Ethan took his sweet time and strolled over while I threw all of Walter's crap into the box at rapid speed.

"You forgot these." His tone was arrogant as he dropped a pair of handcuffs in the box, and then slid the cardboard container back into its place next to the couch. Calm, cool and collected, Ethan sat down just as the door opened.

"Hey, Rose." Walter entered, wearing a preppie ensemble. Dressed in a blue blazer, light-blue button-down shirt, dress pants, and loafers he looked vastly different from the usual Walter who cleaned our toilet and scrubbed the bathtub. The sole thing recognizable was his Ray-Ban sunglasses.

"Nice outfit." The fact that he had matching clothes — let alone this getup — shocked me.

"It's a rental." Walter shrugged.

"I'm Ethan. I live here." Ethan said point-blank, remaining seated.

"So do I." Walter and Ethan sized each other up like two alpha males.

"Since when?" Ethan squinted his eyes and scrutinized our maid.

"Officially? Since last month." I interjected.

"Yeah. Hey you must be the doctor dude." Walter knew all about Ethan.

"Yeah, and you're the mai… actor. Rose has been catching me up," Ethan's tone was beyond gruff.

"A *working* actor, starting next week," Walter's attention shifted to me. "I got a contracted part on *One Life to Give.*" His tone was so matter of fact, it sounded as if he were telling me we were out of Windex.

"Oh my God, Walter, that's awesome." I leapt to my feet and hugged him, although I was puzzled by how blasé Walter seemed about getting a steady acting job.

"Well, it's not Broadway, but hey, it's a great payday." Walter, the true artist, believed working in commercials and soap operas was like accepting a job in the Devil's workshop. It was apparent he'd had enough of being poor, cleaning our apartment and living out of a box and had reconsidered his artistic choices. He removed his sunglasses as his eyes cast downward and he studied the cracks in our wooden floors. "I sold out." He shrugged his broad shoulders again and seemed dejected.

"Are you kidding?" Ethan blurted out, his whole demeanor changed, as he jumped off the couch. "*One Life to Give* is the best!" He gave Walter a rough slap on the back. "I always watch it at the hospital."

"Is Ce here?" Walter ignored Ethan and his congrats, then took off his rented clothes, stripping down to his underwear.

"Rose, maybe we should give Walter some privacy," Ethan whispered, and looked uncomfortable.

"Hey, no worries, man," Walter mumbled.

Walter always hung out in his bikini briefs, so I was oblivious, as he stood almost naked in the center of the room.

"It's cool." He grabbed his ripped, bleach-stained jeans and tie-dyed T-shirt from deep inside the cardboard box. Walter smiled at me, and although technically Ethan and I were in his bedroom Walter didn't care.

"Ce's at the restaurant," I told him.

Two minutes later, Walter was dressed and headed for the door. "I'm gonna go tell her about the gig. Nice meeting you," Walter said to Ethan, then left.

"Wow, *One Life to Give*. We're living with a real-live soap star!" Ethan sounded like a groupie while he bounced on the couch and then sat down.

"Yep, it's awesome," I lied, pretending to be happy for Walter. "Awesome!" I repeated while deep inside I wondered why it couldn't have been me. I would've been ecstatic getting cast in a soap opera and he seemed annoyed and depressed. My career would've been jump-started and Walter thought he was selling out! I hadn't had an acting job since the "Whisper of Opportunity," fiasco. Life didn't seem fair.

"Now you can hire a real maid and Walter can pay for it."

I sat down next to Ethan and closed my eyes. "And maybe he can buy us a new couch, too." We shared my Slim Fast in awkward silence and then, just to make conversation, and for no other conscious reason, I asked, "How's Judith?" Truth be told, I was over Ethan. Absence had not made my heart grow fonder of him and my calm steady voice, without a single trace of jealousy or malice, proved it.

"Fine. Yep, she's good, but…" Ethan hesitated.

"But?"

"Well, she's just gotten too serious about our relationship and I think…" Ethan didn't finish his sentence, but the duffle bags he'd stashed in his room did. Judith was out and Ethan was home.

During his temporary relocation, something clicked in my head and turned off my heart. Ethan sensed my indifference and inched closer on the couch. Then his hand was on my thigh. Our eyes met and I felt nothing. "Yep, you'll be seeing a lot more of me now." Ethan gave my thigh a gentle squeeze before he got off the couch and went into his room.

Without warning, my heart skipped a beat. Nurse Ratchet is out; I could be in! It was a random thought, an involuntary response like a knee-jerk at the doctor's office, and not a resurgence of feelings. I had no desire to revisit that area of our past, I told myself. However, I felt the dead butterflies coming back to life as my stomach did a flip-flop and my heart skipped another beat. But I was over him. Wasn't I?

Two weeks after Walter signed his contract to play James Jetling the Third, the soap opera character inhabited his body. He asked me to call him "James."

"Who?"

"James," he repeated. "Or Sir Jetling, if you prefer," he said, as serious as a heart attack.

"Why?"

Sir Jetling explained that it helped him build his character and pranced around the apartment acting like some blue blood. He put on airs and heavy cologne and like magic transformed into the yuppified snob he now portrayed on *One Life to Give*. "Cherry-O," and "Ta-ta" were now part of his lingo, and he (like Ce) spent hours primping in front of the mirror. Walter had forgotten that fourteen days prior he'd been cleaning our toilet.

It was about that time, on a warm Indian summer afternoon, (after his first paycheck arrived) when Walter and Ce sat me between them on our faded and worn maroon couch and attempted to broker a real estate deal.

"So you see, Rose, it's a win-win situation. You won't pay rent, Ce and I take over the big bedroom, and you sleep…" Walter shot Ce a quick glance.

"You sleep on the couch," Ce jumped in, finishing his sentence.

My mind started racing. "Where? Here? On the couch?" The notion of sleeping right next to Ethan's room made me nervous as an unexpected bevy of butterflies resurged inside my stomach. "I don't think it's a good idea."

Ce reminded me how Ethan was at the hospital most of the time and suggested I sleep in his bed when he isn't home. "I'm sure he won't mind." She concluded while flipping her hair over her shoulder.

"He might not mind, but …" I started sweating.

"But what?" Ce snapped at me. Jolting up off the couch, she put her hand on her hip and waited for an explanation. "What's the big deal, Rose?" Ce persisted while her blue eyes bore right through me. "Why not?" She stamped her foot.

"You know," I whispered.

"Know what?" She sounded clueless.

"Ethan and I…" I mouthed.

"Because of Ethan?" She laughed. "Are you kidding me? C'mon, Rose, that was nothing. You were stoned."

Since she viewed people as disposable, how could she understand that kissing Ethan meant more than just smooching with our roommate? I remembered her initial reaction to my news and cringed with embarrassment. "Ew, you kissed him? His teeth are so gross." After that comment, I didn't need anymore of her opinions and kept silent. Even if she knew the depths of my feelings about Ethan, and the details of that afternoon, she still wouldn't understand my trepidation. Ce never looked back at her defunct romances, and she assumed no one else did, either. "When a relationship is over, it's done. It's buried and never revisited." This was the mantra that she'd recited so many times that she almost had me believing it too.

"You're right," I felt defeated. Surely a few butterflies weren't enough to warrant a conversation with her. "You're right," I repeated, even though more of the insects were sure to arrive.

"C'mon, Rose! That was one stinking time. And ew! I still can't believe you even kissed him. His teeth are so disgusting."

Again with the teeth! "He can't help that. It's from tetracycline."

"I don't care who he inherited them from; they are just friggin' horrid."

There was an awkward silence, and then Walter intervened. "Hey, Rose, we're trying to help you with your acting career. If you're serious you can't spend all your time being a waitress at Mikos. You need to get out there. You need to be available for auditions and gigs."

He had a point.

"Walter's right, Rose. You could waitress anywhere!" said Ce, as if that would make me feel better. Then she flung her arm over my shoulder while a victorious smile crossed her face.

"I just..." felt numb and outnumbered. I hung my head down, unable to speak.

Ce reassured me that it was going to be fine, but I knew in my gut that it wasn't. But she always got her way and wasn't backing down and letting this go.

"Why not think about it for a few days?" Walter cranked up the newfound charm he'd acquired on the set of *One Life* and took Ce's hand. "Let's get some air, baby," he mumbled while coaxing her toward the door.

"Yes, let's get ice cream!" Ce squealed. They left and headed for the Carvel on Twenty-third Street while I retrieved a chocolate flying saucer from the freezer.

In a brain freeze moment, I picked up the phone and called my mother. I told her about the new living arrangement Walter and Ce had suggested. My vulnerable state of mind let the words, "I feel kinda hesitant" slip out of a mouth full of ice cream.

"And with good reason!" Mom yelled. "The 'cot boy' moves in, and now *they're* throwing you out of *your* bedroom? Come home, Rose. You can always teach drama at Coral Gables Elementary School."

Why did I mention this news to her? She was too old (fifty-three seemed ancient) to understand how twenty-something's lived here in New York City. I was able to keep my non-relationship with Ethan secret from her all this time. Why did I have to tell her about this? Why was I such a glutton for being trampled on? Me and my big mouth.

A week later, and against my better judgment, I put a plaid sheet down on the couch and called it "home."

The day after I relocated to the living room, Ethan vanished again. On rare occasions, I'd see him pop in out of a corner of my sleep-filled eye. I'd pretend to snooze while watching him traipse across the living room wearing nothing but an old brown, tattered towel. I felt like a voyeur spying on him while he strutted in and out of the bathroom, and I wondered where he'd been sleeping, and with whom.

One morning, I worked up the courage to ask. "Do you have a new girlfriend?"

"Why?" I heard Ethan's smirk in his voice.

"Just curious."

"Curiosity killed the cat," he said.

"You've hardly been here." He didn't answer and headed into his bedroom. "So, where've you been?" I shouted through the thin wall that separated my "bedroom" from his.

"I'm on a different rotation."

"Oh," I said, trying to sound casual. Minutes dragged on like hours as I waited on the couch for his return. "Are you back with Judith?" I asked into thin air.

"Nope, just making the rounds." Coming out of his bedroom, he looked sexy dressed in his green scrubs and Nikes. He flashed me a cocky smile.

"Oh." I whispered and felt the swarm of butterflies play tag inside my stomach.

Ethan combed his hair, checked himself in the living room mirror, then grabbed his cigarettes off the dining table and was gone.

Chapter 13
Careful What You Wish For

The red, orange and yellow leaves that ushered in fall with their glorious brilliance were gone. The temperature had plummeted and I felt the cold November wind whip around the buildings while I went to one audition after another. No longer saddled with the responsibility of rent, I felt a great sense of financial freedom and spent most of my time pounding the pavement. I relinquished all but one of my waitress shifts and went to countless casting calls.

Persistence paid off when I landed a part in an Off Off Broadway play. Hesitant at first 'cause the play was being produced at the Thirteenth Street Theater, on Thirteenth Street: a double whammy of unluckiness. To top it off, the title of the play was "Doom." Yes, the name of the play, in conjunction with its location on the unlucky street numbered thirteen, created a trifecta of fears. I was going to blow off the callback but changed my mind after talking to Ce.

"Are you kidding me, Rose? That is so ridiculous! Not even *I* would come up with such stupid reasons." Once again, the conversation was all about her.

"I didn't ask what you'd do. This is about me, and I thought *you* of all people would understand."

"Understand? About your phobias? I understand about the unlucky elevator, your lucky pen, even the friggin sidewalk cracks, but Rose, this is different. Getting acting jobs is why we came here in the first place. Just let it go already. Besides, Walter used to live there. Remember? And nothing terrible happened to him."

Ce's attention turned away from me and toward the living room mirror. "Just let it friggin go," she said then began her make-up application.

"I wish I could get over my phobias, but it's not that easy." I paused and waited for her to respond. "Ce?"

She'd stopped listening. Once she looked into the mirror, not even a fire alarm could tear her away. Knowing she was lost in Ce Land, I grabbed my headshot and left for the cursed callback.

Two days later, I got the message that I'd been cast. I was elated at first and replayed the message over and over on my answering machine. But the next day my stomach clenched with cautious anticipation while walking up a path covered by decaying leaves and fallen tree branches. "It's an omen," I thought when I saw the dead squirrel, and my fears about the play being jinxed returned tenfold. "Thirteenth Street Theater" read the sign in front of the shabby wooden door where the dead squirrel lay. "Thirteen - another bad sign," I whispered while my hand grasped around the freezing doorknob. "Another bad sign," I repeated while a cold wind slapped me in the face. The temps were in the teens, but I was sweating and my heart raced as thoughts of fleeing bombarded my mind. If it were a dead crow, the absolute symbol of death, I would've punted without a second thought. "It's just a dead squirrel," I justified, then forced myself to open the creaky door and enter the drafty cold hallway leading to a small room adjacent to the theater. I sat down on a wobbly stool between two other girls: a beautiful African American to my left and an Asian gal on my right. I sensed an eerie feeling of deja vu. Diversity casting, I thought, as flashbacks of "A Whisper of Opportunity" replayed inside my head. We sat in silence while the minutes dragged on. Three sets of eyes focused on the decrepit wooden door and waited for the director's arrival. "What am I doing here?" I whispered and counted my eye blinks.

I watched a gray mouse scurry across the floor and disappear under the door. Was that a sign of another born-to-lose experience in progress? The two space heaters positioned at opposite ends of the room didn't make a dent in the cold and I shivered inside my coat. A single florescent bulb hanging from an exposed wire threw off dim light and cast scary shadows on the broken brick walls. I made a mental note to wear thermal underwear and bring a flashlight for the next day's rehearsal.

When the director threw open the same door the mouse had made a getaway under and waltzed in, I fought the overwhelming urge to bolt. He called the rehearsal to order. "I am Osvaldo." He paused as if expecting applause. "Velcome. We have six short veeks 'til opening night, so let's make the most of our time."

He stood in front of us while over-articulating in an effort to conceal his lisp-laden Spanish accent. Draped in a large overflowing black cape, and wearing a black turtleneck, torn jeans and faux black lizard skin boots, Osvaldo, just like my acting teacher Stephan, appeared to love the sound of his own voice. His eyes were the palest shade of blue and never blinked as he stared straight ahead while pontificating. "When I was six years old, my family moved from Barcelona to a small town in Ohio."

I thought, *Who cares*? I stopped listening and resumed counting my eye blinks instead. Forty-five minutes later, Osvaldo was still elaborating about the specifics of his life as I continued to zone out. A change in the rhythm of his voice forced me to snap to.

"I took a cargo plane to New Jork and found this theater." His eyes welled with tears. "Edith was kind enough to grant me a couch to sleep on and…."

I prayed his long-winded spiel with more information than I wanted to know was in wind-up mode and handed him a tissue.

"I am delighted to be on this directorial journey with jou." Tears streamed down his face as he took the tissue, wiped his eyes then blew his nose.

I sighed in relief and thanked God when the history of Osvaldo concluded.

He tilted forward as if ready to take a bow, but decided not to. "Are there any questions before we begin?"

Please, dear God, don't let anyone ask a question! I was curious whether he knew Walter but certain his answer would take another forty-five minutes, so I refrained from asking. It must've been my lucky day because the two other cast members seemed anxious to keep Osvaldo from any more over sharing and kept silent too.

Osvaldo made a sweeping gesture while moving the cape out of his way before sitting backward on the lone metal chair. "Let the game begin, then!"

The read-through took an hour-and-a-half. "Doom" had received a prestigious playwright award, but sounded like it was written by an amateur, avant-garde, Edward Albee wannabe. Worse than the writing of the play was the discussion that followed.

"Ve must not let the darkness of this existential work color our interpretation," Osvaldo began as he sat hunched over in his directors chair.

Color our interpretation? There was nothing to interpret; the play sucked.

"Ve must tread gently and keep it light." He yanked his cape from under his thigh, and then crossed his legs.

"I don't understand what this play is about," Devon (the Asian girl cast as 'Doom Future') was brave and spoke out for us all.

"This is a spiritual journey of hope. Full of faith and love, hidden beneath the masquerade of gloom and doom covering it up," Osvaldo stared at us. Three blank faces stared back.

"Huh?" was all Tanya (the African American gal cast as 'Doom Past') said.

"It's the meaning behind vhat you *don't say* that's important." Osvaldo sounded defensive about the script that was his directorial début. "You girls need to go home and look between the lines for the true meaning of 'Doom.'"

I didn't need to go home to find answers. I knew right there in that freezing room the exact meaning of "Doom." My gut feeling to run for the door continued. Get out while there was still time to escape. But, I ignored it and remained seated on the uncomfortable stool, watching our Batman attired director and listening to more of his batshit.

Devon and Tanya wanted more information and tried asking more questions, but Osvaldo stonewalled them. "Ve'll discuss all of this tomorrow after you've had time to read the play at least three times." A moment later he stood up, gathered his papers then stuffed them into a plastic bag functioning as a folder. "Alrighty then, tomorrow at ten."

He pulled the hood of his cape over his head and flew out the door as if he were running late to catch a train or a ride in his batmobile.

Rehearsals began the next day in the theater. "Is the heat not working in here, either?" My thermal underwear itched, and I felt chilled.

Osvaldo stared past me, and pretended like he hadn't heard me.

"It feels like a meat locker in here," I whispered and looked around the dilapidated 900-square-foot theater for heating vents.

"Edith only turns the heat on for performances," Osvaldo said a few moments later.

"What if all the actors catch pneumonia and can't perform?" Doom Past asked.

"I don't have health insurance." I sneezed.

"Neither do I," the other two dooms said in unison. Osvaldo ignored us while positioning three stools on the empty stage.

"Sorry I'm late." All eyes (except Osvaldo's) focused on the soft-spoken, tall and lanky boy wearing a plaid beret as he entered from backstage. "I got stuck in the train." Disheveled and inaudible, he looked lost in our Twilight Zone.

"I was wondering where the hell you were." Osvaldo stopped arranging the stools and folded his arms. "Put the middle stool a little upstage," Osvaldo told the boy still dressed in his coat. "This is Felix, our stage manager." Our director introduced the frail-looking beret boy.

"Hi," he said hunching his shoulders forward and then jumped onto the stage. Felix placed the stool as Osvaldo walked to the apron of the stage and leapt off. A few moments later he returned and shoved a script into Felix's shaking hands.

"Ve're on page seven," our Marty Scorsese-wannabe director told him.

"Yep. Sure. OK, got it. Places," Felix muttered.

"No one heard you, Felix! From the buns, dear boy, from the buns!" Osvaldo directed.

"Places!" Felix screamed, then left the stage. Removing his coat but leaving his beret on, he slumped into a front-row seat, looking bewildered.

Two weeks into rehearsals, I was still having serious doubts and frequent panic attacks. "This script is so awful! I can't even memorize my lines," I complained to Ce, who'd stopped by Mikos at the end of my one waitress shift. We sat in the back booth smoking cigarettes and waiting for Walter to join us.

"Bummer," Ce said as she chomped on ice from her empty iced-tea glass. "You're not thinking of quitting, are you?" Her eyes opened wide.

"I've thought about it."

"You can't even think about quitting. It's great experience. The play can suck, but you could be outstanding!" Ce ate the leftover lemon slice on the side of the glass.

"Doomed if I do, and doomed if I don't." We were laughing when Walter showed up.

"What's so funny?"

"Life. Life is a goddamn laugh riot," I said.

Walter looked at me with those dark, dreamy bedroom eyes that had seduced Ce and persuaded me to relocate my sleeping quarters to the living room.

"How's the play going?" He slid in the booth next to Ce.

"Oh, it's, ugh, going." I averted his stare by fishing in my purse for another pack of cigarettes.

"Rose is thinking of quitting," Ce blurted out as Walter kissed her neck. "Walter, stop." She giggled. "You're tickling me." Walter ignored her and continued gnawing on her like a vampire. "Walter," Ce was playful and pushed him away while I fixated on the purple blotch he'd left, "tell Rose not to quit the play!"

"What? No way. Didn't you just get the part?" Walter asked in his melodramatic soap opera, America-wants-to know, voice.

"Yeah, but I..."

"I'm hungry." Walter's normal voice returned, the telltale sign he was agitated. And hungry. "Where's the waitress?" He looked around while Ce nuzzled against his arm.

"Tell her not to quit," Ce repeated.

"Yeah, you have to go on, Rose," Walter said half-heartedly while looking around for the waitress. When Walter was hungry, he was cranky, and nothing else mattered. Ce volunteered to go find her and left us alone.

The nasty vibe coming from across the table became unbearable, so I tried small talk to distract Walter from his hunger pangs. "Do you know this guy named Osvaldo?"

"Yeah, I know him." Walter rolled his eyes. "I don't Know, KNOW, the dude." Walter sounded defensive. "He slept on the other couch when I was crashing at the theater." His eyes darted around the restaurant "Where is that friggin waitress?" He focused on me for a split second then asked me how I knew Osvaldo.

"He's directing the play."

"Maybe you should quit."

"Why?"

"The guy's whack."

"Yeah, he's a little out there, but..."

"More than a little. The dude is bat shit crazy."

The waitress appeared and placed what I knew was a basket of three-day-old bread on the table and took Walter's order. Walter devoured two pieces in less than a minute and reached for a third as Ce returned.

"I had to whiz." She slid in the booth next to me and picked up a butter knife. Using the knife as a mirror, she applied lipstick. Walter continued cramming bread into his mouth as if he hadn't eaten in a week.

"I think he owned some movie house in Ohio," Walter said in between gulps.

"Who's from Ohio?" Ce asked, putting the lipstick away and admiring her reflection in the butter knife.

"Osvaldo," Walter said. "They shut down the movie theater 'cause too many people complained about him."

"Why?" Ce and I asked in unison.

"He was a cross-dresser, and I'm guessing the people in that small town couldn't handle it."

Ce started laughing, and I felt more discouraged than ever.

"Fantastic!" Walter said as the food arrived. He finished his hamburger in four large bites while Ce and I picked at his fries.

How could I look at Osvaldo tomorrow without imagining what he'd look like wearing a pink chiffon dress or gold brocade pantsuit? How could I concentrate knowing his secret? I was doomed.

Chapter 14
Light the Lights

"Rose, are you with us?" Osvaldo's voice startled me. "That's the second time you've missed your cue!"

Now that Walter had let the cat out of the bag (rather, the queen out of the closet), it was impossible to look at Osvaldo without wondering whether he was wearing boxers or string bikinis underneath his jeans. Why hadn't I followed my instincts and bailed when I saw the dead squirrel? The familiar mantra of "What next?" returned to haunt me.

"Sorry, I got distracted." I'd become obsessed thinking about Osvaldo's underwear, which made focusing during rehearsals a challenge. "I'm good now."

"We have less than a month until opening night, girls, and missing cues is unacceptable," he lisped.

The next few days of rehearsals were torturous and dragged on. I suspected the other two girls felt like I did. Contrary to most situations shrouded in doom when people sometimes bond and ignore their differences, Tanya and Devon kept their distance.

Tanya was always the first to arrive at the theater. I'd say "Good morning," but she'd never answer. Keeping her head buried in some Sidney Sheldon novel, using the book as a shield, she'd pretend not to hear me. I'd sit two rows behind her, drink my Dunkin' Donuts coffee and wait for the rest of our odd squad to arrive. "She's not a morning person." I'd justified her aloofness, but when she continued ignoring me all day, day after day, I took my head out of the sand and saw her for the rude moody bitch she was. She was all about herself and had a giant chip on her shoulder.

"Run off the changes on page seventeen through twenty," Osvaldo's voice boomed as he paraded into the theater barking orders at poor Felix. "Then give 'em to the girls." Our stage manager trailed behind the big black cape and tried to catch the papers Osvaldo flung into the air.

A few minutes after Batman and Robin's entrance, Devon rushed in, thus completing our circle of doom. "Oh good, I'm not late!" She plopped her pink knapsack on the stage apron, pulled out her script, and immersed herself in the pages. She seemed so focused, so professional, but just like me, she still didn't know her lines.

Same shit, different day. Every day.

But one day the gulf seperating us closed. The three of us were sitting in the back row of the theater sharing some stale pretzels during a break. While food connected us for a moment, Devon asked, "Is this play as bad as I think it is?" Her eyes were as wide as saucers. It was the first time any one of us dared discuss the quality of "Doom."

"No, it's worse. Much worse," I reassured her while munching pretzels, grateful for the chance to commiserate.

Tanya kept silent but listened.

"I'm not inviting anyone to the play. Are you, Rose?" Devon asked.

"My roommates are coming. That's all." The day I was cast, I was impulsive and shared my spectacular news with my entire address book. After the first day of rehearsals I called all those people back and lied that the play had been canceled. But Ce, Walter, and Ethan knew the truth, and keeping them away from opening night was impossible.

"Positions," Felix whispered as we rolled our eyes. I threw the empty pretzel bag on the floor and dragged my feet back to the front of the theater, finding my place on the freezing stage.

The next morning, my alarm hadn't yet sounded, and it was still dark outside when the phone rang.

"Rose?" Even with his hoarseness, I recognized Osvaldo's accent on the other end of the phone. "We are canceling…" (*the play, oh, dear God, it was too good to be true*) "Rehearsals for today and all of next week." It was the third week in November and flu season. The entire cast was sick, except for me.

I was beyond ecstatic being doom-less, even if it was just a short reprieve. I slipped on my lucky gray sweat pants and did a happy dance in my head, but my happy dance didn't last long.

"Roooose," Ce's voice croaked from the bedroom. "I'm siiiick."

"Shit," I whispered.

"Could you go to the drugstore and get me some Robitussin?"

"And some Tylenol, and tissues," Walter's voice echoed, followed by loud coughing.

"Damn." The last thing I wanted to do was play nursemaid but I bundled up and headed for the door like any good little people pleaser would. "Bye!" I yelled into the sick ward.

A week's reprieve from "Doom Ville" was better than good; it was off the charts friggin fantastic. I smiled as I rode lucky elevator number 1 down to the lobby. Once outside I literally ran into my friend Mitch, from acting class.

"Oops. Oh my God, Mitch! I'm so sorry." He lay flat on his back, smiling as he looked up at me.

"Are you alright?" Maybe he had a concussion.

"I'm more than alright. I am sensational!"

Mitch grabbed my extended hand and hoisted himself up.

"What are you doing here?"

"My agent's apartment is a few blocks over, and I had to pick up my contract." Mitch waved a manila envelope in the air. "I'm so excited!" He brushed some dead leaves off his sleeve. "My first film gig!"

"Oh my God, that's great!" Hugs and more cliché congratulatory comments followed. "Let's celebrate!"

"Oh yes, let's!" Arm in arm, we crossed Second Avenue.

I popped in and out of the nearby drugstore, and a moment later we stood in front of the coffee shop. "I'll be back in a minute." I told Mitch.

"Where are you going?"

"I need to bring these meds to my sick roomies." I held up the little brown bag.

"Can't they wait a few minutes? They're not dying, are they?"

He was right. They'd live. And besides, I needed a cup of coffee. Mitch pulled the door open, and we walked into the coffee shop.

"Miss Rose! So good to see you." The waiter who was used to seeing me dressed in a bathrobe and slippers handed us two menus, then sat us in a back booth.

"Tell me more about this movie." I lit a cigarette.

"It's ultra-low-budget, and the filming will take place in Canada." Mitch was vibrating.

"That's fantastic!" I was happy for him.

"It shoots next week." He beamed.

"Congratulations!" Thrilled and overjoyed. "No one deserves it more than you." Except for me.

"Thank you, Rose. That means a lot to me." Mitch reached across the table for my hand.

OK, maybe I was just a little happy for him and a lot jealous. That didn't make me a bad person. Did it?

The waiter brought over two large mugs and left a giant silver coffee pot on the table.

"I'm over the moon about this," Mitch said while filling my cup. "The only bummer is giving my boss at my day job such short notice about leaving. It's just for a week, but still..."

"Don't worry. I'm sure there are plenty of waiters who could cover your shifts."

"I'm not a waiter." A strange indignation filled his voice while he filled his coffee cup.

Since Mitch was an actor, I just assumed he had the same pay-the-rent gig as the rest of us. "You're not?"

"Nope." He sipped his coffee. "I retired from schlepping food two years ago. I, my dear, am a nutritional consultant."

"A what?"

He reached into his coat pocket and handed me his ID badge from work.

"Mitch Panella – N.C.," I read the badge out loud. "Wow, I'm impressed. I didn't know you were a nutritionist!" I handed him back his ID.

"I'm not. I'm a nutritional consultant." He laughed out loud while putting the ID back into his pocket.

"What's the difference?"

"Beats the shit out of me. To tell ya the truth, I'm not a 'real' nutritional consultant, either. Mostly I answer the phones, file papers, fill vitamin orders and run errands for the doctor."

"Is he a 'real' doctor?"

"He says he is."

"And you're a pretend nutritional consultant. Isn't that illegal?"

"Who knows? I don't do anything nutritional. It's more like an acting job; my costume is a white lab coat and a name badge. People think I'm important," Mitch justified. "What a joke! I work five days a week and haul in about six hundred bucks. Cash." In the '80s, that was a small fortune.

The waiter appeared at our table and asked if we were ready to order.

"Oh, we're good with the coffee." Mitch, too excited to eat, answered for both of us. The waiter took our menus and walked away. "Yep, it's a great gig. I do my job and don't ask any questions."

"What kind of questions?"

"Sometimes, the doctor asks me to do some weird-ass errands and well, as much as I'm tempted to know specifics, I just do what I'm told and keep my mouth shut." Mitch tapped a spoon on the edge of the table and changed the subject. "Hey, he lets me leave for a few hours during the day if I have an audition. He never hassles me. Most of the other people who work there are actors, too."

"Sounds like a fun place to work."

Mitch's demeanor grew serious. "Dr. Berber's been great, and I feel bad just leaving him in the lurch. Even for a week. Would you happen to know anyone who's looking for a week of work?"

Adrenalin rushed through my veins as I considered the possibility of hanging up my waitress apron. Even though it was just one shift a week, I was sick of slinging hash at Mikos. Mitch's eyes sparkled. "What about you, Rose? You'd be a great nutritional consultant!" It was as if he'd just read my mind.

"Me?"

"Oh, abso – friggin –lutely!"

Fate had intervened, and I said yes. This random meeting with Mitch while I was "Doom"-free wasn't an accident. It was a sign! The universe was pointing me in another direction and I had to obey or else.

Fifteen minutes later, we hugged outside the restaurant.

"I'll call you later, after I've told the office manager about you." Mitch smiled and I felt reassured. "It will work out great. You'll see." He hugged me again and winked.

I watched him cross the street heading west and couldn't help remembering how he'd stretched the truth about the bee gig. Was this nutritional consultant gig along the same lines as "beedom?" I dismissed the eerie memory of Ce and me standing on street corners dressed as bees freezing our stingers off. I closed my eyes and saw the bee head rolling down the sidewalk, and gasped. I shuddered as my eyes popped open. "No. This is different," I convinced myself as I got a Tums from my purse and chewed it while my head returned to its favorite spot in the sand.

A few hours later, while heating up some Campbell's chicken soup, the phone rang.

"You start Monday!" Mitch sounded ecstatic.

"Start?"

"Yeah."

"Don't I have to meet the office manager and..."

"No worries, Rose. I told Lucinda all about you. It's cool." Mitch's words were hauntingly familiar and I felt dizzy.

"Doesn't she wanna interview me first?"

"Rose, they trust my judgment, and you're in, kiddo! You're in!" Mitch sounded confident. "Besides, they're short-staffed, and if you can't cover the week..." Mitch's confident tone turned to panic.

"Fine, I'll do it. No problem. Don't worry. Go be a film star in Canada." I scribbled down the office address.

"Please be on time, Rose."

"Yes."

"The phone system is a little tricky, but you'll get it. Don't worry if ya disconnect a few people at first."

His forced laugh made me nervous. "Got it." My hands started to cramp, and I fought the sudden urge to hang up the phone.

"And remember, don't ask questions. No matter what."

"Yep, no questions." I hung up and broke out into a cold sweat. What was I getting into?

Chapter 15
Follow the Yellow Brick Road

Monday morning, I walked through the massive dark-green tinted glass doors leading into the waiting room. "Oh my!" Had I just been transported to the Land of Oz? It wasn't just the bright colored rainbows covering the massive walls, or the forest-green doors making me feel like Dorothy. It was the entire décor. The plush, dark-green drapes that billowed to the floor framing the oversized windows and the framed autographed picture of Judy Garland hanging on the wall next to the ladies room door gave me the feeling I wasn't in Manhattan anymore. I peeled off my scarf but remained in my coat just in case I needed to make a quick getaway. The emerald-green velvet couch was soft and comfortable as I sat and waited for Lucinda. Upbeat music filled the room, and a hint of lavender scented the air. Funny, Mitch had never mentioned Dr. Berber's obvious obsession with all things Oz. Perhaps he thought this décor was normal. Whatever. I pulled my poppy-seed muffin from the Dunkin' Donuts bag and nibbled my breakfast and sipped coffee. My left foot tapped to the beat of a syncopated jazz tune when I heard a high-pitch voice call out my name.

"Rose Gardner." The small pass-through window that connected the waiting room to the office opened, and a blond girl poked her head out.

"Yes." I shot up and threw my half-eaten muffin into a nearby trashcan while downing the remaining coffee.

"Lucinda will see you now." The blond woman, clad in a pale-green lab coat with a small but obvious baby bump jutting out, opened the door leading into the office area. More rainbows adorned the walls, and forest animals were painted on the low overhead ceiling.

A tiny, dwarf-sized dark-haired woman emerged from behind a lavender door. "I hope you haven't been waiting long." Lucinda reached up to shake hands.

"I just got here," I lied.

"I'll take your coat." She seemed sweet and smiled while extending her tiny arms.

"Oh, thank you." I removed my coat and placed it in her outstretched arms. It nearly covered her while she scooted over to a closet.

"Ready for the tour?" Her eyes were bright as she led me down a long hallway and I followed behind, careful not to step on the heels of her red patent-leather shoes. "Over here are the six treatment rooms." The six neon-green doors would've seemed odd under different circumstances, however the décor in the waiting room and the front office had prepped me to expect anything.

"The lab is back there, on the left." She pointed to the far end of the corridor. "We do all our own testing right back there. Phyllis!" she screeched, and a young woman wearing a rainbow colored facemask poked her head out. "That's our lab tech."

Phyllis nodded at me, then vanished back into the alcove. "She's backed up today. We've been swamped since Dr. Berber was on Phil Donahue."

"The talk show?"

"Yep, he's promoting his new book." Lucinda sounded like a proud mother.

He writes books? Another thing Mitch neglected to mention.

"And right in back of the lab is the lunch table." Lucinda paused and looked up at me. "I'm sorry, am I going too fast? Do you have any questions?"

Several, but I remembered Mitch's strict warning and shook my head.

We walked back to the front office past the lavender door that she'd come out of earlier.

"What's in there?" I couldn't help myself.

"That's Dr. Berber's office." Her face lit up again while speaking his name as if it were sacred. "His office is off-limits, unless you're invited in." How I wanted to ask her why but adhered to Mitch's warning.

Lucinda's walk was sprite as she unlocked another neon-green door.

"Another treatment room?"

"Oh no." She giggled. "This is where we stock vitamins and other medications. You'll work in here today, Rose. Just fill each vial according to the label." She pointed to the multi-colored bins containing thousands of pills all lined up in perfect order against a rainbow-covered wall.

"Wow!"

She diverted my attention to a second set of bins on the opposite side of the room. After a brief explanation about the color coding of the vials, Lucinda demonstrated what a monkey could do without any problem. "Simple dimple." She smiled. "Tomorrow I'll teach you the phone system."

She left, and I began my first task at my new job as a nutritional consultant. Seated on the little steel chair that was set on four wheels, I rolled myself from one bin to the next. Of course, this wasn't in Mitch's job description, either. And where were all the other actors and models who worked here? Friggin stung again! "It's just for one week," I whispered as I took a vial from the first bin and then rolled across the room to the bin containing the green pills. "One, two, three..." I counted as I started another mindless job as pill filler.

By midweek, I was promoted to answering the phone.

"Good job." Lucinda clapped her child-sized hands. "It takes most folks a few hours to learn this system, but you got it in fifteen minutes. Impressive Rose." She disappeared behind the lavender door, and a few moments later, Dr. Berber walked out. He avoided me and walked into a treatment room.

"Dr. Berber wasn't thrilled about Mitch's sudden departure." Lucinda sounded apologetic. "Although it's just for a week, Dr. Berber gets possessive. Introducing you would've just called more attention to Mitch's absence."

"I understand."

"Sometimes, when he's upset he can be a little... ummm... moody."

My new mantra, "Don't ask," resounded in my head. I didn't care whether I met the mysterious doctor, anyway. Over seven feet tall, he was the largest man I'd ever seen. His towering height and broad stature cast giant ogre-like shadows on the walls. "Don't ask," I repeated to myself while I watched him lurch through the hallways en route to treatment rooms where eager patients awaited.

"Here you go, Rose." The week had whizzed by. On Friday afternoon, Lucinda handed me my paycheck, which I stashed in my pocket. "Thanks for filling in. Have a great weekend." Her smile was infectious and I smiled back.

"You, too." I'd been "Doom"-free for a week and mentally patted myself on the back for working forty hours in a straight job. Before heading home, I made a pit stop into the Judy Garland bathroom and looked at my check. Five hundred and fifty dollars. Oh my God! This was the most money I'd ever seen at one time. Now the strange décor and the peculiar vibe that permeated the office didn't matter, and I felt a weird sadness that today was my last day in the Land of Odd. "I'll fill in for you anytime," I'd tell Mitch. Hell, it was easier than schlepping food at Mikos. I could deal with painted rainbows, a little person, a giant doctor and even a few flying monkeys. Couldn't I? The letdown feeling lingered as I walked through the lobby. Even though it was just filling pill vials and answering the phone, I felt a sense of accomplishment. I walked out the office doors and turned around to take one last look at the large brass plaque on the building: "Dr. Berber, MD." Goodbye, Oz; hello, "Doom."

Chapter 16
The Show Must Go On

"We missed a valuable week of rehearsal," Osvaldo barked when the crew reconvened Monday morning. "We need to work extra-hard now to make up for lost time."

"Extra hard" translated into three more weeks of grueling ten-hour days, working my ass off for free.

Each day seemed like an eternity, and I felt like quitting "Doom," but I'd made the commitment and couldn't bail. During one of Devon's monologues, I zoned out thinking about Dr. Berber's office and realized how much I liked the consistency of a real job. And receiving the nice big paycheck at the end of the week made it sweet. Maybe being an actress wasn't for me anymore.

The morning of opening night arrived. I got to the theater a little after eight and sensed a different vibe. The heat was cranked up and after a few minutes I was suffocating inside my winter coat. "Where is everyone?" I flung my fiber-filled blanket styled coat onto a nearby seat, and then looked around for my cast mates. I saw Osvaldo and Felix huddled in the corner of the theater and overheard them talking with a new person.

"You see it's no complicated." Osvaldo's Spanish accent always slipped out when he was nervous. He was pointing to the ceiling as Felix stood next to him writing a mile a minute on a yellow legal pad.

I overheard the stranger say she understood the lighting board, and how to run the two spots. The guy, (or was it a girl?) was our lighting specialist. "I'm sure I'll get it down after one run through." Something about the voice seemed familiar.

"Here." Felix handed the androgynous person a legal pad and disappeared backstage.

He/She said thank you while Osvaldo patted them on the back.

"No sweat. This will be easy." They seemed confident.

One by one, the other cast members arrived and slumped into the audience seats.

"Settle down, people," Osvaldo shouted to a silent theater. "Felix!" he screeched. Felix came lurking around from backstage. "Introduce

Bobby to our cast, and call places."

"OK," mumbled Felix.

"Must I do everything?" Osvaldo screamed then threw his arms in the air. It was only twenty minutes after eight, and Osvaldo was already keyed up. He had opening-night jitters. "Everything!" He shouted then stormed out of the theater and headed to the bathroom to throw up.

Felix looked like a deer in the headlights when he brought Bobby center stage while Osvaldo's retching echoed throughout the theater. "Um, this is Bobby, and she's running the lights." Felix's soft-spoken, inaudible voice was no match for Osvaldo's loud heaves. "That's Devon." He was shaking like a leaf while nodding toward the apron of the stage. Devon, still trying to learn her lines, didn't look up from her script.

"Tanya." Felix pointed to the second row where Tanya sat eating, drinking, reading and not responding. As usual.

"And that's..." Felix was about to introduce me when Bobby interrupted.

"Rose?" Bobby blurted out, sounding surprised.

"Bert? I mean Roberta?" I thought I needed to throw up, too.

"I'm Bobby now," said my ex-roommate with the powerful fists.

I remained seated, faked a smile and sipped my coffee as "Doom" continued living up to its name. I looked at Roberta dressed in her flannel shirt and knew that seeing her was a bad sign. Very. Whenever our paths crossed, something terrible happened. Screwed again, I thought and added her to my long list of bad omens.

After a grueling eight-hour rehearsal, we took an hour break. Too nervous to eat the peanut butter sandwich I'd bought from home, I chain-smoked instead. Opening night was just minutes away and I was petrified.

"Is it warm in here? Or is it me?" Beads of sweat sparkled on Devon's powdered forehead.

"Edith has the heat cranked up," I said. "It's a sauna. I'm sweating bullets."

"Better than being in a damn meat locker!" Tanya seemed calm and cool as she teased her hair.

Osvaldo appeared backstage wearing a red sequined cape, a face full of make-up and red stiletto heels. How could he walk in those things?

"Break a leg, girls." He gave us a group hug, and my heart raced as

I watched him teeter back and forth in his shoes. Then, maneuvering his way to the door that separated the backstage from the audience, he blew us dramatic air kisses. "We have a full house," he said, as if that were a good thing.

"Places," Felix whispered.

The curtain opened as Tanya, seated center stage, began her six-minute monologue. Spotlights came up on Devon and me, seated on stools at opposite ends of the stage in front of the prosceniums. (The staging, reminiscent of the Greek chorus in "Antigone," would've made Sophocles turn in his grave). Frozen like a statue, I felt sick to my stomach when I peered into the audience and caught a glimpse of Ce, Walter and Ethan in the second row. They were sharing an oversized carton of Milk Duds and a giant bag of popcorn while passing a paper bag back and forth, which I just knew held a beer (or a bottle of tequila). Behind them, sat Osvaldo with what looked like the entire cast of "La Cage aux Folles."

Tanya finished her spiel, and inappropriate laughter erupted from the direction of where my roommates were seated. "Focus," I thought, as the play continued. Although the intermittent laughter was intrusive (as were the occasional "shush" and a few random audience comments) "Doom" was going along without a glitch. I remained in character, even during the stigmata scene when Ethan's unmistakable burst of hysteria caught my attention. I was a trooper and ignored it. I stood in tableau while fake blood poured from my palms, and didn't flinch. I tuned out Osvaldo's "shut ups" and stayed focused while picking up all my cues on time. I remembered all my lines, and was able to block out the sights and sounds of my friends behaving as if they were at a circus. The visual of Osvaldo and his gal pals seated in the third row was also ignored. I was a professional, full-fledged, living-in-the-moment actor, making my theatrical debut on a New York City stage! I smiled inside, feeling on top of my game, and connected to my inner doom-gloom.

All that ended when I smelled the smoke.

Oh my God, I thought, almost forgetting to say my line, which concluded the first act. I exited the stage after the green velvet curtains were drawn, signaling intermission. Polite applause ensued but wasn't audible over the sounds of fire engines.

"Get out, now!" yelled two firefighters rushing around backstage. We didn't waste time asking questions or grabbing our belongings.

"Run for jou life! Run for jou life," we heard Osvaldo shriek from the audience. "The theater is burning."

I grabbed Felix, who looked like he'd gone into shock, and we made a swift getaway out the back door. Tanya and Devon were already outside, crying.

I raced around to the front of the building and ran into an empty lobby wondering where the hell everyone was. I glanced inside the theater and saw the audience still seated. They looked bored as Osvaldo, playbill in one hand and red stilettos in the other, hauled ass screaming as his entourage followed. People thought Osvaldo's hysterics were part of the play. But that changed when thick smoke filled the theater, and audience members began coughing.

"The theater is on fire!" someone screamed and suddenly the aisle was packed as people panicked and pushed their way to the one exit. I stood by the door, scanning the crowd and tried to spot my roommates as people shoved past me.

"This way!" I heard Ethan yell and watched him jumping over seats. Ce hung on to Walter's T-shirt while they played leapfrog over the rows in front of them. Within a few minutes, the audience had made a departure, leaving the theater empty, as more firefighters arrived.

Defective wires connected to the faulty heating system had been the culprits; no wonder Edith never ran the heat. Opening and closing night became one in the same as the New York Fire Department stormed the stage. The plush velvet curtains that had opened forty-five minutes before were now closed permanently on "Doom."

Thank God.

Chapter 17
Would've, Could've, Should've.

If it hadn't been for the fire, I would've been furious with my three so-called friends who laughed like hyenas during my dramatic debut. Instead I felt ecstatic, relieved to be done with "Doom." I'd been a real trooper. I didn't quit the play, and even though I'd almost been burned alive, I felt wonderful.

Three days later, after the thrill of survival subsided, Ce, Walter and Ethan's constant laughter irritated the hell out of me. Ce was the worst offender.

"C'mon, Rose, you told us the play sucked. Why are you so upset?" She was unloading Chinese food, (delivered two hours earlier), out of a large paper bag.

"You guys were supposed to be supporting me!" I reminded her while placing the fried rice next to four soggy egg rolls.

"Oh please, Rose." Ce tried brushing me off then handed me the cashew chicken.

"Why didn't you stop laughing after Osvaldo told you to shut up?"

"You heard that?" Ce's big blue eyes opened wide as she raised her eyebrows and feigned surprise. "I can't believe you could hear anything over all that laughter." She giggled and handed me a large container of wonton soup.

"Shut up!" I'd had enough. "It was my first performance in a real New York City play. It was *my* night!"

"And your point is?" Ce's insensitive indifference infuriated me.

"The play might've sucked, but we worked hard, and you could've used a little self-control." I wanted to dump the soup on her head.

"It wasn't just me. The whole audience was laughing!"

Was that supposed to make me feel better? Ce's face scrunched up while she continued defending herself, but I wasn't listening. If she'd been onstage and I had laughed at her, she'd have never spoken to me again. Didn't Ce realize how hurtful she'd been? She wasn't stupid, although sometimes she was a pro at pretending to be a "duh." Our friendship had seen its ups and downs and now I wondered whether other people's best friends acted like her.

"Oh get over it, already!" Ce used a dismissive tone and gave me some chopsticks. My blood boiled, and I fought a sudden urge to stab her with them. Lucky break for Ce that Ethan came out of the bathroom and she smiled with relief when she saw him.

"Need any help?" Ethan eased over to the table and shoved an egg roll into his mouth while he evaluated the spread.

"Sure." Ce handed him the half-empty paper bag, and he placed the remainder of our Christmas Eve feast on the table.

Ethan was on winter break from the hospital and around the apartment all the time. Sometime between rehearsals and opening/closing night, my romantic thoughts and feelings of lust ended. The butterflies were dead again. We were in pre-hug-and-kiss mode, and I couldn't have been happier to feel absolutely nothing.

"Waaaaaalter!" Ce yelled toward my old bedroom. "Dinner." The three of us stood in the dining area, plastic ware in hand, and waited for the soap star's entrance. "Walter! The food's getting cold!"

Getting? It had arrived two hours ago.

"I'll be out in a minute." Walter was always on "Walter time," and a minute could've meant an hour. My stomach growled while we looked in the direction of the closed bedroom door and waited.

"Oh, let's start without him!" Ce said. Just like Walter, hunger made her irritable. "Who cares if it's Christmas Eve? I don't know what he's doing in there." She pointed to their bedroom. "And I'm starving!" She started piling food on the special red holiday plates with Santa's face in the middle when Walter strolled out of the bedroom.

"Finally," Ce snorted as Walter bypassed the table and headed straight to the large fake poinsettia, serving as our Christmas tree/Chanukah bush. We watched him place three large envelopes underneath our faux tree in the corner of the living room.

"What are those?" Ce's eyes sparkled. She walked to the faux tree and handed off her plate of food to Walter.

"Holiday gifts." He smiled, flashing his newly crowned teeth while taking the plate of food from Ce. "Thanks, Darlin'!"

"Gifts?" Ce wasn't hungry anymore, as gifts always trumped food. "Waalter!" Ce stood on tiptoes, threw her arms around his neck and planted a big smacker on his cheek and almost knocked the overflowing plate of food out of his hands. "What did you get me?"

"You'll have to wait 'til tomorrow," he teased. "Let's eat." Walter walked over to the couch and sat down, but Ce fixated on the gifts.

Ethan and I sat on the floor across from each other and ate in silence. Isn't that what all Jews and one Gentile do on religious holidays? If the ratio were reversed, we'd be getting ready for midnight Mass. If the theater hadn't caught on fire, I'd be onstage.

Ethan kept looking at his watch in between bites of fried rice.

"Going somewhere?" I asked.

Walter stopped wolfing down his food and asked Ethan if he had a hot date.

"No and no." Ethan replied. I couldn't help smile as I watched him try to use his chopsticks to eat fried rice. But then I grimaced when the rice fell off his chopsticks and Ethan, being Ethan, picked the runaway bits off the floor and ate them.

Ce's eyes stayed fixated on the gifts. "C'mon, why can't we open them now?" Walter didn't answer. She picked off an egg roll from his plate, nibbled on it and then sat down on the floor by me. "Rose, you wanna open your present tonight, don't you?"

I was on my fifth spare rib and pretended not to hear her while licking sauce off my fingers.

"Don't you, Rose?" she persisted.

I continued eating and didn't answer.

Ce seemed irritated by my silence and jumped up and ran back to the tree. As she shook, smelled and held the envelopes up to the lamp, trying to see what was inside, she reminded me of the Chelsea back in Miss Dundee's kindergarten class. "Hey, we all got the same thing," she concluded like Columbo. "Oh come on, Waaaaaaalter, pretty please?"

"It's Christmas Eve. You're supposed to wait 'til Christmas morning. Isn't that right, Ethan?" Walter seemed to be counting on Ethan to back him up in his little holiday game of teasing Ce.

"Religion is just a load of crap. A marketing bonanza for the retail industry." Ethan sounded like Scrooge. "What's the big whoop? What does it matter when you open the stupid gifts? Tonight, tomorrow, next Tuesday?" Bah humbug! He wasn't interested in a male bonding moment with Walter and acted as if he had a stethoscope stuck up his ass. I wondered what the hell was bugging him before I remembered I didn't care. A minute later, he disappeared into his room and shut the door. Ce continued nagging Walter, and I tried tuning out her repetitions of "please" and "why not?" while I cleaned up the remnants of our holiday feast. Five minutes later, Ethan emerged from his cave holding a wrapped gift.

"Is that for me?" Ce, filled with way too much holiday spirit, almost knocked Ethan down as she grabbed the gift out his hands.

"This is for Rose." Ethan grabbed the package out of her hands, and Ce shrugged. "Your gifts are…" The doorbell rang, and Ethan, for the first time all evening, smiled. "…Arriving right now." He placed the wrapped package on top of Walter's gifts, and then headed to the door.

"We deliver," announced the stranger on the other side of the door.

Ethan cracked the door and left just enough room for a bony hand, holding a small crumpled brown paper bag. Ethan took the bag and then put some cash into the outsider's hand. The hand disappeared, and Ethan closed and chained the door.

"Happy holidays." Ethan's mood had improved. He smiled and put the bag next to the other gifts.

"I'm sure it's Christmas morning somewhere," Ce whined, running over to see what Ethan placed under our tree. Now it was Ethan's turn to be badgered. "Oh, Ethan, can we pleazzzzzzze open our presents?"

"Well, I don't care, but Walter's mind seems set." Now that Ethan's gift had arrived, he was ready to join Walter's game of egging on Ce.

I looked at the presents under our tiny, wannabe tree and felt guilty. I'd been so consumed with "Doom," that I'd forgotten all about the holidays. I half-smiled at Ethan and said, "Your gifts are… on the way."

"That's right. Rose and I ordered you guys gifts and they should be here soon." Ce piggybacked her lie on top of mine.

"Yeah, sure, along with the second coming," Walter laughed.

"The what?" Ce and I asked.

Walter ignored our question and lit a cigarette. "Look, if you wanna open the gifts now, go for it. Knock yourselves out." Seated on the couch, blowing giant smoke rings into the air he was the epitome of arrogance.

"Oh goody! I love presents. C'mon, Rose." Ce hugged me, forcing me into the holiday spirit. Her exuberance was contagious, and I'd forgotten that an hour earlier I'd contemplated giving her a wonton bath while stabbing her.

Ce took charge and handed Ethan and me the envelopes.

"Let's open 'em at the same time, at the count of three," she instructed. "Ready? One..." Before Ce got to "two," she'd torn open her envelope, and its contents fell to the floor.

"Plane tickets?" Ethan looked confused, holding his opened envelope.

"To Las Vegas?" Saying I was stunned would be an understatement.

"To Las Vegas!" Ce screamed, picking her ticket up off the floor. "Oh my God, Walter! Did you win the lottery?" Ce jumped up and down.

"No." Walter's smugness was so irritating. How could Ce be so enamored with someone who looked in the mirror more than she?

"No? Then how could you afford..."

"By getting a weekly paycheck, my darling." Walter cut Ce off.

When had Walter gotten so arrogant?

"Duh, I meant, oh, Waaaaaaaaaalter! You *know* what I meant!" Ce covered him with kisses as Ethan and I exchanged blank stares.

"Calm down, woman!" Walter peeled Ce off him.

"What's up with this, Walter?" Ethan asked.

"Turns out we're filming some location shots in Vegas, on the strip. The head of production is a buddy of mine and said the condo they rented is empty for three days before we start shooting. He offered it to me. So, I thought, let's all go."

Ethan went into his room and returned with a black appointment book. "When is this happening?"

"The flight's tomorrow at five-ish, and then you guys have to clear out of the condo Sunday. That's when the other people from the show get there."

Ethan checked his book and smiled. "I don't go back to work 'til Tuesday. Count me in."

"Rose, your play got canceled so you can go, too!" Ce answered for me while Walter walked over to our tree and held up the crumpled bag that had been delivered earlier.

"Ethan, buddy, who's this for?" Walter asked.

"You and Ce," Ethan's tone sounded apologetic. Perhaps he felt outshined by Walter's gift.

Ce grabbed Ethan's present from Walter, opened the bag and sniffed. "Jamaican gold. Thank you so much, Ethan. Now, who's got the papers?"

"Do you still have your bong?" Walter asked.

"Somewhere. C'mon, Walter, help me look for it." Ce gripped the bag and headed to the bedroom. Walter followed and closed the bedroom door behind him.

"This is for you, Rose." Ethan took the remaining gift off the table and handed it to me. For the first time in months, our eyes connected.

"Thanks, Ethan." In all the excitement, I'd forgotten about the lone gift still on the table with a card marked "Rose" on it. I took my time opening the gift, carful not to rip the wrapping.

"Uh, thanks, Ethan." I said holding his gift, a hard covered book, called "The Power of Positive Thinking."

"It's a great book." Ethan's eyes met mine again while an uncomfortable silence hung in the air.

"Well... thanks." Why did he give me this? I had no interest in self-help reads and would've preferred something by Sidney Sheldon. I broke our gaze and pretended to look over the table of contents.

"Hey, now you have something to read on the plane!"

"That's right." The plane.

"So ya won't be bored."

"Great." I looked up from my pretend reading and saw Ethan grinning from ear to ear. Perhaps now that he'd seen what a great actress I was he had newfound respect for me. Maybe, just maybe, he saw me in a different way.

"Why do you care how Ethan sees you or what he thinks?" Ce's voice rang in my head.

Oh yeah, I forgot. I didn't care. I was past that. The butterflies were dead (weren't they?) But if that were true, why did the past few minutes feel so wonderful?   "Oh, Ethan, thank you."

I hugged him. It was an innocent, non–butterfly, thank-you hug. Yep, I'd won the battle of loving Ethan, and the dead butterflies proved that.

"Night, Rose." Ethan pushed the hair out of my face and kissed my cheek.

"Night, Ethan." I held up the book as he meandered slowly toward his bedroom. "Thanks."

Ethan lingered in the doorframe, and then turned around and stared at me. The uncomfortable silence returned, but this time it spoke volumes and filled the room. After a minute, Ethan said, "You're welcome, Rose." He hesitated for another minute, and then closed his door.

Walter and Ce never returned from the bedroom. The party was over, and I sat down on the couch and opened his card. "Never give up! Love, Ethan," was scrawled in small, barely legible handwriting on a three-by-five white index card. I felt a familiar flutter of something in my stomach. Probably just gas, I thought while reading Ethan's card again. I don't care, I reminded myself, while re-reading the card over and over and over as my stomach did flip-flops. Even though I remembered how long it took me to get off the emotional hamster wheel of loving him, I now felt a flicker of those old familiar feelings. Memory had no sense of logic, or time. "It's just gas," I said, as I felt my stomach do another flip. Just gas, I tried convincing myself. Just gas, I prayed.

Chapter 18
Viva Las Vegas

We'd been airborne for fifteen minutes when the plane started shaking.

"Oh my God." I grabbed Ethan's arm for dear life. "Are we gonna crash?"

"Relax, Rose." He cradled my hand in his. "It's just a little turbulence." He leaned across me and pulled up the shade on the airplane window. "See all those clouds?"

"Yeah," I fibbed, too nervous to focus.

"When the plane rides over them, the plane shakes."

"Really? We're not gonna crash?"

"I promise." Ethan's hand remained firm, wrapped around mine and felt reassuring. I calmed down about flying, but the butterflies in my stomach made me nervous in other ways. I closed my eyes and sighed. It was crystal clear now that last night's gas theory was wrong.

Two hours into our flight, while I cleaned out my purse and Ethan sat engrossed in a crossword puzzle, I heard banging.

"What's that noise?" I grabbed Ethan's arm again as my purse fell off my lap and onto the floor. "Do you hear that?" Ethan didn't answer. "Where's it coming from?" I stood up, and my eyes darted around the plane. "There it goes again! Where is that noise coming from?" My heart pounded.

"The bathroom," Ethan said. His eyes never left his puzzle. "Sit down, Rose."

Ethan pulled me back into my seat while my I fixated my stare towards the bathroom. "It sounds like someone's stuck in there." I reached up to ring the call button for a flight attendant.

Ethan grabbed my hand in midair. "Don't."

"Why not?" The muffled noises continued.

Ethan smirked, and told me to trust him that they don't want any help. "It's all good." He reassured me.

"How do you know?"

"I've been on this flight before."

"Oh."

"And I've been in *The Mile High Club*, myself."

For a moment, I wasn't sure what the hell he was talking about and then the light bulb turned on in my brain. "Oh!" I'd thought having sex in an airplane bathroom was just an urban myth. Hell, I couldn't even get laid on the ground, so what did I know? The noise subsided, and a young woman emerged from behind the bathroom door. A few moments later, an older, bald man came out of the same lavatory and followed her up the aisle. The sight of their flushed, sweaty faces creeped me out.

Ethan finished his puzzle and closed his eyes while I flipped through the December issue of *Cosmopolitan* magazine. Five minutes later, his head rested on my shoulder and he began to snore. I felt a deep sense of contentment listening to him and watched him sleep.

It wasn't long before the plane started shaking again and felt like it was falling out of the sky. "Ethan!" I shouted.

"Turbulence," Ethan said with his eyes still closed. The violent jerking continued while flight attendants hurried to their seats. I had a death grip on Ethan's hand and continued freaking out.

"Oh my God." Panicked, I felt like I was gonna barf.

"We're not going to crash, Rose." His eyes opened wide. "I swear." He smiled and took my other hand.

The roller coaster sky ride continued for another half-hour and then I felt a drop in altitude.

"Dear God! Ethan we are going down. I can feel the plane…" I dug my nails into his arm and buried my face in his chest.

"We're starting to descend." Ethan laughed while he leaned me back into my seat and tightened my seat belt.

I clenched my teeth and shut my eyes, holding my breath until I felt the wheels of the plane touch down on the tarmac. It wasn't until the plane started its taxi to the gate that I breathed a sigh of relief.

"I told you so." Ethan winked and we deplaned.

We found Walter and Ce inside the airport terminal, situated in front of a slot machine. Traveling first class had its advantages. Ethan and I were not so gifted and flew to Vegas seated in stowage, in the last row, next to the Mile High Club. The trek from the back of the plane into the terminal took almost an hour.

"It's about time," Walter growled, glancing at his watch.

"Looksee Looksee, Rose!" Ce jumped up and down while she held out a fistful of coins. "I'm up two hundred bucks." Her face was beamed.

"Wow, there are slot machines in the airport?"

Ethan smiled. "They have 'em in the bathrooms, too. They're all over this town."

"Wanna sip?" Ce took a cocktail glass off the top of the slot machine and handed me her martini. I took the drink but felt guilty sipping alcohol in the middle of an airport.

"Passenger Williams, please report to the check-in counter at Pan Am," blared a loud voice over the crackling intercom. The airport announcement competed with the loud clinking of coins as they poured out and clanged against steel.

"This place is awesome!" Ce loved airports, especially airports with slot machines.

Ethan asked me to watch his bag while he went to the bathroom, then dropped his small carry-on next to me and wandered off.

"God dammit!" Walter pounded the side of the video poker machine with his fist. "I wanna get outta here."

His overreaction attracted the attention of two middle-aged women who stood nearby. Their eyes widened as they stared at him.

"We have to wait for Ethan," I said.

"Shiiiit." Walter looked at his watch and ran his fingers through his hair.

The two women whispered to each other while they approached Walter. Then, the overweight woman spat out "You're Ja... Ja... James Jetling!"

"Oh my God," screeched her friend in a thick Chicago accent.

"You *are* him, aren't you?" The friend seemed a little less sure of their star sighting and reached into her handbag to retrieve rhinestone eyeglasses.

"James Jetling the Third," Walter confirmed.

The star-struck, middle-aged women acted like they'd stumbled across the Messiah. Walter gave them his autograph as Ethan returned from the bathroom. We watched Walter pose for a picture and then he looked around to see whether any other fans wanted to meet his starnass.

"Let's go." Ce rolled her eyes. "C'mon, I wanna get outta here already." Her joyous mood vanished. "Waaalter, I'm tiiired," she whined. Was she jealous of Walter's notoriety?

Walter hugged both women and flashed his cosmetically enhanced smile as the two groupies giggled like teenagers and left.

We walked through the airport and looked for an exit while Walter looked around and strutted like he was hoping he'd be recognized again. (He wasn't.) We got into a cab, and twenty minutes later arrived at the condo.

"Wait here," Walter said. He opened the door and got out with Ethan. I watched through the backseat windshield while the guys unloaded our bags from the trunk and walked toward the building.

Ce had been silent during the cab ride. "Walter thinks he's such a star," she snorted.

"Well, Walter is a star, Ce."

"It's just a stupid part on a dumb soap opera," she snipped while fishing for a cigarette in her oversized purse.

"That counts."

"Whatever." Ce took out her last cigarette and threw the empty crumpled pack on the floor. "It's not like he's in the movies." She lit up and took a deep drag off of her cigarette. "It's not like he's Richard Gere, for God's sake."

"No one is like Richard Gere, but Walter is, well he's kinda a star." Why couldn't she be proud of him? I was, and I didn't even like him.

"Yeah, in his own mind." We shared her last smoke in silence until the guys returned a few minutes later.

"To the strip," Walter said in an English accent and hopped into the front seat next to the driver.

"Cherry-friggin-Oh," Ce muttered as Ethan climbed into the back and sat next to me. He slammed the door shut, and the cab sped away.

It wasn't long before we hit an endless sea of bright neon lights. "Oh goody, goody we're here." Ce had gotten a second wind and was recovered from her bad mood. Thank God.

"This OK?" the driver asked, pulling up next to a casino.

"Sure." Walter paid the cabbie, and we got out.

"What's going on?" I asked Ethan as I saw mobs of people on the street and cramming the sidewalks.

"It's Vegas, baby!" Ethan put his arm around me, and a chill went up my spine. "C'mon, Rose, let's get something to eat. I'm starving." He hugged me tight and then guided me around the three bums lying in the middle of the sidewalk.

"Looks like Manhattan." I giggled and tried convincing myself that it was a friendly hold Ethan had on me while we weaved in and out of tourists while Walter and Ce lagged behind. I might've told myself that Ethan was just acting like a brother, but my butterflies didn't buy it.

I did a double take as six Osvaldo look-alikes strutted ahead of us. "Are those men or women?" I yelled to Ce over my shoulder.

Ce yelled back, but I couldn't hear her over the noise. Ethan and I continued walking and stopped in front of a huge building that looked like a circus tent.

"What is this place? Is it a circus?" My Coral Gables bumpkin was showing.

"No, silly, it's a casino." He laughed.

I stared at the large building shaped like a circus tent, named 'Circus Circus,' but it wasn't one. "Hmmm... too bad. I love the circus."

Somehow, Ce and Walter had long since disappeared into the crowd. Ethan assured me they hadn't been abducted and that they were gambling. "We're in Vegas, remember?" Besides, they already ate on the plane," Ethan reminded me while I heard one of our stomachs growl.

"They served cordon bleu on fine china," Walter had told us during the cab ride from the airport.

"Yeah, they always use fine china in first class," Ce interjected.

"And crème brulee for dessert," Walter added

Ethan and I hadn't touched the disgusting food offered in coach and we were beyond starving.

We left the circus-style casino, walked a few more blocks, and then turned a corner.

"Do you know where you're going?" The lights were less bright on this off-the-beaten-path side street.

"Absolutely." Ethan led the way and smiled as we entered the glitziest dump I'd ever seen. "Seymours. I love this place."

Really? Seymour's was old and dinghy, and smelled like mildew. The multi-colored neon lights that flashed on and off were dizzying. Maybe their illumination did exude a certain charm for an all-night, all-you-can-eat, $3.99 buffet, but they gave me a headache.

"Here ya go, Rose." Ethan handed me a white ceramic plate and then piled food on his own platter from the buffet line. I walked behind him, wary of the multiple trays of mixed concoctions and took some cantaloupe and raisins. I didn't wanna risk getting food poisoning on my first night in Vegas.

A few minutes later, Ethan left the buffet line and headed toward a table in the back, near the kitchen door.

I joined him a few moments later but he was too mesmerized his food to notice me. "Oh baby! Come to papa." He said to his veal chop. Then he picked up a piece of greasy fried chicken with his fingers and looked me squarely in the face. "Ya want a bite, Rose?" He dangled the breast in front of me.

"Uh, no thanks."

I was silent and watched him consume the massive quantity of food in less than fifteen minutes. "Isn't this place amazing?" Ethan grabbed a fork and dug into a mountain of Mac 'n cheese.

"Amazing!" I echoed and picked at my cantaloupe.

"Oh, Rose, you have to taste this!" He stuck a forkful of bright colored yellow crap two inches away from my mouth.

"Uh, no thanks." I waved his hand away and felt nauseated. Ethan might've had a cast-iron stomach, but the funky smell coming from his plate made just breathing difficult. "I'm good,"

We never found Walter and Ce as we meandered the Vegas Strip after leaving Seymour's. It was the wee hours of the morning when we walked through the door at the condo and heard our roommates inside their bedroom, arguing. As we reached the living room their quarrelling ended with an abrupt "Fuck you" from Ce.

Ethan and I looked at each other and I felt a familiar flutter, as we awkwardly stood three feet apart, not quite sure how to end the evening. After a few minutes of silence, Ethan took a step toward me.

"Nite," he whispered and half-smiled. He took another step and then stopped as if he'd hit a brick wall. "See ya tomorrow" he whispered while his eyes stared at the floor before he turned around and headed to the upstairs bedroom.

I cursed my butterflies and found my room downstairs next to Ce and Walter's. I thought about putting on my nightgown but felt too exhausted. So I climbed, fully dressed into the full-size bed with the bright red comforter and fell fast asleep.

Chapter 19
Girls' Night Out

The next day, I dragged myself into the living room at four in the afternoon. Between the time change (it was three hours earlier in Vegas than in New York) and all the previous night's excitement, I was discombobulated and could've slept for days.

However, Ce would have none of that.

"You can sleep when you're dead." She tossed her hair over her shoulders and looked at herself in the mirror.

"Is Walter still sleeping?" Exhausted, I lay down on the couch.

"No. He and Ethan took off about a half-hour ago." Ce brushed her hair and posed, watching her reflection from the corner of her eye.

"Where'd they go?"

Ce explained that Ethan wanted to show Walter Fremont Street."

"Where's that?"

"In 'Old Las Vegas.'"

My eyes hurt, and I felt jet lagged, but I ignored all those signs telling me to go back to bed. "Are we meeting them?"

Ce yelled a resounding, "Hell no," while checking out her stomach, or lack thereof.

"Why not?" Whether I liked it or not, the butterflies were back.

"Why do ya think they built all these beautiful *new* casinos, Rose?"

Old, new, what the hell was the difference? All of Las Vegas was new to me.

"Why do you think they built all these fabulous new hotels?"

Was this a quiz?

"Because Old Las Vegas sucks." Ce spun around and faced me.

"Isn't Vegas just Vegas?" I'd never even seen a casino before last night.

"Well it's not!" Ce lit a cigarette then snarled she wouldn't be caught dead on Fremont Street.

"Why?"

"It's full of sleazy people. Bums, hookers, strip and tittie bars. The streets reek of urine."

"Sounds like where we were last night." Manhattan had its share of vagrants, too, downtown in the bowery. Countless cardboard boxes doubled as residences. Shopping carts functioned as closets. The homeless blended into the fabric of the city and were a normal part of Manhattan. But in Vegas, against the backdrop of neon lights, the homeless stuck out like a sore thumb. "Ya mean Fremont Street is worse than 'New Vegas'?"

Ce assured me it was ten times sleazier.

How was that possible? "Then why would Ethan take Walter there?"

"They're guys, Rose," she snipped in a nasty tone.

"Oh." What the hell was bothering her?

"Guys like that stuff." She flicked her ashes on the floor. "Besides, Walter is getting on my nerves. I'm glad he's not here now."

My eyes burned, and I considered going back to my room and sleeping the rest of the day away, but I knew that wasn't an option. Instead, I rested my head on the couch and closed my eyes. I'd almost drifted off to sleep when I heard crying. "Ce." She didn't answer. I heard another sob and bolted upright. "Ce?"

"Oh, Rose, why couldn't it be *me* on the soap opera?" She was lying in the middle of the kitchenette floor, sobbing.

I jumped off the couch and stood next to her as she curled into a fetal position.

"It's not fair!" she wailed while tears dripped off her chin. "I should be the one giving autographs. I should be filming on location here in Vegas, not him."

I grabbed some paper towels off the kitchen counter. "It's not fair!" Her voice was hoarse and she sounded like a five-year old who'd lost her favorite doll.

"Here" I handed her a paper towel with my right hand and coaxed her upright with the other. I lit a cigarette, then sat down beside her on the cold, avocado-green, linoleum floor.

Her shoulders slumped as she wadded up the paper towel and wiped her eyes. She blew her nose several times and wept while I sat silently, supplying her with Bounty. "Thanks, Rose." she murmured "I'm soooooo glad you're here. I'm so lucky you're my best friend." Her crying ceased for a moment, and I'd hoped she'd finished. Then her eyes became glassy again and the next round of tears began. "I'm sooo glad you're here," she repeated.

"Me too." Not. I wasn't glad or happy to be sitting next to her during her cry-fest, handing her towel after towel until the roll was empty.

If it hadn't been for the knock on the front door, God only knows how long I would've sat on that sticky floor enabling Ce to dwell in her misery.

Through the peephole I saw a man chewing gum and holding a large box. "FTD," said the voice on the other side of the door.

I used caution and cracked opened the door. After signing for the delivery, the messenger boy pushed a large box through the narrow door space and then left. "This is for you," I told Ce while I shut and locked the door.

Her recovery was instantaneous. She jumped up, grabbed the long box out of my hands and ripped it open.

"Oh my goodness! Roses!"

Oh, the healing powers of flowers.

Ce placed the box on the kitchen counter and read the card out loud. "You are my forever star." She smiled and looked at me. "He still loves me." She sounded surprised.

"Of course he still loves you."

Her confession followed. "I said some nasty things to him. I told him…"

"Yeah, I heard you guys when we came back last night."

"Did ya hear me remind him how he used to clean our toilet?" Ce giggled.

"I missed that one. Yep, that's pretty low."

"And he *still* loves me." Ce smelled the red roses, bundled and held together with a plastic tie.

Wonder of wonders, her misery was gone.

I scoured the kitchen cabinets, looking for something to put them in.

"Ain't love grand, Rose?"

How would I know? I found a giant pitcher stashed in the back of the top kitchen shelf and filled it with sink water.

Ce's left eye twitched while she handed me the flowers and one by one I counted them out loud. "One, two, three, four…" Her tic was a telltale sign that she had something up her sleeve. Or that she was lying. "Twenty-four." I put the last rose in the vase and stood for a moment, admiring the flowers and wishing someone had sent them to me instead.

Her twitch ceased and she seemed recovered while suggesting a special girls' night out.

"What kind of girls' night out?"

"It's a surprise!" That was Ce code for 'I haven't got a clue, but I'm working on it.' "Go shower."

An hour later, we walked out of the condo and stepped into Ce's surprise: an oversized white stretch limousine.

"Oh my God!" Shocked, I climbed into the backseat of a car that I'd only seen in the movies. "This is so amazing." I smiled at Ce while the driver closed the doors.

"Here." Ce handed me a pair of dark, oversized sunglasses. "Put these on."

"Why?"

"So no one recognizes us." We giggled, and I felt like a celebrity behind my Foster Grants while riding in a limo with tinted windows. Ten minutes later, we arrived at the entrance of Caesars Palace.

The driver opened my door. "Madame." He extended his white-gloved hand, and I felt like I was going to a movie premiere.

"Thank you!" Once outside the limo, the enormous casino dwarfed me back into a Coral Gables bumpkin. I removed my movie starlit glasses and waited for Ce as she paid the driver.

"Ready?" She stood beside me a few moments later and reapplied her red lipstick while I stared at all the bright lights. Then I reached into my handbag and pulled out ten singles. "Here, Ce. Take this to help pay for our ride."

Ce waved my money away and laughed. "No worries, Rose, tonight is on Walter" she said, then flashed an American Express card in the air. "Viva Las Vegas!" Ce said, and stashed the lipstick, sunglasses and Walter's credit card into her small rhinestone clutch. "Let's go." She headed toward the casino, and I tried to keep up with her breakneck pace, but my size eight feet stuffed into her size six black stilettos slowed me down.

"Hurry up," she yelled while I trailed behind her and watched her walk into Caesars Palace like she owned the place.

Chapter 20
What Are the Chances?

Heads turned as we approached the roulette table. No doubt they were all looking at Ce. Dressed in hot-pink leather pants, a matching sleeveless leather vest and stiletto heels dyed the exact color as her ensemble, she looked like a model on the cover of "Welcome to Vegas" magazine - or a hooker. If ever I felt self-conscious and insecure, it was at that moment. Once again, she was a Rolls Royce and I was my father's Oldsmobile. I stuffed my insecurities down into my borrowed dress. "You know how to play this game?" I asked.

"I know how to play *every* game," Ce piped up as a drunk, middle-aged guy sporting a full set of hair plugs sidled beside her.

"How yous doin,' Blondie?" he slurred.

Ce was calm and cool and told him to drift. He shrugged his shoulders and walked away.

"Ya gotta be direct with these creeps!" Ce spoke as if she were teaching a course in casino etiquette.

"Color me," she told the croupier and handed him a hundred dollar bill while I stood behind her feeling awkward. I caught a stranger sizing me up and down and to my surprise, I liked it. Maybe dressed in one of Ce's too-tight micro-mini black dresses advanced me to mid-sized, luxury car status instead of my fathers Oldsmobile. If only Ethan could see me now. I watched Ce as she put chips on several numbers etched into the green felt that covered the lined table. I heard the dealer call for all bets down, as a little ball spun 'round and 'round on a large black-and-red numbered wheel. Just as the little ball bounced from number ten to thirty-one, I heard a familiar laugh. I looked across the table, and standing at the other end was our long, lost roommate.

"Pam!" I screamed.

"Rose? Oh my God, Roooooose!" she screamed back.

Ce's eyes never left the wheel and then she cheered as the ball of fortune landed on zero.

"Oh my God," we yelled while I ran toward Pam as fast as Ce's painted-on dress allowed. We squeezed each other tight and jumped up and down acting like over-excited five-year-olds.

"What are the odds?" Pam screeched.

"I can't believe it," I screeched back. She looked chic, dressed in a black satin jumpsuit accessorized with a white shimmering shawl that matched her Gucci purse and shoes. "Ce's here, too!" I said, after several more exchanges of "Oh my God!" and "This is so amazing!"

"Ce's here? Where?" Pam's eyes darted around the casino.

"Over there." I pointed toward the far end of the roulette table. Just then, a loud round of cheers exploded.

Pam squinted her eyes, trying to find her in the crowd.

"Right there. Where all the noise is coming from."

"I can't see her."

"She's there, at the end, next to the wheel. That guy keeps blocking her from view. She's there. I can hear her." Ce's whistles were unmistakable.

Once more, Pam's eyes scanned the table. "Nope, don't see her." She shook her head and gave me another hug. "I'm so happy to see you, Rose."

We'd lost complete touch. I'd called her several times but to no avail. Feeling frustrated by a recording assuring me her number was disconnected I'd given up trying to find her and hoped that one day she'd call me. Back in the 1980's there wasn't FACEBOOK and Big Brother might be peeking, but wasn't always watching.

I'd exhausted all available resources and it seemed as if she'd fallen off the face of the earth. But now here she was. What *were* the chances?

"Oh my God! Pam!" Ce's voiced pierced through the crowd. She'd no doubt seen Pam out of her peripheral vision but didn't make a move to leave the game. "Paaaaaaaaam!" she screamed, while throwing chips all over the table. "I'll be there in a sec." She waved. "Ooohh, c'mon number ten," Ce roared as the little silver ball spun into motion.

Pam covered her ears and told me she couldn't stand the noise.

"There's a little bar at the other end of the casino." I suggested.

"Yeah, let's go there. My ears are ringing from this racket."

"I'll be right back." I walked over to the far end of the table and found Ce seated next to the creep with the hair plugs, whom she'd told to drift a half-hour earlier. "C'mon, you can come back later." I tugged at the back of her pink vest in a futile attempt to pry her away from the game.

"I'll lose my spot." Ce wasn't budging.

After three minutes of trying to persuade her to join us, I gave up. "We'll be in the bar," I said and walked away.

"Oh my God. I'm up five thou," Ce yelled at my back. "I'll be there when I... " Ce stopped talking midsentence while the croupier called for final bets.

"Feel like it." Pam finished Ce's unspoken thought. "Same old Ce."

"Yep, same ole Ce."

Pam frowned and shook her head again. "Seems she's *too* busy for me." Her voice dripped with sarcasm.

I looked at her and thought, what's wrong with *her* legs? She could've walked over to the table but didn't. Then I remembered. It had been a year since Pam left but seemed like yesterday. I recalled all the tension between them during our roommate days and me always being in the middle of their emotional tug-of-war. The more I remembered our history as roomies, the more Pam not taking a single step in the direction of the roulette table made sense. She wasn't going to be the one to initiate their reunion. After all, Ce symbolized the competition, (the other actress) and their rivalry would remain. It was the Ce of Manhattan who made Pam's move to L.A. an easy decision.

Ce's choice to stay planted at the roulette table wasn't a shocker, either. Thinking Ce would ever forgive Pam for stealing that job away from her in college was delusional. She still mentioned it and would hold that grudge until she died. And how many times had I heard her mantra: "If I can't be a movie star, then I want to marry a millionaire?" Ce hadn't scored either but still wanted to be rich. Playing roulette with the money she'd advanced from Walter's American Express was too good an opportunity to pass up.

"Ce, what if you lose? Walter will be soo..."

Ce told me she needs money to make money, and assured me she wasn't going to lose. So there she sat, determined to win millions while Pam and I hovered in the background.

"Oh, who cares?" Pam laughed.

"Who cares?" We linked arms and walked through the casino looking for the bar. For a moment it felt like when we walked home together from Mikos along Third Avenue after one of my waitress shifts, back in the good old days.

The bar walls were covered with maroon velvet and reminded me of our DNA couch. The leather booths that lined the back area were black. Unlike the bright lights in the casino, the lighting inside the bar was dim. I almost fell when I didn't see the step leading down into the booth. Wearing Ce's stilettos didn't help as I stumbled, but caught the end of the booth before face planting on the floor.

"Here?" I asked Pam, before I took off the shoes and caught my breath.

Pam nodded and we sat down across from each other. Five minutes later we were sharing a carafe of white wine. Again, I felt like we were back in New York, sitting in a booth at Mikos.

"I called you a million times," I told her.

"I moved." Pam seemed guarded as she traced the rim of her wine glass with her index finger and stared down at the table. The feeling of being grounded in the good old days vanished and I felt like I was sitting with a complete stranger.

"Why did ya move?" I tried reading Pam's face. It used to be like a well-marked map, but tonight she wore a poker face.

"Do you still live in L.A.?" I pressed, more curious than ever about her disappearing act.

Pam shook her head and sipped her wine.

"No?" I waited for her to continue, but she didn't. "Why'd ya leave L.A.?" I took a sip of my wine and waited for her to say something. After a few minutes, she spoke.

"I couldn't stand it anymore." Her eyes met mine, and I could see a little bit of the old Pam still in there.

"I've heard L.A. can be pretty weird." I finished my first glass of wine and poured another.

"I didn't just leave L.A.; I left showbiz." She downed the rest of her wine and looked away from me. "The empty promises, the lies, the constant struggle. It was just too much disappointment."

"*How* did you leave?" I wanted to know her exit strategy in case I, for real, got into showbiz and wanted to leave, too.

"I cut up my union cards, moved out of Los Angeles and got a job as a receptionist in admissions at Paradise Valley Hospital," Pam said in complete monotone.

"Valley Hospital? Where is that?"

"San Diego."

"You live in San Diego?"

Pam explained that she lived near the big city. She decided to make a clean break with all things show business. She shook her head and sighed. Pam might've left the business, but she still had the drama going on.

"Why didn't you call? Let me know where you went?" None of what she was saying made sense.

Pam squirmed a little and looked uncomfortable. A long silence hung between us before she spoke again. "I cut ties with all my theater friends." Her eyes met mine.

"What does that mean, 'cut ties?'" Was that her way of letting me know she'd dumped me?

"I did a kind of twelve-step program." Pam gave a long-winded explanation about the concept of Alcoholics Anonymous. Then she said, "I applied those principles to change my life." A long pause ensued. "I'm a recovering thespian."

"Oh." I felt hurt. I'd always thought we were more than just theater friends.

As if reading my thoughts, she said, "Of course, we're more than theater friends." She smiled as a tear rolled down her cheek. "I just needed to sort things out."

I forced a smile. "Well, cheers to your recovery and your new life." I raised my glass to hers. It was apparent a new-fangled Pam sat across the table from me. I felt saddened by how much she'd changed. "Have you met any doctors at the hospital?" If any subject would bring back the Pam I knew, that would.

"I'm not into doctors anymore," Pam answered a little too casual for me to believe her.

Who was this woman? This shocked me more than her news about being a recovering thespian. "Is that part of your twelve-step deal?"

"Kind of. Not really. I'm just over them. That's all." My fear that the old Pam was forever gone was now confirmed. "They're such assholes. All of them." She emptied the last bit of wine in the carafe into her glass.

Yep, Pam had changed, in an extremely scary, Stepford-friend kind of way.

"The one good thing that came from dating all those jerks was my realization that if all those idiots could become doctors, then so could I!"

Who *is* this person?

"Yep, I applied to medical school and I start in the fall."

This was way too much information on just a single carafe of wine. I signaled the waitress just as Ce waltzed into the bar. Plugs, the guy she'd sat next to at the roulette table, the same guy she'd initially told to drift, trailed behind her.

"I am sooo sorry, Pam." Ce hugged her while she slid into the booth beside her. Pam was stiff and didn't return the embrace.

"Who's your friend?" She asked, noticing Plugs ten feet away.

"Oh that's Lucky."

"Lucky?" Pam repeated.

"Yeh, Lucky." Ce confirmed. Then, "Can ya believe that's his real name?"

I stifled a laugh and watched Pam rolling her eyes while Ce beckoned him over.

The stranger came closer to our booth and sat down next to me.

"Lucky?" I blurted.

"That's my name. What's yous, doll face? " The middle-aged, short, stocky guy with obvious hair plugs stared at my chest. Lucky looked anything but lucky; like a reject from a "Godfather" movie, his thick New Jersey accent didn't help. Neither did the stench of alcohol that surrounded him. "Dom Perignon OK for yous?"

Ce giggled and said, "Oh yes, please."

"You got dat?" he asked the waitress, who now stood at our booth. She nodded and walked back to the bar. "How yous guys doing?"

Neither Pam nor I were in any mood for small talk with Lucky or any other stray that Ce might've befriended. We remained silent.

Ce told Lucky we needed to have some girl time, and promised she'd catch up with him later. She batted her eyes and as quickly as Ce had called him over, she now brushed him off, but not before getting his credit card to pay for the champagne.

"You can bring it back to da roulette table later," Plugs told Ce while handing her his MasterCard. Lucky's right shoulder twitched while he winked at Ce then left.

"Isn't that the guy you told to drift?" I asked.

"He's a nice boy," Ce said defensively.

Boy? He looked older than my father.

"You can't always judge a book by its cover," she said self-righteously, then changed the subject. "Oh my God, what are you doing here Pam?"

"Business. My boyfriend's attending a convention, and I came with…"

"Oh, a medical convention?" Ce blurted out and lit up a cig.

"No. I'm over doctors."

"Huh?" Ce's cigarette almost fell out of her mouth.

"I've dated enough doctors to know they all suck." Pam's eyes squinted, and her nostrils flared. "They want to be with you when it's convenient for them; on their time schedule."

"No more doctors?" Ce was having a hard time processing this info.

"I got sick of being on call. They striiiiiing you along, then dump you when you get too close." Pam's eyes started tearing. Ethan's face flashed in front of me.

"Oh," Ce said.

"Then when they're ready to commit to a serious relationship it's the bimbo who's around who gets to be the doctor's wife."

"Well what kind of convention, then?" Ce asked.

"A plumbers convention." The sparkle returned to Pam's voice and she smiled.

"Excuse me?" Ce gasped.

Pam spent the next fifteen minutes telling us all about her boyfriend, the plumber.

Ce stared at our former roomie in disbelief.

"And he's so loving and kind. He is Mr. Wonderful!" Pam gushed. "And so generous. Check out this bracelet he found in someone's sink drain." She showed off the sparkling diamond bangle next to her Cartier watch.

Ce wanted to know if he'd given her the watch too and spun it around on Pam's small wrist.

"Yep, he found that in a toilet." Ce pulled her hand away and mouthed "Gross" at me.

It was evident from Pam's smile how proud she was of her jewelry collection and of her boyfriend, the plumber. She looked at the face of her expensive, diamond-encrusted toilet treasure and with Meryl Streep flair, announced: "Oh my God, I can't believe it's so late. I was supposed to meet Jonathan a half-hour ago… I gotta go." Pam pulled her shawl around her and stood up. "Goodbye, my friends," she said dramatically and made her exit.

Ce and I stood up, and the three of us hugged. For another brief moment, it felt like we were all back in our apartment.

"Goodbye, Pam," I said and continued our hug long after Ce sat down and reapplied her lipstick.

"Bye-bye, Rose," Pam said, then turned on her Gucci heels and left.

Ce and I looked at each other in amazement.

"Wow." I sat down, still stunned that I'd run into her.

"Wow!" Ce parroted. "Can you believe that watch?"

Chapter 21
The Date?

The next afternoon, Ethan was sprawled out on the couch when I stumbled into the living room. "Hey, Rose." His voice rasped while his eyes remained glued on the television, as he scarfed down Cracker Jacks.

"Where's Ce?" I walked into the kitchenette and poured some luke-warm coffee into a chipped mug. I lit a cigarette and wondered whether Ethan had heard me. "Ethan?"

"Oh yeah, here you go, Rose." Ethan's eyes remained fixated on the screen as he stretched his arm over the back of the couch and handed me a post-it.

'Went to Reno', the note began. 'Don't know when we'll be back, so don't wait for us. Love, Ce. P.S. We may get married. Just kidding (I think).' It was obvious she didn't tell Walter about her extended use of his American Express card and all the money she'd lost. She was off on yet another Ce-capade.

"I guess we're on our own." I sipped my coffee and smoked a cigarette. Breakfast of champions.

Ethan muted the television, turned around and swung his bare arms over the back of the sofa. "It's our last night in Vegas. Let's do it up right." Our eyes locked.

What was his definition of right?

"Pick a casino. We'll have dinner and see a show. Whadda ya think, Rose?" His eyes bore through me before he refocused his full attention on the TV and upped the volume.

The only casino I knew was Caesars Palace, thanks to Ce. "Great. I love Caesars." Ethan shouted over 'The Price is Right.'

I walked over to the couch and sat down. Ethan handed me the half-eaten box of Cracker Jacks in exchange for my cigarette. "Great," he repeated and smiled.

The butterflies in my stomach amped up into full gear. 'Dinner and a show' repeated inside my mind as I nibbled a handful of caramel-coated corn. 'Dinner and a show.' Was this a real date? The possibilities of what could happen on an actual date with Ethan Schwartz were exhilarating!

"Doctor's are all creeps. They string you along and then dump you." Pam's words haunted me, and fear reared its ugly head and turned off the butterflies' engines.

"Shut up," I whispered, then left Ethan and Bob Barker alone in the living room. "Shut up," I repeated as I headed to the bathroom for a long soak in the tub.

Three hours later, bathed, coiffed and dressed in the previous night's Casino attire, I entered the living room.

"You are smokin'." Ethan wolf-whistled.

I almost whistled back when I saw him. He looked sizzling dressed in skin-tight black leather pants, black turtleneck, off-white leather jacket and black lizard boots. He'd put some gel in his hair and looked more like a punk-rock star than a medical student.

I took a deep breath. "Ready?"

"You betcha. But first," he handed me a shot glass. "A toast. To Vegas." We clinked glasses.

"To Vegas," I repeated, and downed the shot, feeling it burn the back of my throat.

He poured himself another and began refilling my shot glass.

"I'm good." I told him, but he was insistent. Already light-headed from the first shot, what difference would another make? Besides, Ethan had already refilled my glass and I didn't want to be a party-pooper. "Cheers," I said then downed the second drink.

I might've been a little tipsy from the tequila, but I was aware of Ethan's hand gripping my thigh in the backseat of the cab. The ride seemed shorter than with Ce the previous night and before I knew it we were at Caesars. Ethan tipped the driver twenty bucks and caught me before I fell on my face while exiting the cab. Damn shoes!

"Allow me." Ethan stood me upright, and we walked arm in arm through the entrance of the mother of all casinos. I felt the Vegas vibe, a feverish energy that never dulled. Ethan was on an adrenalin high as he strutted his stuff. Looking like Mr. Las Vegas, he walked through the massive doors into the casino lobby. I was startled when he stopped short and engulfed me in his arms.

"C'mon, be my lady luck." He cupped my face in his hands, and his piercing steel-gray-blue eyes bore through me. It was at that moment I jumped back on the hamster wheel and knew I was doomed to love him forever. I'd never ever be happy with being just friends.

"Over there!" he pointed into the gaming area then griped my left hand and sped up his pace. "Rose, walk faster," he shouted above the noise while pulling me behind him. "There's only one seat left." Ethan let go of my hand and made a beeline to the single available spot at the blackjack table. He sat down between two bleached blond transvestites, and I felt invisible as Ethan handed the dealer a thousand dollar bill. I stood behind him and peered over his shoulder and heard my stomach growl. I'd not eaten anything since the Cracker Jacks, except the lime in the tequila.

"Busted," the dealer said five times in a row. Each win was celebrated with shots of Patron, the Rolls Royce of tequila. I felt ready to barf. Ethan seemed unaffected by the alcohol and kept drinking and winning.

"I'm going to the bathroom," I told him. He didn't turn around and acknowledge me because his eyes were fixated on the ace sitting on top of the dealer's card. I heard the croupier say "Insurance," while he waved his hand over the table. "Ethan, I'll be back in a few minutes." I watched the back of his head nod then zigzagged across the floor into the ladies room. The room was spinning and I soon knew why casino bathrooms had couches. They were for sleeping on post vomiting. The cool faux leather soothed my sweaty face as I lay down and passed out.

"Rose? Rose Gardner?" I felt someone shaking my shoulder.

All of a sudden, I was stone cold sober and looked up at the stranger who knew my name.

"Is your name Rose?"

I nodded my head, still wondering how this woman knew me. Where the hell was I? And how the hell did I get where I was?

"Your boyfriend is looking for you. He's outside the door."

Boyfriend? What door?

The stranger in the silver sequined mini-dress raised her eyebrows and gave me a concerned look. She asked if I was okay.

Was I? I didn't know.

"C'mon, Sleeping Beauty. He's worried about you." She helped me sit up, and I realized I'd passed out.

"I'm fine."

She nodded and left while I wobbled a bit then stood up and walked over to the large ornate mirror in front of me. I fluffed my hair and rinsed my mouth with the Listerine sitting on the counter top next to the black and gold marble sink. I'd gotten my second wind, and my pace quickened as I left the ladies room, ready for more casino action. Ethan was leaning against a huge column and rushed over when he saw me.

He grabbed me by my shoulders. "Rose, I've been looooking all ooover for you! Are you OK?" he slurred.

"I'm fine."

"You were goone sooo long. You never shudda leff."

Ethan was sloshed.

"You're my lucky charm, Rooose. Dooonchaaa ever leave meeeeeee again, Rosie. Ever."

Very sloshed.

"I started loooooosing after you left." His eyes looked bloodshot.

"Everything?"

"Almost, but I passed the 'Wheeeeel of Fortune' on my way to fiiiind you and... voooooooila." Ethan flashed a stack of hundred dollar bills. "Let's bloooow this joint." He took my hand, and we headed out of the casino to find a cab.

Once inside the cab, I told the driver the address while Ethan drew me into him. The cab sped off as Ethan's mouth found mine. We devoured each other with a passion I'd never experienced.

"We're here," a strange voice said ten minutes later. The driver had stopped the cab, opened the passenger door and was waiting for us to get out.

Ethan handed him a fifty-dollar bill. "Keeep the change."

Once outside the condo door, he fumbled with the key.

"Give it to me. I'll do it." I put the key into the lock as Ethan pressed his body against my back and cupped my breasts from behind.

"There." I opened the door and almost fell down as Ethan bit the back of my shoulder. Somehow, Ethan managed to take my dress off while he slammed the door shut with his foot. By the time we reached the couch, I was braless, and Ethan was stark naked. In a frantic frenzy we fell onto the couch and most definitely crossed the line past "just friends."

Afterward, I was silently nestled inside Ethan's arms, wondering whether I'd dreamt the last hour of the evening. I was afraid to speak 'cause if this was a dream I didn't wanna wake up. Besides, hadn't we said enough already?

I heard him whisper my name over and over while he pursed his lips against the back of my neck and we spooned in each other's arms. "Rooose." His voice was low and soft as he repeated my name several times. He ran his finger from the nape of my neck along my spine and rested his hand on my lower back. His movements were slower now, more controlled, as he slid on top of me and touched my face with his. My entire body trembled as I felt an intense physical and emotional connection lying beneath him. Somehow our souls had united in an alternate universe.

"I looove you, Rose." Ethan whispered. "Myyyyy Rose." He rocked me gently.

How I wanted to believe him. "You're drunk."

"I knoow, but I still loooooove you."

I wanted to tell him I loved him, too, as he stroked my hair. I wanted to say I've loved you since our first innocent hug while our faces pressed together and I felt your breath on my neck. I almost told him that I would love him forever but held back, terrified that if I said the words out loud I'd jinx everything. And so I remained silent.

Chapter 22
The Crash

I'd ignored my gut feeling and gotten sucked into an alternate universe where pigs could fly and Ethan realized he loved me. What transpired between us stayed in Vegas, trapped within the walls of condominium No. 1211.

Even before our plane lifted off the tarmac, Ethan began backpedaling. "Cheers." He forced a tight-lipped smile while he opened the silver flask he'd brought on board and took a swig. "Rosie... Rosie...." Ethan drinking at ten-thirty in the morning was the first red flag. Still a little drunk from the previous night, he slouched in his seat and dropped his arm over mine on the armrest. "Are you nervous about flying?"

"Not right now. We haven't taken off yet. Are *you*?"

"Me? Nervous about flying?" He forced a laugh and then stared out the window, focusing on luggage being loaded onto the plane. "You know, Rose, we were both very, very, very, drunk last night," he spoke at a deliberate slow speed, and never took his eyes off the window.

"One of us still is." The second red flag shot up as the safety video came on and the cabin doors were locked and secured. All the fibers of my being wanted to run off the plane, but it was too late.

"The point is..." He turned away from the window and looked down at the floor.

"What?" Both flags flapped in the breeze while my heart sank, and I waited for him to confirm my worst fear.

Ethan paused for what seemed like an eternity. His eyes looked up from the floor and past me into the aisle. "The point is that I do love you, Rose."

My heart raced as I hung on to a final thread of hope like a life raft.

"But I can't love you the way you want me to."

"Why?" I asked feeling ready to barf.

"Because I like you too much and would hurt you too much if we..." He stopped talking mid sentence and stared down at his feet.

"If we what?" I couldn't bear the endless pause that spoke volumes.

"Continued." Ethan whispered, his eyes still glued on the floor.

"Continued? Loving each other?" The plane rolled back from the gangplank as the wormhole leading to that alternate universe where Ethan and I had spent the night as soul mates closed forever.

"Screwing each other." His voice was low and I couldn't hear him. But I didn't need to because his body language said it all. He couldn't see my eyes well up as he stared at the back of the seat in front of him. The plane turned and headed toward the runway and I envisioned him spread eagle, chained to the tarmac in harms way. After two minutes of unbearable silence, Ethan spelled out what I'd known but denied all along. He took another swig from his flask. "I can't screw people I like and respect or care about." His eyes pierced through mine.

"Why?"

He hung his head, and repeated, "I don't know" several times. His eyes fixated on the floor as tears dripped down my face.

"Was that all just a lot of crap you said last night? The standard bullshit men say while screwing women?" My voice cracked as I fought back more tears. Ethan was my first, and without previous experience in pillow talk, I believed that his "I love yous" were genuine.

Our eyes met. "I DO love you Rose. I just can't love you full time. The way you deserve to be loved."

"Why?"

"I have no interest in being in a serious relationship, or getting married. Ever." There was another horrible pause as the plane gained speed on the runway, but I was too stunned from the pain of Ethan's words to remember to be afraid. Just as the wheels of the plane left the ground, Ethan said, "You knew that," as if I'd tricked him into bed. As if it were my fault he'd confessed deep feelings for me.

Just eight hours before he'd whispered, "I've loved you since the first time we played Scrabble," while I'd lain in his arms. "I can't believe we've waited so long to be with each other," he'd said. Had I imagined him telling me that we were soul mates? I'd worn him down and got through his emotional armor and now I was paying the price.

My body was being pushed into the seat as the plane climbed higher and higher and for the first time in my life I was comforted by the weight. Without the g-forces holding me down, I was afraid I'd shatter into a thousand pieces and be sucked up into the plane's air-conditioning system. After several minutes, the plane reached cruising altitude, and the pressure ceased. Rather than fall into pieces, as I'd feared, rage held me together.

"You bastard." My light-headedness vanished long enough for me to get up and walk to the back of the plane. I found an empty seat and collapsed.

"Asshole," I heard some woman say.

"Yeah, what a jerk! Better off without him, honey," said another. It was apparent that our voices carried past our row. I had been duped again, this time thirty thousand feet in the air, with a small audience to boot.

Ethan walked to the back of the plane and crouched down in the aisle next to me. "I knew this would happen, Rose."

I ignored him.

"Why can't we just go back to the way we were?" Ethan hated being ignored. "Why can't we be just friends?"

I stared straight ahead in a semi-catatonic state and pretended to be deaf.

"Rose? Rose!" Ethan shook my shoulder.

A flight attendant approached us and asked if everything was okay?

"No, everything is not OK. Everything sucks. But thanks for asking." I answered.

The flight attendant blinked her eyes several times, and seemed stunned.

"This man is bothering me," I told her in a monotone voice.

"Where is your seat, sir?" She glared at Ethan.

"Rose." Ethan ignored her.

The flight attendant asked to see Ethan's boarding pass and tapped her foot.

He slid into the empty seat across the aisle from me. "Oh, yeah, my seat is here." He told her with cocky arrogance.

"No. His seat is up there." I pointed toward the front of the plane. After a few more minutes of stonewalling him, and at the flight attendant's insistence, he left.

I turned the overhead vents to full-blast and the cold air hit my face, helping my rapid breathing return to normal. My body stopped shaking, and I felt steady enough to reach into my purse and grab a cigarette.

The flight attendant who had escorted Ethan back to his seat stood in the aisle, offering me her lighter.

I lit my smoke and returned her Bic while she placed a plastic cup of wine on the tray in front of me.

"It's on the house." She smiled.

"Thank you." She disappeared up the aisle as I nursed my wine and dragged on my smoke. I closed my eyes, and visions of the previous night paraded through my head.

When the plane started descending into La Guardia, I'd scrutinized each microsecond of my love tryst with Ethan Schwartz and never noticed the turbulence. Normally I would've feared for my life but my head pounded and I was too consumed with regret to worry about the plane crashing; all the while, hoping and praying it would. I was in a complete grief-stricken stupor while I thrusted forward as the wheels touched the tarmac. Once the seat-belt sign turned off, people scrambled for their belongings and began exiting. I waited 'til the plane was empty before I stood and reached for my suitcase.

"Here, let me help you with that." The kind flight attendant that had given me the free wine pulled my suitcase from the overhead storage bin.

"Thanks." I mustered a smile. She carried the case up the aisle as an unspoken camaraderie passed between us.

"Good luck, honey," she said, handing off the case.

"Thanks. I'll need it."

I walked through the airport as fast as I could, lugging, and half dragging, my suitcase by a well-worn handle. The walk seemed endless as my eyes focused on the concrete floor. I prayed I wouldn't run into Ethan. When I passed through the doors leading outside to the cabstand, the freezing air hit my face like a brick. A cold shiver went down my spine when I spotted Ethan at the front of the line. His back was to me, but I knew it was Ethan as I stood a dozen feet away and heard his loud laughing.

"Of course! Radiology! That's where I know you from," Ethan told the tall blond woman with whom he was flirting.

My face blazed. I felt nauseous and dizzy. I'd heard enough. I did an immediate about-face and walked right back inside the terminal. The empty chair by the luggage carousel became my refuge as I plopped down watching the bags tumble through the chute and circle 'round and 'round on the conveyer belt.

'I don't want a serious relationship,' he'd told me on the plane and didn't waste a second proving his point. How could I have been so stupid? 'You knew that, Rose, and slept with me anyway.' I put my hands over my ears as if that could drown out our conversation. I sat motionless for a long time before my head cleared for a moment and I knew without a doubt that I couldn't be Ethan's roommate anymore. Or friend. Or anything.

After what seemed like hours, I joined the long line of people waiting for cabs. Wet snow was falling and the line was slow but I didn't care. The man in front of me kept checking his watch and seemed impatient but I wasn't in a rush to get home.

A large yellow and black cab pulled up and stopped at the curb. "Cab? Hey, lady?"

I nodded my head and the driver got out and stowed my suitcase in the trunk as I took my time getting into his cab.

"Manhattan," I told the cabbie while I settled into the backseat of the large checker.

"Happy holidays," the driver's voice quipped over the music that blared from his tape deck.

I'd forgotten New Year's Eve was the next day. Under normal circumstance, I'd have pages of resolutions on hand: stay on diet, stop smoking, become a star... the usual. This year I made a single resolution, and vowed to keep it.

No more Ethan Schwartz. I'll tell him "You need to pack your stuff, take your cat and relocate. Just get the hell out of my life! I can't be your friend."

"What, miss?" The cabbie turned his music down and looked at me through his rearview mirror.

How loud was I talking? "Oh, nothing." I spent the rest of the ride obsessing in silence. Seeing Ethan with that woman drove his point to my core and I was seething. Paradoxically, the rage I felt calmed me as I sat in the back of the cab and structured a plan to resolve my horrible situation. The calmness soon ended and my stomach did flip-flops as the cab drew closer to my apartment building.

"Happy New Year," the driver said again after he brought my suitcase into the building and placed it by the elevator bank. Happy friggin New Year. Right. I paid the fare and waited for the lucky elevator, which never arrived.

"All the elevators are shut down for repair, except number three," the doorman shouted across the empty lobby. Figures. I pulled my bag inside the unlucky elevator and held my breath until I reached my floor.

Light streamed from underneath the door. Had Ethan beat me home? I unlocked the door and walked inside. Pirate, who usually hid, sat in a corner by the dining room table.

"Meow," his head tilted as he rubbed his fur against the front of my legs. I put down my purse and picked up Ethan's cat.

"Your father's an asshole." Pirate jumped out of my arms. Just like his father, he hated being held. I reached into my purse to grab a cig and noticed a single key lying on top of a piece of paper... and I knew. I raced to Ethan's room and found his door open and all his stuff gone.

"Oh my God!" I felt blindsided as I looked at the stripped-down bed and empty room. I knew we'd never end up happily ever after, but never thought he'd take his stuff and leave. "No, no, no!" The scenario I'd devised in the cab ride home had me in charge of his departure and included, one more heated argument and perhaps some great good-bye forever sex. Instead, there was a note left under his key.

'It's for the best.' I read his cold words a hundred times and the trauma I'd experienced on the plane returned tenfold. I sat down on the floor in the corner of the dining room where Pirate had been situated when I arrived, and started crying.

"It's not fair!" Pirate, sensing my pain, came out from under the couch and crouched in front of me.

"I wanted to be the one to give him the boot," I stroked Ethan's cat and cried. "I wanted to throw his ass out!" Pirate's eye opened wide, and he curled up in my lap and purred. "It can be our little secret that I didn't."

Chapter 23
The Burn

A quote by Mother Theresa popped into my head. "I have found the paradox that if I love until it hurts, then there is no hurt, but only more love." Bullshit. I guess Mother T. never had a roommate like Ethan. If she had, her words might've been: "Loving may cause isolation, depression and pain." I walked into his room and smelled a hint of Aramis cologne while another quote filtered through my brain: "The truth shall set you free." Really? Knowing the truth did not set me free. Knowing the truth sucked.

I held Pirate while circling the bare room in slow motion. Every trace of Ethan Schwartz was gone except an old athletic sock scrunched into a ball next to the nightstand. "How the hell did he pack up so fast?" Pirate looked at me like I had four heads. "Where'd he go?" I circled the room several more times until I felt dizzy and then squatted down in the doorframe and stared at the hole in the wall.

He probably shared a cab with that blond bimbo from the cab line. I could just hear him: "I just need to make a quick pit stop."

"Meow," Pirate agreed with me.

"Oh, no prob, I can help you," she had volunteered. I visualized the two of them grabbing all his clothes from the dresser, leaving the drawers half-open. I could picture him giving the room a final once-over to make sure he left nothing behind.

"Wait Bimbo," I imagined him telling the girl, whose name he didn't know. "I almost forgot!" Then he'd gathered his baseball caps and videos, all neatly stashed on his nightstand. "OK, that's it... let's blow this pop stand." I bet they'd made a quick, clean sweep of it as if the apartment were on fire. She must've offered to share her bed with him, too, and without hesitation Ethan accepted. "Great, I was gonna check into a hotel, but..." And in my visualization he stared at her the same way he'd often looked at me with those steel-gray eyes piercing through her and...

"Stop!" I shouted and stood up as Pirate leaped out of my arms, leaving a long scratch while he ran for cover under the couch. "No more Ethan Schwartz!" I wished I had the strength to punch another hole next to the one already there.

I needed Ce, even though she'd play judge and juror when I told her the truth about Ethan. "Oh my God Rose, Oh good lord!" she'd repeat several dozen times while shaking her head. Her judgmental comments would make me feel ashamed but she was the one person I felt comfortable pouring my heart out to.

When Ce arrived home three days later, she had her own news to share.

"Can you believe I'm married?" She glowed as she stared at her three-carat cubic zirconium.

"Yep." My eyes avoided hers as I stared at a ball of cat hair clumped on the floor. The last thing I felt like talking about was her nuptials.

"Really?" She frowned and looked disappointed that her news wasn't earth shattering.

"You left a note for heaven's sake."

"Oh, yeah... I forgot." She held her ring finger up to the light. "Did you think I was kidding?"

"Sorta."

"So did I." She giggled and then looked at me. "Rose, you're not upset, are you?"

I hadn't showered in days and wore the same long T-shirt I'd put on the first night I returned from Vegas. I heard Ce talk but her words made no sense. I had my own news to deal with.

Her eyebrows arched and she seemed concerned about my feelings. "Oh no, Rose, you look upset, don't be mad."

"Huh?" I couldn't focus.

"Don't be mad about me and Walter eloping!"

I wasn't. Why was everything always about her? I was too traumatized to give her elopement a second thought. "I was a little hurt," I lied.

"I knew something was wrong the minute I came home."

My eyes welled up with tears, and my body started trembling.

"Oh, Rose, you're being a baby. Don't be upset." Ce lit two cigarettes on one match and handed me a smoke. "Rose? I'm sorry, I didn't think..." The rapid apologies tripping off her tongue sounded sincere. She was a good actress, but not that good.

I walked away from her and sat down on the couch. Sobbing, I buried my face in my hands.

Ce sat next to me. "Rose, we can have another ceremony, at City Hall, and you can come to that. You can be my maid of honor." She hugged me.

"I'm not crying about thaaat." I couldn't speak.

"You're not? Did someone die? Oh my God, Rose, who died?"

"No one." I whispered.

"Then, what's wrong?" she gasped.

"No!"

"Rose, please, please, tell me what's wrong." She pulled my hands away from my face. "Rose, tell me what's wrong!"

"Ethan," I whispered, too embarrassed to look at her I kept my head bowed and eyes glued to the floor.

"Ethan? What about... Where is he?" She raced into his empty room. "Oh my God, Rose, you didn't!"

I stopped crying, and the silence that followed spoke volumes.

"Oh my God," Ce shrieked again. "You slept with him, didn't you? Jesus, Rose, you did! Were you friggin stoned?" She shook her head in disgust.

"We weren't stoned," I whimpered. "We were drunk, and... and "

"And what?"

"We didn't sleep together just because we were drunk."

"Then, why?"

"I slept with Ethan because... I have... I have feelings for him." I closed my eyes and felt Ce stare at me in disbelief.

"You do? Ew... Rose... For real?"

I nodded, and the humiliation I'd tried to escape flourished as hot tears stung my face.

"But Rose, Ethan is a big creepo. You slept with him? For reals?

I nodded.

"And instead of being grateful, the asshole bails?"

"He didn't bail. I threw him out." I choked on the words and then cried. She put out her cigarette and sat down beside me on the couch.

"Tissue," I whispered.

Ce bolted off the couch and scurried around trying to find some tissue. I hadn't left the apartment since coming home and there wasn't a single paper product anywhere. Ce reached into her purse and pulled out a sock.

"Here, Rose. It's clean." She held the makeshift handkerchief while I blew my nose.

We sat together, both of us silent for a long time. Ce had her arm slung around me and held back more Ethan bashing and 'You shoulda nevers.' For the first time in an eternity, my friend from Coral Gables - the Chelsea I knew from kindergarten and moved to Manhattan with - had returned. The money chasing, star-struck imposter who'd invaded her body but never touched her soul had vanished, and I had my best friend back.

She wrinkled her nose. "The litter stinks. Or is that you?" She sniffed and laughed. "Jeez, Rose, you reek! C'mon, I'll run a bath for you." She got up off the couch, grabbed my hands and pulled me to my feet.

"No!" I stopped short. The sheer horror of how filthy our tub was shocked me into decision-making mode. "I'll take a shower instead."

The water was steaming hot and felt good as it poured over my back. Each hot droplet exploded as it hit my skin. I poured shampoo on my head and scrubbed my hair until it was squeaky-clean. After a while, I turned off the hot water and let the cold water shock my system back into some kind of reality. "No more Ethan," I repeated over and over as I attempted to scrub all memory of him away with the large bar of Ivory soap.

"You OK in there?" Ce banged on the door. "Rose?"

"I'm fine," I whispered back. "I'll be out soon." Both lies.

My skin looked wrinkled as I got out of the shower and dried off with an oversized bath towel. "Where did this come from? It smells clean." I wrapped the plush towel around my body as Ce knocked on the door again.

"Did you find the towel?" She screamed through the door. "I took it from the hotel... Rose? Rose... can I come in? I swiped a bathrobe for you, too."

Before I could answer, Ce opened the door and walked in wearing a white terry-cloth bathrobe over her leggings. "Here, Rose. Now we can be twins!" She handed me the luxurious robe with "Heart's Palace" monogrammed in gold letters on the front.

"Thanks, Ce."

"Walter stole one, too, in black," Ce bragged.

"Where is Walter?" I sat down on the toilet seat bundled in the cozy terry-cloth robe and combed out my mangled hair.

"He's still in Vegas." Ce picked up the bath towel off the floor and shook it out. "They had to do some re-shoots today, so he's taking the red eye home tonight." She started wiping off the steamed-up mirror and spotted a large zit on her face. "Shit!"

She stormed out of the bathroom declaring she couldn't see Walter with a zit on her face and just like that our conversation was over.

For the first time since returning from Vegas, I slept through the night. Upon waking, I saw Walter's huge Army surplus duffle bag planted in the middle of the living room. Even though he was earning tons of money and could well afford high-end luggage, he was adamant about keeping his old beat-up canvas bag.

"Throw out that disgusting bag and get something cool, like a Burberry or Cartier suitcase," Ce had complained.

"It keeps me humble," he'd replied. Now His Humbleness was back from Vegas. Still half-asleep, I schlepped into the bathroom, threw some cold water on my face and heard the two of them talking through the thin bathroom wall.

"It'll just be for a little while," Ce whined. "C'mon, Waaaalter."

"Hey, I don't know baby…"

"Oh Walter, pleazzzzzzzzz!"

"Jeez, I don't know."

"I'm worried about her."

There was a long silence, and then I heard laughter.

"Shit, woman, how can I say no to you?"

After I'd washed up and brushed my teeth, I opened the bathroom door. There they were, waiting in the hallway.

"Rosie!" Walter flashed his "I'm ready for my close-up smile," stretched out his arms and then hugged me.

"We thought you were gonna sleep forever," said Ce, examining her split ends while we congregated in the tiny hallway wearing our matching stolen bathrobes.

"Hey, you too!" Walter laughed and pointed at my robe.

"Yep, me too." I pulled the belt tight around my waist and forced a smile. In an awkward moment of silence, it dawned on me that I hadn't seen him since Vegas. "Congratulations!"

"Oh, umm, yeah." Walter smirked and pinched Ce's butt.

"I'll order in the coffee." Ce giggled and went to the phone while Walter strutted into the living room and started emptying out his well-worn bag.

I lied on the couch and closed my eyes. I'd only been awake for twenty minutes but felt exhausted. The doorbell rang and my heart raced.

"Rose, can you get the door?" Ce yelled from the bathroom.

For a moment I envisioned Ethan had returned. "I've thought about it, Rose, and well... I can't live without you."

The bell rang again. "Rooooooooose, it's the coffee."

Walter made no effort to answer the door and I knew if we were to be caffeinated, it was up to me to get the goods. I dragged myself into the kitchen and took the last bill out of the Maxwell House coffee can, which served as our emergency fund container. The can situated in the corner on our kitchen counter was a sweet reminder of the one time we'd used our coffee maker.

I opened the door and the delivery boy, who knew his way blindfolded to our apartment, stood in front of me holding two bags.

I took the bags and handed him ten bucks. "Keep the change."

"Thanks." He stuck the money in his jeans pocket. "Nice robe, Miss Rose."

I took a coffee out of the bag and left the surplus on the dining table. Pirate joined me as I sat on the couch and drank my coffee through an opening in the plastic lid. A few minutes later, Ce grabbed a coffee and sat down next to me.

"Rose, we have something to tell you." Ce looked at Walter who was still unpacking his duffle. "Isn't that right, Walter?"

"Yep, that's right." Walter didn't budge, and his eyes stayed focused on the remaining paraphernalia in his case.

An alarm went off in my head as I waited for more bad news. I could feel the adrenaline pumping through me so fast that I no longer needed a caffeine buzz.

"Whaaat?" Trepidation filled me to the core as I set my cup on the floor.

"Walter and I insist you take our bedroom, and we'll move into Eth... I mean..."

"It's OK, Ce, you can say his name. I won't freak out."

"We'll move into the other room." They stared at me and waited for my reaction.

I breathed a sigh of relief. "Thank you," I said and hugged Ce as a tear of gratitude rolled down my cheek. I knew by their forced smiles this wasn't a heartfelt offer. However, I needed as much distance from

Ethan's old room as possible. Heartfelt or not, I took it. I needed to heal.

Chapter 24
The Rescue and Recovery

"Ethan never changed. He's the same old tetracycline-stained teeth asshole he's always been since day one." Ce sneezed while she opened the dusty Venetian blinds in my "new" bedroom. Their stuff was still strewn all over the room but Ce had changed the bed sheets. Thank God. "You just didn't wanna see the true him," she insisted as she plopped down on the bed beside me.

"I guess you're right."

"Guess? C'mon, Rose, how could you be so depressed over that loser?" Ce's attention shifted. "Have ya seen the remote?" She searched the top of the bed and patted the blanket.

I was depressed 'cause I'd stuck my head in the sand like an ostrich and blind sighted to the real Ethan. My eyes were wide shut as I'd fallen in love with Ethan Schwartz; crème de la jerks. "The remote's on the dresser," I mumbled.

Ce jumped off the bed, found the remote and clicked on the television while I stared out the window, watching the snowfall. Yes, I was friggin depressed and devastated but felt grateful to no longer be sleeping on the DNA couch next to Ethan's old room.

Ce peeled the blanket down and slid underneath the cozy quilt beside me. She switched from one program to the next. I heard Rod Serling's voice boom, "You are now entering the 'Twilight Zone'." Entering? I'd been living there for months. I rolled over onto my right side, put a pillow over my head and went to sleep.

The following week was a blur. I took hot showers then cocooned in my bathrobe while I hibernated like a bear in the dead of winter. Sometimes I'd hear Ce and Walter's low whispers and the sound of the telephone as it rang nonstop. With each ding-a-ling, my stomach clenched, and my heart did a flip-flop. I hoped it was Ethan calling to say he'd changed his mind.

"Wrong number," or, "Nobody," Ce responded when I asked who'd called. "Here ya go, Rose." She smiled and handed me the January issue of *Cosmopolitan* magazine.

I placed the magazine with the pile of literature on my nightstand. "Thanks, Ce," I said and lay in bed shrouded in my bathrobe from

Hearts Palace Hotel while the unread newspapers and magazines collected by my bedside. I had zero interest in anything while Ce seemed hell-bent on her mission of "Resurrecting Rose."

"Wanna play?" She fanned a deck of cards in front of me. Hows 'bout a rousing game of Old Maid?"

Seriously? "Uh, no thanks." I blew my nose, and Ce shook her head and left the room. My complete lack of enthusiasm didn't derail Ce's mission to pull me out of my funk. An hour later she returned toting our large brown and white backgammon set.

"I don't know how to play."

"I'll teach you." She placed the board in the middle of the bed and set up both sides of the game piece by piece. "OK, I'll be white, and you're brown." She sat cross-legged on the bed holding the dice in her hand. "Now the first thing," she began.

"Maybe later."

"C'mon, Rose. It's piss ant easy."

"No. I'm just too tired." Maybe I had a terminal disease.

"How could you be tired? All you've done is sleep."

Maybe I had cancer. Or perhaps it was just syphilis.

"How could you be so tired?" Ce repeated.

"I just am." Epstein Barr was all the rage; maybe I had that.

"Oh, alright, Rose." She shrugged her shoulders and packed up the game. "We can play later." Ce walked to the bedroom closet, then wobbled on tip-toes as she tried placing the backgammon set on the top shelf next to Scrabble. "Holy shiiit," she screamed as she lost her footing and the Scrabble game fell on top of her before landing on the floor. "Damn it!" The box had opened, and all the pieces fell out and scattered about. Seeing the letters strewn all over the floor set in motion a flood of memories, and I curled into a ball and pretended to be asleep while Ce asked me to help her clean up the mess.

Walter made valiant efforts to bring me back to life, too. "This has been circulating 'round the set." He had a sheepish smile as he handed me the self-help book.

I stared at the words on the cover: *I'm OK, You're OK.* "No, I am not OK. I may even be dying," I whispered after him as he left the room. I was anything *but* OK. Lying in bed, listless and staring at the television while dwelling in complete misery was the complete opposite of being OK.

By the end of the second week, Ce had run out of steam. She'd done everything short of putting on a clown costume in a futile attempt to cheer me up. Now she made it clear that she'd had enough of the whole situation and that her role as Florence Nightingale was over.

"C'mon, Rose, you can't just lie around in bed all the time." She pulled the covers off me. "Make a god-damn effort!"

"I can't." I pulled the blanket back on top of my head.

"If you don't get out of that friggin bed, you're gonna get bed sores!"

I didn't answer.

"Rose? Rose! Do you wanna get bed sores?" She persisted.

"I don't care."

A long silence ensued.

"Maybe I should call your family and…"

I took the covers off my head and sat up.

"Ha, gotcha!" She giggled. She knew the last thing I wanted was any family member, especially my mom, to know about what had been going on. I hadn't even told them I went to Vegas! I could just hear Mom's reaction. "You went where? You could've been killed in a plane crash!" After all, hadn't I learned my fear of life from her?

"There are a lot of prostitutes in Vegas," Dad would say. "I hope you didn't catch any diseases."

"You went on a vacation and didn't take me. You are such a selfish bitch, Rose." Nope, I couldn't risk dealing with "sister dearest," either.

Ce and I stared at each other for a long time before I put my feet on the cold wood floor and stood up.

"Do I need to slap you? Enough, Rose! The guy had friggin stained teeth for God's sake!" We looked at each other and I had the strangest urge to laugh as a wave of relief came over me. It wasn't an instantaneous recovery, but it was a start.

The days dragged by and once I'd gotten past the initial trauma of being "Ethanized," Ce no longer doted on me like a bird with a broken wing. Instead she and Walter spent a lot of couple time and it was soon clear that three was a crowd.

"I wub you, Wawa." Ce's pet name for Walter was nauseating.

"I wub you more, Ce Ce." He licked the side of her face like a cat.

"Meow," Ce purred, confusing the hell out of Pirate. Their pet names and private jokes were getting on my nerves. They were so happy and I was so jealous. All had changed now that they'd tied the knot and I felt like a stranger in my own apartment.

The most tangible change was the addition of the *New York Times* delivered to our front door daily. Perhaps Walter had developed a newfound interest in the world outside *One Life to Give* because neither Ce nor I read the newspaper. Ever. When I saw the real-estate section isolated from the rest of the paper, I knew something was up. I could've asked Ce straight out whether they were apartment hunting but decided against it; my head felt too comfortable in the sand.

Then Ce decided to start shoveling the sand away.

"Walter loves the Upper West Side." Ce looked at Walter and I caught her mouthing the words "say something" as he dug his hands deep into his corduroy pants pockets.

"Yes, indeed. The West Side is happening. Those pre-war buildings… they just don't make apartments like that anymore."

I pretended to read a magazine while I caught them exchanging glances.

"You know, I'd love to have a bedroom with western exposure," Walter plodded on.

"Western exposure? How about a bedroom with a friggin window?" Ce added.

"A bedroom with lots of windows, in a pre-war building! Yes, that's the ticket." Walter and Ce were determined for me to take the bait and ask the sixty-four-thousand-dollar question. I wouldn't bite.

They'd drop less-than-subtle hints, and I'd change the subject. "Who wants Chinese?" I'd ask, hoping they'd forget about moving out. Even though their marital bliss made me feel like a third wheel, the last thing I wanted was to live alone or have to find a new roommate. I refused to connect the dots and played dumb for several weeks until Ce got up here nerve to tell me what I already knew.

"Now that we're married Walter wants to get our own place." She blurted the news out without taking a breath.

"Yeah, I figured." I held up the latest issue of the *New York Times* real estate section, which had several apartment listings highlighted in yellow.

"I was afraid to tell you." Ce's eyes watered, but I remained emotionless. After all they'd been drooping mega hints and I'd had time to mentally prepare for the imminent reality of what was coming down the pike: they were moving out.

Two weeks later we stood in front of our apartment building shivering in the twelve-degree arctic blast while the movers loaded up a large steel truck.

Walter's stuff was contained in two cartons and one wardrobe. The remaining twenty-five cartons and nine wardrobes held Ce's clothes and worldly possessions. It took the two guys from Moshie's Movers three hours to pile in all their stuff. They were loading the last wardrobe when Walter reached for my arm and put an envelope in my triple-gloved hand.

"What's this?" I asked him.

"A check. It should cover the next two months' rent, 'til you find a new roommate."

I stuck the check into my jeans pocket as the reality of needing to find a new roommate sunk in. Shit.

"That about does it," one of Moshie's Movers told us as he handed Walter some papers.

Walter looked through the paperwork while Ce threw her arms around me.

"Oh, Rose, I'm sooorry," she wailed as she hugged me.

"Nooo, don't be sorry. I'm happy for you." I faked a smile and hugged her back.

"Geez, we're just moving across town. It's not like we're moving to to Australia." Walter had zero patience for drama, unless he was getting a paycheck for it.

"I know, but I feel soooo sad." Ce used the edges of Walter's flannel shirt to dry her tears.

I felt sad, too, and frightened. I knew everything would be different. For the first time ever, I'd be in complete charge of my own life. No Ethan, no Ce or Walter to fall back on. In my heart of hearts I also knew that Ce talked a good game and her good intentions were just that, intentions. She was an "out-of-sight, out-of-mind" person and it would be up to me to initiate phone calls and keep in touch. But if our friendship were unconditional, did it matter who called and when?

Our arms were flung over each other while we walked to the corner and Walter flagged down a cab. "Seventy-second and Amsterdam," he told the driver as Ce climbed in.

"I'll call you as soon as we get the phone put in," Ce promised.

I watched the cab speed up the street, with Ce waving through the rear window. I forced a large smile that belied my tear-drenched face and waved back.

Chapter 25
Moving Forward

The March wind whipped around the buildings as I stepped off the Fourteenth Street bus then headed to acting class. "One, two, three, four," counting the blocks 'til I reached the studio provided a great distraction from the frigid weather and how much my heart ached. "Thirteen, fourteen, fifteen." I stopped and caught my breath. The wind had died down as I made the final turn and traveled half a block up Bank Street. "HB STUDIOS," the door read. "Has that inscription always been there?" I walked up the short cobblestone path and yanked open the heavy door. A blast of heat hurled from inside and hit my face like a fireball. "Geez!" Sweating, I unwrapped my scarf from around my neck and pulled off my coat before melting into the floor.

"Welcome back, Rose." Stephan half-smiled as he slinked by. He wore the exact ensemble I'd seen him dressed in two and a half months prior: baggy denim jeans and a blue-and-white-checkered shirt.

I returned the smile, careful not to make direct eye contact. My eyes remained focused on the floor as I found a seat in the last row of the designated smoking section. Slinging my coat over the back of my chair, I glanced around the room. Not a single face looked familiar. Was I in the right class? Had I gotten the day mixed up? My hands felt clammy and my stomach tied up in knots just as Mitch walked through the door. Thank God! At last, someone I knew.

"Mitch!" I waved frantically.

"Where the hell have you been?" We hugged as the class monitor took attendance. "Where's Ce?" Mitch scanned the room before he sat beside me. "Is she in the bathroom?"

"No, she's…"

"Let me guess, she's in Paris?" He put his hand on his hip.

"Nope."

"Taiwan, uh, Timbuktu?"

"Neither." I giggled.

Mitch pondered for a moment. "Is she in jail?"

"No!" I shrieked and felt Stephan's eyes bore through us like laser beams. Our game of "Where's Ce?" ended.

"I hate to interrupt you, Mitch and Rose, but I'd like to start class.

If that's all right with you two?" His voice dripped with sarcasm while my face flushed with embarrassment.

"Sorry," I answered, looking down at the floor. So many changes had rocked my world but a few things remained the same. Stephan's sarcasm was still intact and oddly comforting.

However, getting comfortable in my chair was impossible as I twisted and turned. The chair felt harder than I remembered and focusing on the two scenes and three monologues that were showcased was challenging.

"Do you have ants in your pants?" Mitch whispered during Stephan's final critique.

I smiled and rolled my eyes.

"Tennessee Williams would be turning in his grave." Stephan's harsh and ruthless comments brought the poor girl to tears. I felt bad for her but I was relieved that it was her getting the harsh critique and not me. Even though I'd been in Stephan's class for more than a year, I hadn't yet showcased a scene. Between *Doom* the play and doom my life, I hadn't had the time, motivation, courage or stamina to chance Stephan's unkind, wrist-slitting criticisms. Deep inside I was too terrified.

"Let's go to the Whitehorse and grab a drink," Mitch suggested after class was finished.

I hesitated. I hadn't been to our after-class hangout in months. "Umm..."

"C'mon, Rose, I'll buy. We need to catch up and I have some exciting news to tell you."

I'd never been to the bar without Ce, and for the first time since she'd moved out, I missed her. Terribly. "I dunno... I have to..."

"Have to what? Whaddaya have to do at ten o'clock at night?" His eyes twinkled. "Oh, c'mon, Rose. Just for one teeny weenie glass of wine. Pretty please?"

"Oh. OK." I was reluctant but wrapped my plaid scarf around my neck while Mitch helped me put on my bulky down coat. We braced for the cold as we left class and walked arm and arm up the dark side street leading to the bar. The streetlights flickered, except for the one in front of the old tavern. The two lanterns positioned at the entrance of the Whitehorse were welcoming. Mitch opened the massive front door, and we walked inside the New York City landmark. Many famous authors sat in the same chairs that Mitch and I flung our coats over. Countess literary greats once inhabited the Whitehorse Bar, drinking scotch or vodka while they penned their masterpieces.

Seated in the same chair that Ernest Hemmingway might've sat in gave me the chills. I watched Mitch while he walked back from the bar, careful not to spill a single drop of red wine. "So, what's the big news?"

Mitch placed a wine in front of me and then sat down. "First, tell me where Ce is." He grinned.

"Ce is living on the Upper West Side, and she's married." I took a long sip of wine.

"To a millionaire?"

"Nope, to a soap star."

"No shit!" Mitch sat up straight and inched his wine glass toward mine. "Here's to Ce and her soap opera husband." We clinked glasses and exchanged smiles.

Mitch was so funny, warm and sweet. He was also so caring. He would be the perfect boyfriend. "Too bad you're gay."

"Whaaa?"

Had I said that out loud? "Oh nothing, I was just thinking – what a nice day."

"Oh." He wrinkled his nose as a perplexed expression crossed his face.

He was so kind. "I'm lucky to have you as my friend," I said.

"Me too, Rose! Me too."

I felt calm around Mitch. After being snapped out of my comfort zone of Ce and Walter, it was time to reconnect with people who made me feel safe and loved. I downed the last bit of wine from my glass and smiled. Yes, Mitch would be the ideal boyfriend if only he weren't gay. Why was it always something? I set my empty glass on the table.

"Got any other dirt?" Mitch leaned his head halfway over the table, and his eyes searched mine.

"Well. Sorta. About Ce's husband." Pausing increased the tension and the fun I was having while I milked my news.

"Well?" Mitch waved his hand. "What already?"

"You know him."

"The soap star? I do? How? Have I ever slept with him?"

Mitch's candor about his sexuality was refreshing and reminded me (again) why Mitch could never be my boyfriend. AIDS had shoved so many gays into the closet that it would take a blowtorch to get 'em out. But Mitch wasn't like that. He was authentic and always himself no mater what.

"People need to get a freakin' grip" he'd said when the media reported on the new "gay disease." Homophobia was on the rise as people reverted to old behaviors reminiscent of the '50s. Panic-stricken, they'd forgotten all about the sexual revolution of the '60s and promiscuity of the '70s. It was the 80s and being openly gay was not socially acceptable.

"Remember Walter?" I said.

"Walter?" Mitch took a sip of wine and his eyes flashed as a look of recognition appeared on his face. "The guy from acting class?"

"Yep."

"He was Stephan's old class monitor. Hey, didn't he live at some theater?" Mitch cocked his head.

"Yes, same guy."

"Didn't Ce and him do that scene from *Cat on a Hot Tin Roof?*"

"Close. *A Streetcar Named Desire.*"

"Yeah. *Streetcar*. That's it! He's hot. Ce married him? I thought he was gay."

"Mitch, you think everyone's gay."

"True enough. A boy can dream, right? So did she marry him before or after he became a star?"

We both knew the answer to that and laughed out loud.

"OK, I've shared, now it's your turn." I lit up a cigarette and waited. "Well?"

"Well what?" He feigned forgetfulness for a moment and then exploded with excitement. "I've been cast in the touring production of *Seven Brides for Seven Brothers*!" He clasped both of his hands together, and then stretched his arms upward.

"That's fantastic! Are you playing a bride or a brother?"

"Ha ha, funny." After a moment he lowered his arms, then rested both elbows on the tabletop. "Now, here's the exciting part, concerning *you!*" He cradled his chin in his hands and grinned.

"Me?"

"Lucinda asked whether you could cover for me. She likes you a lot Rose."

"Lucinda? Oh, from Dr. Berber's office." How could I have

forgotten her?

"You've been requested. That is, if you're free."

Hmmm. Yep, I was free and almost broke. Timing, for once, was on my side.

Chapter 26
Return to Oz and the Wizard of Weird

The next morning, Pirate's loud purring awoke me from a coma-like sleep. "Good morning, kitty," I whispered. We'd become close over the past months, and he no longer hid under the couch or retreated to a corner in the living room. As I relocated him from his favorite sleeping spot on top of my head to my stomach, his compact body stiffened with disapproval. "That's better." I stroked the underbelly of Ethan's ex-cat and realized that the passage of time and my feline companion had helped heal some wounds. The butterflies were at long last dead, but I still missed Ethan.

The phone rang, and Pirate and I looked at it on the nightstand. Like Pavlov's dog, my heart skipped a beat. I had stopped answering it, letting the machine pick up while I pretended that it was Ethan calling. It was a harmless fantasy. Imagining that it was Ethan on the other end of the line, spewing his regrets about leaving, comforted me. Even though the "I love and miss you" was imagined, it helped heal my heart and kept my head comfortable in the sand.

After the phone stopped ringing, I removed Pirate from my stomach and bolted into the bathroom. After a five-minute shower, I threw on some black pants and my lucky white button-down shirt. "Bye, kitty kitty".

"Meow," Pirate answered as I headed out the door.

Although four months had passed since I last worked for Dr. Berber, I felt confident about my return to the medical world. After all, I'd worked there before. With that full week's worth of prior medical expertise, I was competent to handle any health care situation. Wasn't I? Well, I was competent to fill pill vials. A surge of self-confidence filled me as I pulled open the green glass front door and stepped inside. This time, already familiar with the "Oz-ities" of the decor, I was amused instead of shocked.

"Hello, Rose!" Lucinda's sweet voice filtered through the lobby. "Welcome back." The door leading to the office flew open and moments later Lucinda stood smack dab in front of me with her arms outstretched. "I'm so happy you've returned." Her swift appearance was startling.

"Thank you." I bent down and hugged her. "It's good to be back." I walked through the office to hang up my coat.

She smiled while holding a large tray covered by a white lace doily. "Have a muffin!" She held it under my nose. "I baked them from scratch, and they're still warm." Her cheerful voice was a welcome change from temperamental cooks screaming "Order's up" from the back of a hot, greasy kitchen.

"Oh. Thanks."

"They're blueberry." She followed me to the closet, and I felt her eyes on me while I stashed my coat. "You're early. Sit and relax before we start the day." She smiled.

I took a muffin off the tray. "Are these fresh blueberries on top?"

"Oh, of course. I never buy frozen." She sounded a bit insulted.

Fresh? Frozen? Who cared? It appeared that Lucinda did. "The berries are so large. They look like miniature cherries." I picked a berry off the muffin top and examined it. "I didn't know blueberries were in season." I tried sounding savvy.

"And homemade fresh blueberry preserves throughout," she gushed.

"No way." I popped the oversized berry into my mouth, and then took a slow bite into the muffin. "Wow. This is hands-down the best breakfast ever!" After devouring the rest in three large bites, I sighed. "That was delish!"

Lucinda grinned, and then nibbled her muffin as I reached for another. A moment later her happy demeanor darkened and her brow furrowed. Were seconds frowned upon? I put the muffin back. As I watched Lucinda examine her hand I realized her sudden mood shift had nothing to do with the muffins, so I took another off the plate.

"What's wrong?"

"I'm not sure I like this nail polish." She held up her tiny fingers. "Whaddaya think, Rose?"

"Pretty." Her nails were teeny. I tried hiding my amazement and nodded my approval. "Mauve is the new hot color for spring." I'd never met a little person before and felt ashamed how her size unnerved me at first. Four months ago, I couldn't help equating her to all the stereotypical clichés I'd heard about little people. But now, while sitting together chitchatting over breakfast, I felt relaxed and comfortable. The only physical difference I noticed was that Lucinda's nails were longer than mine, and impeccably manicured.

"Today's a big day," she announced while covering the rest of the muffins.

"Why?"

"You're going to 'officially' meet Dr. B." Excited anticipation filled her voice while my stomach felt queasy. She took the rest of the muffins into the lobby and placed them on the table. "He scheduled your meeting for ten o'clock." The phone rang, and she hurried back into the office. "Good morning," her lyrical voice sang out. "Dr. Berber's office."

"Oh." My neck stiffened as I felt the blood drain from my face and the familiar feeling of dread returned.

Lucinda covered the phone with her hand. "Just be yourself, Rose. Doctor B's gonna love you. It'll be easy-peasy." She smiled, winked and then resumed her call.

At ten sharp, I knocked on the lavender door.

He'd never spoken to me and I'd expected his voice to be loud and his tone, abrasive and brash. I felt surprised by the soft, warm voice that belied his large stature. "Come in. It's open."

My hand shook as I turned the brass doorknob and entered his private domain. Dr. B.'s office, which Lucinda regarded as a shrine, smelled like pickles. The deli smell that permeated the air faded by what I saw on the wall right behind The Great Wizard. It wasn't adorned with rainbows or forest animals, as I'd imagined. Instead, it was exposed red brick, hosting more paraphernalia than the Hard Rock Café. I stood dumbfounded, feeling like I was peering into a giant scrapbook of my boss's life. The torn ticket stubs tacked up next to playbills, alongside of faded black and white photos of old cars, grabbed my attention. My jaw dropped as I scanned numerous newspaper and magazine articles interspersed among framed photos. An assortment of bright colored baseball caps formed a border around the enormous scrapbook strewn on the wall. My expectation of more "over the rainbow" décor had been thrown a curve ball.

Dr. Berber watched as I fixated on the wall behind his oversized head. "Pretty darn impressive!" he said.

"Oh my, yes!" Impressive in a weird, Twilight Zone kind of way. The wall was like an accident, hard to look at, but impossible to look away from.

"They are my patients," he said proudly. "Some of 'em are celebrities. Others just nobody's." He chuckled.

The only celebrity I recognized was Liza Minnelli. My idol. The not-so-recent photo of her dressed in a get-up from *Cabaret* hung dead center on the brick wall.

"Sit." He gestured toward a chair in front of his enormous cherry wood desk. Seated, Dr. B. was still twice as big as I was. I felt nervous and buttoned the top of my lab coat and sat down.

"So, you're Mitch's friend." His smile vanished and his tone grew cold. It was obvious that he was still pissed about Mitch's departure. Again.

Not able to find my voice, I nodded.

He removed a doily hiding a stack of fries. "French fry?" He dipped a well-done steak fry into a mound of ketchup and offered it up. "Here. Have one. Just the right amount of salt and ketchup; that's the key to perfection."

I took the French fry from between his large fingers and forced it down my parched throat.

"Don't tell my patients." He laughed. "After all, I am the great and powerful Diet Doctor."

And modest.

"So, have you read my latest book? And if you haven't, why not?"

My face flushed. What book?

"Here's your own special copy of *Star Powering Your Diet*." He removed the hardback from a large stack on the floor and then signed it with a purple marker.

"Oh. Thank you." I opened to the front flap of the cover and read the inscription: 'for you, Ruth. Welcome'.

Ruth? I contemplated telling Dr. B. that my name was 'Rose' not 'Ruth' but kept silent.

A moment later, Dr. B. was out of his chair, looking giant-like as he walked over to a shelf of more books near the red brick wall.

"This is my first baby." He removed a large book off the shelf and kissed the cover. Then he leaned on the front edge of his desk for support while he opened it and proceeded to read numerous pages out loud. Twenty minutes and several passages later, he'd finished.

I left his office with my wrong name, signed copy of *Star Powering Your Diet* and a headache.

Planted right outside of Dr. Berber's door, Lucinda managed to startle me. Again. "So?" Her eyes sparkled with anticipation.

"You were right. It wasn't so bad. I think he liked me."

Her eyes squinted and her tone grew serious. "Did he share his fries?"

"Yes." (One counted as a share, didn't it?)

"Oh, he definitely likes you!" She let out a sigh of relief. "I was a little worried because he was so fond of Mitch. I kept my fingers crossed that he wouldn't hold that against you." She walked into his office and shut the lavender door behind her.

And thus began a new chapter in my life, full time employment. Working from nine to five every day was challenging. However, something about having a regular routine felt good, and it wasn't long before I was well integrated into the Land of Odd.

Another Monday morning rolled 'round, and I smiled as I rode the crowded train to work. The claustrophobic feeling that always accompanied a packed subway car was nonexistent. Looking forward to starting my third week on the job, I raced to the door of the subway car as the train screeched to a stop. Once out of the stifling station, I smelled the flowers that signaled spring's arrival. My winter coat felt suffocating as I walked the four short blocks from the train to the office.

"Your hair looks amazing!" Lucinda raved as I walked through the lobby door.

"Thanks. I needed a change." I pulled off my coat and headed to the closet. "Do you really like it?"

"Oh, yes. Absolutely."

"You don't think it's too short?" I put away my coat.

"Oh, no. Not at all. Now you can see those cheekbones." She smiled. "It suits you, Rose. Perfectly."

I walked over to the reception desk and lifted up the large doily covering Lucinda's muffins, grabbed one and headed off to fill the pill vials.

By the end of the month I'd gained five pounds, so I had to cut back on the muffins. When the blond pregnant girl, who'd kept a cool distance from me, went on maternity leave I was promoted from pill-filler to receptionist.

"The most important thing to remember is your attitude," Lucinda began.

"Attitude?"

"Yes, attitude. And lots of it." She winked. "Janice came by it naturally and was a pro at being cold, distant, and borderline rude."

Rude? "Oh." My stomach hurt.

"Dr B.'s wealthy and famous patients don't want to engage in friendly conversation." With a nobody, I thought. "Or be asked for autographs." Especially by the nobody receptionist. "Anonymity is their priority." Lucinda's voice lightened up as my panic-filled eyes met hers. "You'll do great, Rose."

"I'll try."

"I have complete faith in you." She squeezed my hand and headed back to the lab. "You're an actress, Rose! Act!" she yelled from halfway down the hall.

A month after my promotion, I was proficient at keeping my personal feelings under wraps and acting like an ice cube.

"He's running a half hour late," I told the star quarterback of the New York Giants. No apology. No warm and fuzzes. "Have a seat." I slid the glass window separating us shut and took a deep breath. How I wanted to engage in conversation. "Oh I'm so sorry," I wanted to say to the handsome football player, but forced myself to keep to the script.

By mid-summer I had the role of Dr. Berber's cool, indifferent receptionist down pat. I was proud to wear a lab coat, and wore my name badge pinned onto the lapel. In a crazy way, I felt part of the medical profession and could've won an Academy Award for playing the part of a pretend nutritionist / receptionist. For the first time since moving to Manhattan, I was grounded. A new clarity of purpose and power replaced obscurity and fear. Not even the shorthaired woman knocking on the opaque glass one morning early in August could rattle me.

"May I help you?" I slid the pass-through window open.

"It's Liza with a 'z'," said the stocky woman behind the oversized dark sunglasses. She turned around and walked back into the empty waiting room. My jaw dropped as I peered into the lobby through the half-open glass and watched "Liza with a z" pace back and forth. Her name was listed on the schedule as Liza Z., but I hadn't connected the dots. Sure, I'd seen her picture on Dr. B.'s wall but I never expected to see my idol standing right in front of me. How I wanted to call my mom. "You'll never guess who's standing less than ten feet away from me!" Or Ce. (She was a big Liza fan, too.) Or anybody for that matter.

My body was drenched with sweat as I lost my cool. Liza with a Z was in the house and it took disciplined restraint not to talk to her. "I loved 'Cabaret' and saw 'The Sterile Cuckoo' five times!" I screamed in my head. I'd managed to put up a damn good cold front for all the other patients but now I felt my fake icy exterior melting. It was Liza Minnelli, for God's sake. How I wanted to ask for her autograph.

"Rose. Rose!" How long had Lucinda been standing next to me? "Dr. B. is ready for the next patient."

I felt light-headed. "Would you mind showing her back? I feel a little dizzy."

"Sure." Lucinda went into the waiting room and hugged "Liza with a z." I watched them walk into treatment room No. 3 and was grateful that Lucinda took her into that treatment room instead of me. Why? Because just like the elevator, treatment room number three was unlucky too.

Chapter 27
Working Girl

Two days before Labor Day weekend, it hit me, Summer was over. It had flown by like the A train at 42nd Street while I was immersed in working full time for Dr. B. Receiving hefty paychecks had compensated for a nonexistent acting career. Contrary to what Mitch told me, I didn't have free time to pursue the passion that had driven me to New York. I still went to acting class and I was content with that little bit of theater experience. Day after day, I wore my white lab coat to work, where the patients treated me like I counted. They said "please" and "thank you," making me feel appreciated and purposeful. I took meditation classes at the Y, which helped me feel settled and confident. Forcing myself to stay away from Lucinda's Monday-morning muffins, I lost the five pounds I'd gained, and an additional seven. Within five months, I'd evolved into a new Rose. People noticed.

"You sound amazing!" Ce gushed on the other end of the phone. "I think you've found your calling."

"Better then slinging hash."

"It's way cool," she said, treating me like I was a rock star.

Ce and Walter had been gone six months and I'd barely noticed. After the first few weeks, my loneliness vanished and I had an epiphany: I loved living alone. No more holes punched in the wall by crazy people or roommates who fled to L.A. and became recovering Thespians. No artistic egos to battle and nobody around who could break my heart. I was content having Pirate as my only roomie.

"What kind of doctor is he again?" Ce asked.

"He's a fancy diet doctor. He treats food allergies, too."

"How?"

"Vitamin therapies and drugs. The patients have all sorts of tests." Lucinda offered me those tests for free, but I declined. If there was something wrong with me, I preferred not to know. Just seeing needles made me wince.

"What kind of tests?"

"Blood."

"Ew."

"Yeah. I still get freaked when I see those red vials. Anyway, all the patients get the exact same blood tests no matter what they're seen for."

"Where do they have the tests done?" Ce persisted.

"Here."

"There?"

"Yes." I paused, anticipating another question. "After Phyllis draws their blood, she takes it back to the lab."

"A real lab? Where is it?"

"In the back, near the lunch table."

"There's blood near where you eat? Gross."

"It's not right next to the lab; it's down the hall. Anyway, I never go in there, and the door's always locked. Just Phyllis is allowed access."

"Who's Phyllis?" Ce's inquisitive mood and her endless questions were starting to get on my nerves.

"She's the lab technician and the nurse."

"Is she a midget, too?" Ce laughed.

"No. She's normal size and the polite and correct name is little person." I cringed. "Just so ya know, Lucinda has a rare kind of dwarfism called skeletal dysphasia. That's the medical term." I felt smart and defensive.

"Does Lucinda have step stools all over the office?" Ce giggled again. "And ask you to open doors 'cause she can't reach the knobs?" Her laughter sounded vulgar.

Why had I even told Ce that Lucinda was a little person? "No, she can reach the doorknobs all by herself." Her comments were tasteless and not amusing. Not only wasn't I laughing, I was pissed. "Lucinda is capable of doing everything that we can do. And smarter than you and I put together." My face felt hot.

She stopped laughing and asking questions as silence fell on the other end of the phone. Ce knew from the coolness in my voice that I wasn't amused. After a moment of silence she did what she always did when she felt trapped: changed the subject. "Oh, Rose, I miss you sooooo much. We have to get together."

"Sure."

"I'll call ya next week."

As we hung up the phone, we knew our next conversation

wouldn't be next week, or maybe not even next month. And for the first time, I didn't care.

Labor Day weekend was uneventful and I was eager to go back to work Tuesday morning. I was up an hour earlier than usual and spent extra time on my makeup and styling my new short hair with the eighteen-dollar hair products that the stylist insisted were "must-haves." A little gel here, some hairspray there and voila; just forty minutes later I had the same carefree, messy look I loved in the magazines.

"Meow." As I reached down to kiss him good-bye, Pirate backed away as if he didn't recognize me.

The subway car was packed and the air conditioner was broken. By the time I got to work I'd sweated off my makeup, and the hair gel, clumped together with sweat, ruined my 'do. As I passed through the green glass doors, I was hell-bent to get into the "Judy Garland" bathroom. A major re-org was required! STAT. However, something else caught my attention.

"Hello, Rose." Janice, the receptionist whom I'd replaced, was back from her maternity leave, and she was seated behind what had been my desk for the past three and a half months.

"Oh. Hi." She'd caught me off-guard, and I forgot all about fixing my sweat-drenched hair and smeared makeup. My head pounded as I meandered straight into the office and saw her sitting in my space. It was odd that Lucinda hadn't mentioned that Janice was coming back. Seeing her wearing her stark white, just-pressed lab coat and flipping through the appointment book, I feared being demoted to my previous position as a pill-filler. Or even worse, fired.

"Lucinda is in Dr. B.'s office." Janice stood up, and I saw she didn't have a trace of post-pregnancy weight; she looked thinner than I did. Now I had two reasons not to like her. "They want to see you," she said in a cold, monotone voice as she turned down the thermostat to sixty-eight.

Now what? If they were going to give me the ax, why didn't they do it by phone instead of making me schlep in here on the stinking train? "Ohm, Ohm, Ohm," I repeated the mantra I'd learned in meditation class but regardless of the effort to stay focused, my mind raced with thoughts of impending doom. The short distance to the lavender door seemed like a mile. I felt my stomach tighten, as I knocked then was thrown off-guard when Dr. B., all seven-foot-two of him, opened the door.

"Rosy, come in." Although my name wasn't 'Rosy' either, it was better than 'Ruth.' Dr. B. smiled while towering over me. "Nice haircut." He turned around and headed to his desk.

Lucinda ended a phone call and darted over. She stood beside me and slid a muffin in my hand. "It's chocolate pecan swirl, your favorite." She winked as I stared at the muffin. "I'm not taking no for an answer." Her sweet smile and Dr. B.'s crooked half-grin set off a seven-alarm alert in my head. This reminded me of something. But what? The Last Supper? A final meal before an execution? Both images made my stomach lurch.

Dr. B. sat down behind his desk and removed the familiar doily covering his morning snack. "Pickle?" he offered.

"Oh, no thanks." I held up Lucinda's muffin. "I'm good." I picked off a chocolate pecan from the top and popped it in my mouth. What next? Would they offer up a blindfold and a final cigarette?

"Rosy, sit. Please. We want to talk to you." Dr. B.'s tone turned serious.

I sat on the edge of the chair smack dab in front of his desk, cupping the muffin in my lap for dear life.

"Rosy, you've done a remarkable job and now that Janice is back..."

Here it comes. No matter how much I prepared myself, being fired always sucked.

"...I'd like to offer you a new position."

"Huh?" I looked at Lucinda. Her face was luminescent as she nodded her head.

"Oh." Had she been talking to Governor Carey when I walked into the office? Did he call at the eleventh hour and stay my execution?

"Now that Dr. B.'s new book is out, he needs extra help." Lucinda bounced off her chair and stood in front of me, offering up another muffin.

I hadn't touched the first and shook my head.

"I'll take it," Dr. B. volunteered and the muffin went flying over my head. "Nice throw, Lucinda." He gobbled it up in two enormous bites. "So whadda ya think, Rosy? Do you wanna be my personal assistant?" he asked with a mouthful of food.

"Sure. But what will I have to... I mean what does a personal assistant do?"

"You won't be just any personal assistant, you'll be my personal assistant."

OK, what does the personal assistant of a narcissistic giant do? My inner voice asked as my stomach flipped again and my sweat glands kicked into overdrive.

"Here, Rose." Lucinda placed a two-page, single-spaced document on my lap. "It's all listed on this chart, and the corresponding days you'll need to take care of it." She flipped over to the second page and pointed to the print highlighted in yellow. "Those are all the names and addresses."

"Addresses? To where?"

"The dry cleaner, the dog groomer…"

"What isn't listed," Dr. B. interrupted, "are the perks."

"Oh, yes, the perks are wonderful!" Lucinda chimed in.

Complete silence filled the room as Dr. B. walked over to his giant scrapbook on the wall and stared at its contents. "Sometimes I need a companion to go to the theater," he said, "or to a baseball game. Do you like the opera, Rosy?" He turned around and waited for my answer.

"Yes." I guess I did. I'd never been.

"Good. Then it's settled." He walked back to his desk and opened the large top drawer. "Congratulations." He handed me an envelope "Here, this is a little sign-on bonus."

"Open it, Rose. It's a gift certificate, from Bloomingdales!" Lucinda gushed.

I stared down at the elaborate gift certificate for five hundred dollars. "Thank you." Stunned, I stood up and looked down at the spreadsheet that charted my personal assistant duties. "Let's see. Today is Tuesday and Tuesday is… dog groomer?"

"Lilly and Willie were coiffed over the weekend. Take the day off. Celebrate. Go shopping." Dr. B. stretched his arms upward and almost touched the ceiling. "Enjoy, Rosy. Enjoy."

He headed out of his office door and Lucinda followed behind on his gigantic heels.

"Oh yes, Rose, go use your gift certificate at Bloomingdales," she echoed. "It's like no other store in the world."

And so for the first time since moving to Manhattan I was going to have an official paid day off and shop at a department store other than Chuckles or Labels for Less. I was going to shop where our patients shopped instead of some street vendor's clothing rack. My stomach felt fine, I was no longer sweating and life, at that moment, did not suck.

Chapter 28
Over It

It was Monday, October 5, one month to the day since my promotion and shopping spree. Yet my new ensembles and I had gone nowhere. Not to the theater, not to a ball game and certainly not to the opera. Where were those perks? "I'll just wait 'til he mentions it again. I'll wait another month and then I'll remind him," I justified while dropping off some shoes for Dr. B. at the office.

"You've been played, Rose." Dad's voice barked inside my mind. "'Do you like the opera, Rosy? What about baseball?' That was just bait. The bum doesn't even know your name. You can't trust those doctors. Lying pricks. All of them!"

Lucinda was behind Janice's desk sharpening pencils when I arrived.

"When do you think I'll get to go to an opera?" I blurted out a moment after stumbling in. "Soon?"

"Patience, Rose." She slid pencil after pencil into the small electronic sharpener. "All in good time." Her voice was inaudible above the No. 2 wood grinding, but I could still hear Dad's voice as clear as a bell.

"Sucker!" Dad snickered while I stared into space and wondered whether he was right. Lucinda, once so warm and friendly, had become cold and distant. Her subtle attitude shift hadn't been apparent until then. Granted I was out of the office most of the time, so perhaps I'd missed something. But what? She was acting oddly and I felt more like a stranger than a co-worker. Had I done something wrong?

Instead of confronting her, I ignored the obvious bad vibe and uncomfortable feeling. "Here are the shoes." I took them out of their boxes then laid them out on Janice's desk. "Black and brown."

Lucinda held up the two pairs of gigantic Italian imports for inspection. "Perfect. Dr. B. needs these pronto." She took the shoes, which were almost as big as she, and wobbled off, trying not to drop them. Busying myself with a magazine, I waited a half-hour for her return, but the lavender door remained closed. Lucinda disappearing into his office without so much as a "thank you" or "good-bye" was disconcerting, and I wondered whether she was mad at me.

Yes, something felt off. It wasn't just Lucinda's cool reception and quick disappearance. A weird vibe permeated the entire office, but I couldn't quite put my finger on what was wrong and so I just assumed it was my fault, just like I always did.

"Wake up and smell the coffee, Rose," Mom's voice echoed in my head.

I looked around and realized that Janice, who never left her desk, not even for lunch, wasn't there either. And where were the muffins?

"Do you need a brick wall to fall on you?" Another one of Mom's motivational quotes whispered from my subconscious. Perhaps I was being paranoid but the knot in my stomach and Mom's voice in my head told me otherwise. Maybe I did need a brick wall to fall on me 'cause I didn't do well with subtle. "Ohm. Ohm." I closed my eyes and tried a quick moment of meditation.

"Rose!" Lucinda stood in front of me.

I opened my eyes.

"Don't you have to pick up Dr. Berber's dry cleaning?" she asked in a sugarcoated voice. For a moment, the Lucinda of shared muffins and manicure chats returned.

I smiled back, then walked out of the green doors and ignored the pain in my stomach. The early October sun shone brightly and felt warm on my face. I couldn't help but smile when I saw the orange and red leaves blazing on the trees. I walked to Broadway, then turned up Forty-fifth Street en route to pick up Dr. B.'s dry cleaning. The smell was intoxicating as I passed Dunkin' Donuts, so I made a quick pit stop. "Three powdered sugars," I told the clerk. "I'll take one now and you can throw the rest in a bag." I left the store inhaling the first doughnut and reached for the second as I passed the Booth Theater and glanced at the marquee and saw Bethany Vance's picture. I froze. We'd graduated from college together and now she was starring in a play on the Big White Way, while I was picking up dry cleaning for the big white whale. My doughnut fell out of my hand and hit the ground. I missed the smell of grease paint and the roar of a crowd. (OK, not a crowd, and maybe the roar was just bursts of inappropriate laughter.) "It's not fair," I whispered. Pangs of jealousy ripped through me while I lingered in front of the marquee and stared at Bethany's face. For the first time, I resented my job. Working full time sucked. "Maybe I'd be on Broadway, too, if I had time to go to auditions!"

If it hadn't been for the bum throwing up in a garbage can five feet
away, I would've stood there all day, pondering the "what-ifs" of my
life. My face flushed as resentment filled my core and my old mantra,
"What next?" returned. I forced myself to move as the bum leapt over
and recovered my doughnut from the ground.

At the dry cleaners, the clerk handed me three enormous evening
gowns.

"Huh?"

"Just a minute." He walked to the back and took three sequined
jackets off a nearby rack. "I almost forgot 'bout these." He handed
three glitzy jackets over the counter.

"Wait! I think there's a mistake." I tried handing back the gowns to
the curt clerk while he backed away.

"This is a pickup for Dr. Berber, right?" He sounded agitated.

"Yes."

"*Those* are for him." He pointed to the gowns I was holding. "And
so are *these*." The belligerent asshole tossed the matching sequined
jackets across the concrete counter and almost knocked me down.

"But…" I remained steady and caught the jackets before they hit
the filthy floor.

"I remember the gal who dropped 'em off. This midget." He rolled
his eyes and chuckled.

"Little person."

"Yeah, she stumbled around and needed my help getting through
the door. Her face was hidden by all this stuff she carried." The clerk
laughed, and a familiar rage brewed inside.

"Thanks." I took the clothes off the counter and glared at the clerk.
The gowns and jackets weighed a ton. No way I was schlepping on a
subway with this load.

"Hey, lady, this is the ticket," he waved an orange receipt in my
face. "And that's his stuff. We done here?" A line had formed behind
me, and the clerk de jerk was anxious for me to move on. I glared at
him again, and then walked out the door. Did Doctor B. have a
girlfriend the same size as him, I wondered, and looked up and down
the avenue for a cab?

A week later, while waiting in the ornate lobby of the dog
groomer, I realized I hated being Dr. B.'s assistant. But I also hated
being poor. The one saving grace about being at 'Pooches Palace' was
the free doughnuts in the waiting room. "I'm wasting my life," I

whispered while shoving one chocolate doughnut after another into my mouth while waiting for the dogs' coifed return. Carting these mutts to the friggin groomer on a weekly basis sucked! I felt like a trained farm animal, not a personal assistant. An hour and a half and four doughnuts later, the doggie hairdresser handed back the two neurotic toy poodles and we left the salon and headed to the corner of West Fifty-third Street to hail a cab. Personal assistant my ass! I was a glorified errand girl. While holding the two dog cases and listening to them yap, I knew I wasn't really a farm animal. That was ridiculous. Nope, I was Dr. Berber's slave.

Chapter 29
What's Going On?

A few weeks before Thanksgiving, Lucinda told me the news. "Janice took an indefinite leave of absence and we need you to fill in for her."

"Starting when?"

"Today." She half-smiled, then handed me several envelopes. "After you take these to the post office."

"OK."

"They need to be certified."

I took the stack and shoved them inside my purse "Great," I said.

"Good. I'm glad resuming the receptionist role isn't a problem." She winked. "Welcome back, Rose." She patted me on the back.

"Thanks." I smiled, but my joyous expression was not heartfelt. Sometime among the trips to the dry cleaners, dog groomers, and the shoe repair, the thrill of being Dr. B.'s assistant soured. I was sick of schlepping through the streets and in spite of the great money and promised perks, my straight job had lost its seductiveness. I flirted with throwing caution to the wind and returning to my former life as a struggling actress. On the other hand, without a financial safety net, the thought was too frightening.

I left the office and walked down the five long blocks to the post office, pondering the notion of quitting. My stomach clenched, and I knew that today wasn't the day to take such a big risk. It was a Tuesday and I hadn't worn my lucky watch, two indicators that it was a bad time to bail. Besides, they needed me.

"Sitting behind Janice's desk isn't going to further my acting career," I whispered to the ground while waiting in line for the postal clerk.

"Neither is being broke and homeless," Dad shouted through my thoughts.

A half-hour later, back behind Janice's desk, my discontent abated and I felt grateful not to be at the dry cleaners. "It could be worse," I heard the voice of Mom, the eternal optimist, say. I reached into my purse for a Snickers bar and ignored her.

"Why is Janice on leave? Is she pregnant again?"

"I can't talk about that right now," Lucinda whispered while her eyes darted to and fro. "Let's talk later." She walked toward the lab, then yelled over her shoulder, "We'll meet at four."

When had a conversation achieved meeting status?

Later that day, two official-looking men wearing identical suits sat waiting in the lobby when I returned from my lunch break. "We're with the FBI." The tall, dark man approached me while the other, wearing sunglasses, stood beside him flashing his badge. "We need to talk to Dr. Berber and Lucinda Lindsey."

"They're not here," Lucinda bellowed as she flew through the office door leading into the lobby. "Rose, these need to be filed." Lucinda's hands shook as she handed me a stack of manila folders.

"It's important they contact us immediately." The Tommy Lee Jones wannabe flashing his badge sounded serious while Lucinda led both men to the lobby couch and out of earshot.

Five minutes later, Lucinda stood beside me while I filed the M's into the large wall cabinet. "Rose, do not, under any circumstances, give out information to anyone." She shook in her red shoes. "None!" Tiny beads of sweat formed on her forehead. "And if those two men come back, get me. At once!"

"What kind of information?"

"Oh. Nothing. It doesn't concern you, Rose." Her voice softened. "Don't worry." She shook her head. "Just get me!" Lucinda looked frazzled as she walked away, and then slipped behind Dr. B.'s lavender door.

It was the first time I'd seen those men and I wondered how long they'd been lurking around the office. Now I correlated Lucinda's cold shoulder and bad moods to the two strangers dressed in dark suits. Hell, the FBI could bring out the worst in Mother Teresa. Lucinda's transformation was not my fault. It was the government's. A surge of relief powered through me, and I realized a basic truth: not everything was my fault, even things I didn't understand. Discounting the lessons I'd received throughout childhood was hard but I didn't need a brick wall to fall on me; just two men with FBI badges.

The next day, I was determined to wheedle information out of Lucinda. A good night's sleep gave me a different attitude. I sat behind Janice's desk, pretending to be busy. "There's a great new nail salon on Fifty-seventh Street."

Lucinda's head was buried inside a patient's chart. She nodded but didn't look up.

"It's right next to Cohen's bakery." I pulled a bag of pastries from inside my purse. "This is for you." I smiled and placed a blueberry muffin in Lucinda's hand. She could be bribed, couldn't she? Yesterday's insights piqued my curiosity and now I needed to know the truth.

"Rose, I don't have time. Dr. B. is waiting for me." She mustered a weak smile, then set the muffin on the far edge of the desk. "Sorry," she said then headed toward Dr. Berber's office.

An hour later she was back, peering over my shoulder into the lobby. "Is that them?"

"Who?"

"You know, Rose, the men from the other day?" Her voice quivered.

"No, Lucinda, it's the mailman." Now her anxiety heightened mine.

"Oh, thank goodness," she muttered and disappeared. But it wasn't long before she returned. "Rose, I hear talking out there." She tilted her head toward the lobby. "Is it them?"

I peered through the glass partition and saw two men dressed in gray uniforms. "No, it's the exterminators."

"But their voices sound just like those FBI men! Are you sure, Rose? Are you sure?"

"Yes, I am positive. They have spray cans." Was she hallucinating?

By the end of the week, I was convinced that something was indubitably wrong and made another attempt to stop ignoring the obvious. Dr. Berber's office was under a secretive spell that only Lucinda and he were privy to. Pretending all was hunky-dory in the Land of Odd was no longer an option. Dressed in my lucky sweater and wearing my lucky watch, timing was on my side when Lucinda appeared beside Janice's desk the split-second I'd gotten up my nerve. "Uh, can I talk to you for a moment?" My voice squeaked, and my palms were sweaty.

Lucinda said sure, and smiled a little too broadly.

"What's going on here?" I blurted out.

"Dr. B.'s preparing for his book tour." She looked calm and sounded relaxed. "In L.A." Her voice lilted as she pulled up a chair and sat down beside me. Lucinda seemed serene. Maybe she'd taken a Valium. Or was drunk.

"Yes, I know. I don't mean that. It's all the other stuff."

"What other stuff?" My pointed question sobered Lucinda up, and her smile vanished.

"Those men from the FBI, for starters."

"Shush, Rose." Her head spun around, reminding me of Linda Blair from *The Exorcist*. "Please, Rose, just do your job and don't ask any questions." She pleaded in a hushed whisper. "Don't ask questions," she repeated.

Don't ask questions. Mitch had been emphatic. Now Lucinda parroted him and I should've listened to them but didn't.

"Why? What is so…"

"Trust me, Rose, you are better off not knowing." She cut me off. "I wish I didn't."

Just then we heard Dr. Berber's office door open.

"Rose, act busy. Look through the appointment book," Lucinda said in a slow, deliberate voice, and then headed off to the bathroom.

The sound of Dr. B.'s footsteps grew louder as I rifled through the appointment book. A few moments later, I made a bogus phone call and pretended not to notice his large presence behind me.

"Rose, when you're off the phone, call these bookstores and confirm the times." Dr. B.'s beady black eyes darted back and forth scanning the waiting room. "Here's all the information." He placed a stack of papers on Janice's desk, then walked back to his office and slammed the lavender door. I hung up the phone and closed my eyes.

"Rose, please come home. They have nice Jewish doctors in Florida who need receptionists." I tuned out Mom's voice, opened Janice's desk, and grabbed my secret stash of Milky Way bars.

"Do you really need that?" Mom's voice hocked inside my head again.

"Yes. Definitely." Three enormous bites later, the candy bar was finished. "Mmmmm, that's better." After the sugar rush wore off, I felt more depressed than before and slumped in my chair while staring out into the empty lobby that looked like a morgue. Perhaps this is the slow season for diet doctors. Who was I kidding? I tried to put my head in the sand, but it was too late.

The day before Thanksgiving, seated at the counter of Mickey's

Pizzeria, I had a disturbing thought: What if my life were in danger? What if those FBI guys came back and there was a shoot-out? What if a stray bullet hit me in the head and I ended up in the hospital, or worse, in a coma?

"Let's just pull the plug now, " Heather would say.

"Good idea, she's costing us a fortune hooked up to all those damn wires," Dad would agree.

"No!" Mom would insist. "The doctor said there's a chance she'll recover." Thank God for Mom.

I had a revelation in between bites of a greasy calzone: Needing to know the truth was no longer curiosity, it was a matter of life and death. I was an oxymoron, content and uneasy at work, unable to escape my gut feeling that I was in danger yet I enjoyed a cushy job with a great paycheck. But was it worth risking my life for? What if the FBI guys thought I was mixed up in Dr. B.'s mysterious shenanigans and I got arrested? And taken away in handcuffs? And had an awful mug shot taken without makeup and in terrible lighting, to boot!

Why was it always something?

I finished my lunch and then headed back to the office, ready to ask the hard questions.

Lucinda would smile and try to brush me off again. "Don't ask questions, Rose. You don't need to know," she'd say no doubt.

"Yes, I do." No way I'd let her back down. "Where are all the patients? What was the truth behind Janice's quitting? Why do I hear constant whispering? What did those FBI men want? And most important, why aren't there any more muffins?" I rehearsed all the way back to the office, committed to get direct answers. I walked through the big green doors but stopped short in the lobby.

"You're late," Lucinda said while Dr. Berber stood towering over her and shook his head.

"Uh, ummm." I saw my boss as he hovered over Lucinda and lost my nerve and my voice. "Sorry," I mumbled, then lowered my head. *Yes I'd be direct: directly after Thanksgiving.*

Chapter 30
If I Only Had the Nerve

Sometime between my confrontation with Lucinda and Thanksgiving morning, I aborted my plan to dig deeper and get the truth about what was going on at Dr. Berbers Emporium. It was too late for questions. Now quitting, rather than obtaining answers, felt easier and safer. Besides, hadn't I come to New York to be an actress? Did I really want to be another theatrical casualty like Pam? Or Ce? I wasn't completely sure, but after my long, hot shower, I penned a short, to the point, letter of resignation anyway. What I needed was a sign from the universe to confirm my decision. However, I had the flu and reading my own handwriting was difficult, let alone deciphering supernatural codes. Looking for signs would have to wait.

Monday morning I felt much better. I dumped two empty Nyquil bottles into the kitchen garbage can and dressed for work. Now I was more than ready to head back to the office and face the task at hand: fleeing Oz. I stuffed the letter inside a panel of my coat pocket as a wave of nausea washed over me. "Just stage fright," I reassured myself while I flung my coat on and tried to ignore my anxiety.

"Bye, kitty," I shouted while flipping off the kitchen light switch and pretending not to see my hand tremble. I locked the apartment door and a cold sweat ensued as I walked down my hallway and prayed for the lucky elevator. I knew deep inside that resigning was the right move, but nonetheless I was apprehensive. I hated change.

Ten minutes later, positioned on the deserted platform inside the train station, I chain-smoked my Marlboro lights and waited for the train. In between puffs, I checked and rechecked the inside of my coat pocket. I felt the smooth envelope underneath my gloved hand and my anxiety abated (a little), but I was still sweating buckets. My hands were clammy and felt trapped inside the wool mittens, so I ripped them off and stuffed them deep inside my coat pocket.

Adrenalin flowed as I heard the first faint rumble of the subway in the distance. "Friggin finally!" The light from the No. 6's headlight shone at the tunnel entrance, and a minute later pulled up beside the platform.

I hopped onboard and crammed next to people who were all sneezing and coughing. Their symphony of sickness made me fearful of catching some new virus, and so I huddled into a corner and buried my face inside the right shoulder of my coat. Feeling claustrophobic, I gritted my teeth, held my breath, closed my eyes and prayed that we wouldn't get stuck in a tunnel. A few minutes later, the train screeched to a halt, and people pushed and shoved their way out of the doors while I dragged along among them.

"Today's my last day!" I told a filthy pile of half-melted snow heaped next to the subway's stairwell. Smiling, I fought my post-flu exhaustion as I schlepped up the subway station stairs to the street. "Ommm, Ommm." I repeated my mantra, which helped keep me steady on my feet while I walked the few blocks to the office. Nauseous I opened the heavy green glass doors and then stepped inside. I felt like I was going to a funeral, my own.

"Dr. Berber wants to see you." Lucinda's face looked as white as her lab coat. "He's in his office." She rolled her eyes and shook her head, then headed down the corridor leading to the lab.

"Come home, Rose. Elaine Feldman met her husband while working for a proctologist on Miami Beach. I'm sure you could find a job here in no time." I blocked Mom's voice from inside my head as I walked toward Dr. B.'s office door. My legs felt heavy as if my boots were filled with lead while I stood outside his door and rechecked my coat pocket.

"Maybe he'll fire me. Then I won't have to quit." Hating confrontation, I stalled outside the lavender door as my heart pounded. "I can do this. I can do this," I repeated while a forced smile crossed my face and my hand turned the familiar doorknob.

"Come in, Rose," Dr. B. said while he paced back and forth. "I'm breaking in my new Italians."

I stared down at his shoes, which looked like miniature canoes on his giant feet. "Good morning. You wanted to see me?" I felt flushed as I took two baby steps inside his domain.

"Close the door." He continued his gait, then after a minute, stopped dead center in the room. "As you know, I'm heading to L.A. on Wednesday." Dr. B. looked at me squarely in the face, then took his left shoe off and bent it backward with his giant hands. "Eighty-two degrees and sunny." He smiled warmly.

I forced a smile but avoided eye contact.

"Have you ever been to L.A., Rose?" Dr. B. asked.

"No." As I answered, my mind started racing. Maybe Dr. B. was going to make good on all of those promised perks and ask me to go with him. After all, I was his personal assistant. Perhaps I'd misread the whole situation and all was well in Oz. Picturing us seated in first class, jet setting off to L.A., I relaxed a little and for a moment forgot completely about the oddities in Oz, and about resigning.

"L.A. is fabulous!" he said.

I could wear my new clothes. My heart skipped a beat as I took another few steps to the chair in front of his desk.

"Have a seat, Rose. Sit."

I sat down, then noticed the smells of pickles and corned beef, the signature scent of his office, were gone. Perhaps it's a sign! A sign not to resign. For the first time in weeks I felt hopeful and forgot about my life being in danger. I asked, "Did you have a nice Thanksgiving?"

Dr. B. didn't answer but slid his shoe back on his foot then resumed his pacing. My eyes followed him like a Ping-Pong ball. "Rose," he said. "I know how hard you work and I hate overloading you, but…"

But?

"I need this done ASAP." His pacing halted, and he removed a piece of paper off his desk and handed it to me.

I looked at his scribble on the single sheet of lined notebook paper. "Schedule a manicure, pedicure, back wax and facial at The Beverly Hills Hotel." Back wax? My heart sank and I knew unequivocally that the list of spa treatments was for his mystery girlfriend and that she was accompanying him on the tour. The woman whose oversized evening gowns I'd schlepped all over Manhattan would be jet-setting off to Los Angeles (hairy back and all) and not me. So much for signs.

"Doctors! They're all just sons of bitches." I tried to block Dad's taunting out of my head but couldn't.

"Shut up," I whispered.

"What, Rose?" Dr. B.'s stare brought me back to reality.

"Uh… no problem." My cheeks blazed, and my stomach tumbled.

"That's it, Rose. You can go now," he said a bit snarky.

Knowing there wasn't a better time to hand him my resignation letter, I fought the urge to puke, stood up and reached into my coat pocket.

"Uh, one more thing…" he said.

Now what?

"Would ya pick up my lunch from Carnegie Deli? Have 'em double up on the pickles and corned beef. Jeez, I missed that over Thanksgiving."

My hand grasped the letter inside my coat. It was time to seize the moment before my window of opportunity closed. He could get his own friggin lunch. "Dr. B.," my voice squeaked.

"And make sure the corned beef is fatty," he said.

"Dr. B., I need to talk to…"

"I'm starving here! So go now, Rose," he ordered.

I tried to speak, but no words came out. I'd lost my nerve and stood frozen in fear.

"And get a little something for yourself, too, Rosie. Put it on my tab." He winked.

"Sure," I answered while my window of opportunity slammed shut. I looked away so he couldn't see the tears in my eyes and the sweat dripping from underneath my chin.

"Oh, and while you're there, I need you to pick something up for me. From this guy named Lucas," he said as an after thought.

"Lucas?" I wiped the sweat off my neck with the sleeve of my coat and noticed Dr. B. holding both shoes in his hands.

"He works in the kitchen. He has something important for me." He sat down behind his large desk. "When you pick up my lunch, ask the cashier to get him. Lucas will give you a briefcase." He plopped both enormous shoes on top of his desk.

The clunk from his shoes startled me. "Wait… what?" I'd zoned out and didn't have a clue what he was saying. "Briefcase?"

"Yes, briefcase, Rose." His beady eyes bore through my forehead as he spoke with deliberation: "Just - bring – the – case – and – my – lunch - back to the office."

"OK," I said and nodded my head, feeling like a small child.

"OK." He smiled a big toothy grin, reminding me of an ogre.

I shut the lavender door behind me and quickened my pace down the corridor. "Chicken!" sister Heather mocked inside my head as I sped up my pace and raced through the reception area out onto the sidewalk. Forty-five minutes later, while standing in the take-out line that stretched out the door of the Carnegie Deli, I devised another plan. "I'll mail him the resignation letter." Elated, I smiled. This plan would save me from another face-to-face with Dr. B. (And from chickening out, again.) "Why didn't I think of this before?" My spirit felt restored and I did a happy dance in my head.

"Mail, schmail, just leave New York, Rose! I haven't changed a thing in your room." The noise from inside the restaurant spilled into the street and drowned out Mom's voice as I made my way inside, inching closer to the front of the take-out line.

"Next!" the ancient-looking woman sitting behind a steel cash register yelled.

"Berber. I have a pickup for Dr. Berber," I told the cashier. Perhaps this was Dr. B.'s idea of accompanying him out for a fancy meal?

"Berber!" she screamed into the air. "Pickup for Berber!" She yelled again then lit up a long brown cigarette.

While waiting, I almost forgot about the briefcase. "Umm, I also need to see someone named..." I lowered my voice "....umm, Lucas? Dr. Berber said..."

"Lucas!" She yelled in a raspy, been-smoking-since-birth voice. A few moments later, a large, Styrofoam container with Dr. B.'s lunch arrived and so did Lucas.

"You Rose?" His low voice and thick New Jersey accent sounded familiar.

"Yes. You have something for Dr. Berber?"

"It's over dare..."

"Where?"

"Dare." His head jolted toward the back of the restaurant. "Near da can."

I followed him and his noticeable shoulder twitch caught my attention and seemed familiar, too. But it wasn't until we got to the phone banks next to the bathroom that his obvious hair plugs jogged my memory.

I remembered Ce introducing a stranger reeking of alcohol. "This is Lucky..." This couldn't be the same guy from that ill-fated trip to Vegas, could it? The creepy Mafioso-looking guy who Ce nabbed while playing roulette?

"Hey, lady, youz OK?" Lucas stared at me while I remembered that Vegas night. Was this the same guy who later paid for champagne in the casino bar after Pam told me she was a "recovering thespian?"

"Whaa?" My eyes fixated on the rim of his forehead.

"You wanna dis or no?" His voice was gruff.

How could there be two sets of such horrible hair-plugs? What were the chances?

"C'mon, lady, I ain't gots all day." Lucas sounded anxious as he shifted from one foot to the next. "Take it." Lucas extended his arm, grasping the handle of a small black case.

My eyes widened. "Do I know you?" The twitch might've been coincidental but there was no mistaking those plugs.

"I knows a lot of peeps." He shrugged. "I dunno. Do youz know me?" he asked with a poker face.

"No, not really. But yes, I think we've met."

"Hey, doll, I'd remember a cute little piece of..."

"Las Vegas!" I interrupted. Now I was certain. I was one hundred percent positive that Lucky and Lucas were one and the same. Those plugs were as identifiable as fingerprints.

"Las Vegas?" His eyes narrowed.

I nodded as I took the case out of his hand.

"Nope." Lucas shook his head while our eyes met. Then his demeanor changed and his eyes bulged like someone with a thyroid condition. His head lowered while he stared at my breasts. "You don't know *me* and I don't knows *YOU*. Just fageddaboutit." He winced, then disappeared into the men's room.

With Dr. B.'s lunch in one hand and Lucas' case in the other, I walked out of the restaurant, then ran for two long blocks until the Carnegie Deli and the imaginary gangsters chasing me disappeared from sight. Minutes later, the office was in view. Luckily, no one was around when I entered through the lobby doors. Each second seemed endless as I tiptoed down the hallway, then arrived in front of the lavender door that guarded Dr. B.'s shrine. I bent down and leaned his lunch and the mysterious briefcase against the closed door. A moment later, I crammed my resignation letter under the handle of the case and breathed a sigh of relief. "Done," I whispered, and then looked in both directions. Certain that the coast was clear, I bolted out of Dr. Berber's emporium. Forever.

My mission to flee Oz was completed and a tremendous sense of accomplishment bubbled within. "I did it! I did it!" tripped off my tongue while racing toward the subway station. "Yippee. Hooray for me!" My feet scarcely touched the pavement as I flew down the dark stairwell.

My train sounded in the distance, and a moment later it arrived at the platform. With an exuberant bounce in my step I hopped on board and sat down in the middle of an empty row of seats. "Well done," I said as the train pulled out of the station. "Well friggin done!" I mentally patted myself on the back, closed my eyes and nestled inside my warm winter coat, feeling safe. "It's over." A smile crossed my face, and contentment oozed from my pores. However, it wasn't long before the usual act of players living in my head interrupted.

"You did a stupid, brazen thing, Rose. Leaving your job, with nothing else lined up." Dad's harsh words ripped through my mind like a hacksaw. "We're not sending you any money. No siree. Not bailing you out!"

"Oh, Rose, come home!" Mom's imaginary voice pleaded. "Acting jobs can't pay the rent!"

"Yeah, Rose, give up your little hobby," hissed Heather. "You're never gonna be a real actress. Never."

"Fuck off!" I yelled as my eyes popped open and I felt the train screech to a halt. The two teenage girls seated across from me giggled.

"Mommy, that lady said the F word," a child's voice shrieked and I turned my head in her direction. My face flushed with embarrassment while a woman seated three rows behind me shook her head and covered a little girl's ears with cupped hands.

"The F word, Mommy!" the child screamed out again, and I cringed.

"Twenty-eighth Street," the train conductor's voice blared through a loud speaker, drowning out the child's reprimand and the voices of my family inside my head. "Fuck off," I whispered. I zipped up my coat, then walked through the open subway doors and headed home.

Chapter 31
No Laughing Matter

My exhilaration soon faded, and by Saturday it was obliterated. Maybe quitting without a plan (or a financial safety net) wasn't such a great idea, after all.

"Now what, Rose? Prostitution? Like Ce?" Dad creaked. I tried ignoring the seeds of uncertainty he planted inside my subconscious but couldn't. Dark doubts avalanched inside my head, and I spiraled downward into an emotional funk. No job or acting career. What next? What next?

I crawled into bed with three-day-old pizza and pulled the last slice out of a grease-stained box. "What am I doing in New York City?" I asked Pirate. "What the hell am I doing here?"

Pirate spied my pizza and clamored for food, "Meow!"

Some cheese dangled from the tepid slice, and I tore it off. "Here ya go, Kitty."

Pirate gobbled it up and then stalked me for more.

"No more, Pirate. No more." Not in the mood to play "Dr. Doolittle," I ignored him and clicked on the television.

Maybe it's time to call it quits and leave New York. A cold chill traveled down my spine. The idea of another change was overwhelming. I took a large bite from the pizza. "One, two, three…" I counted. Counting was mind numbing and that's what I needed. Twelve chews later, I flipped from channel to channel at rapid speed while Pirate perched on top of the pillow next to me and mewed. "No more!" I told his pleading eyes and he hissed then jumped to the floor. "Where was I? Oh, yeah… fourteen, fifteen, sixteen." The channel surfing combined with counting soothed me and I continued this ritual until something on TV caught my attention.

"Dr. Berber?" His giant face covered the screen. My jaw dropped, and pizza bits tumbled out of my mouth, falling between the crumpled bed sheets. "Oh my God!" A voice-over played in the background but I was so startled that the words were incomprehensible. I leaped out of bed, raced across my bedroom and cranked up the volume.

"Dr. Stanley Berber's death appears to be from a drug overdose. A black briefcase containing several grams of cocaine, three vials of heroin and a half empty vial of Vicodin was found on a nightstand at the posh Beverly Hills Hotel."

My eyes widened as I stood in front of the set and watched the camera zoom in on the exact case that I'd escorted across town a few days earlier. The clandestine meeting with Lucas (aka Lucky) spun inside my head, and my stomach flipped. Had I been Dr. B.'s drug mule? Was I an accomplice? What if the FBI got my fingerprints off that case and I go to jail? That would be worse than being in a coma. Those jail cells were teeny.

"A final cause of death will be determined by the coroner, who will seek toxicology tests. The preliminary investigation turned up no signs of foul play and authorities are tagging his death as an accidental drug overdose or suicide. The famous Manhattan-based doctor also authored several books and was in Los Angeles to promote his latest release."

"The cleaning staff of The Beverly Hills Hotel discovered Dr. Berber's body when they arrived inside the penthouse for routine room maintenance."

The camera refocused on the faces of two petite blonds. "We knocked, but no one answered," the girl on the right side of the screen explained in a monotone voice. "So we opened the door and went in."

"We had to clean the room," the girl next to her added, while she nodded her head and chomped on gum. "There was a strong stench. Like rotten pickles."

"Like some funky deli."

"Then we saw her lying on the bed."

"We thought she was sleeping."

"At first we thought it was a woman." The two girls blurted out together.

"'Cause she was wearing a sequined gown. But..."

"But it was a man." Nervous laughter erupted as the camera swish panned onto the news commentator's stern face.

The camera then refocused on the reporter. "Dr. Berber was under an eighteen-month secret FBI investigation for insurance fraud in addition to practicing medicine without a license."

A moment later the commentator was back on the screen. "Now for the weather," he said.

Just then my phone rang.

"Can you believe it?" Ce said melodramatically. Although it was months since we'd spoken, she blabbed away, like we'd chatted yesterday. "You told me he was a little weird, but a cross-dresser?"

"Yep, pretty weird." Dr. Berber was a fake doctor by day and diva by night. It wasn't weird. It was fucking unbelievable!

Ce continued talking, but I wasn't listening because   fragments of the reporter's words spun inside my brain: "Cocaine. Heroin. A large briefcase. Overdose. Autopsy reports."

"Rose, are you there?" Ce asked.

Dr. Berber was dead. An eerie chill traveled down my spine while I tried processing this information.

"Rose? Are you listening to me?" Ce's voice sounded far, far away.

Dead. My stomach clenched further into a tight ball, and my head pounded. Ever since I was a child I'd been terrified of death. "What happens when I die?" I had asked my dad when I was just five years old.

"Rose, I'm reading the paper. Don't bother me now." Dad sat on his plaid recliner in the corner of the living room and hid behind *The Miami Herald*.

"Daddy, please tell me, do you know what happens?" I stood in front of him, hoping he'd see me through the sports section.

"What, Rose?" he mumbled.

"What happens when I die?"

"Nothing happens" he told me, folding the newspaper in half.

"Nothing? But where will I go?"

"Into the ground." Dad yawned then put the paper on top of the white wicker table next to his chair.

"In the ground? Won't I get dirty?" Confused, I scratched my head.

Dad saw my confusion and explained how the funeral home puts you in a box first, after a Mortician drains your blood. Dad took off his glasses then closed his eyes.

No longer confused, I was horrified. "How will I get out of the box?"

"When you're dead, you're dead," Dad assured me. "You can't get out of the box." His chuckle was sadistic and mean.

"What about the angels? And heaven? What about...?"

Dad shooed me away to ask my mother because he needed to nap.

Two minutes later, Dad stretched out on the recliner, snoring, and I was traumatized for life.

"Rose!" Ce screamed on the other end of the phone. "Are you listening?

"Yes," I answered in a voice befitting a five-year-old.

She blabbed endlessly but I couldn't focus on a single word she was saying until something she said caught my attention.

"Rose, does this mean you're jobless again?"

"Yes, I guess I am jobless." Those words stung as they tripped off my tongue. Then I remembered my resignation letter. "Wait... I already quit."

"When?" Ce asked.

"Wednesday."

"Too bad." She paused and pondered a moment. "You could've collected unemployment."

Ce's concern, like her questions, was irritating. "I gotta go," I told her. Everything had happened too fast and the ice cream in my freezer trumped hearing Ce's take on unemployment benefits. "I'll call you later." Sugar, not conversation, was what I needed.

"I'm coming over. And we're going out."

"No!"

"You're not sitting alone in that apartment and dwelling!"

Ce was right. Dwelling was what I'd planned for the rest of that evening and for the days that followed. "But..."

"Rose, listen to me!"

I was freaked out and trembled as an unexpected sadness engulfed me. We might not have seen eye to eye, but Dr. Berber was my boss.

"Rose? Are you there?" Ce yelled.

"Yes." *But Dr. Berber wasn't. He was dead.*

"I'm coming over and we're gonna go out."

I'd never known a dead person before. "What?"

A take-charge tone filled her voice. "I'll be there in half an hour." For a moment, she sounded like my mother.

"No. I..."

She hung up.

"...Don't feel like going anywhere," I said to the dial tone. I forced myself off of the bed and then dragged my feet into the kitchen. The sudden blast of cold air felt good as I opened the freezer and took out the Haagen-Dazs chocolate ice cream stashed behind an ice cube tray.

I scraped a large tablespoon along the rim of the container and then dug in. The coldness inside my mouth felt comforting and several more spoonfuls followed. I closed my eyes and took a deep breath.

"The man was a drug addict," Mom's voice echoed. "He killed himself! He wasn't even a real doctor." As if that justified his death and would make me feel better. Tears rolled down my face while I finished the pint of ice cream then tossed the container into the trash. I returned to my bedroom on weak legs and spied Pirate curled up in a ball, peacefully asleep on the floor. "In my next life, I want to be a cat."

A half-hour later, my intercom buzzed. "Ce's here. She's waiting for you in a cab," Oscar announced.

I rode the lucky elevator down to the lobby while the news report played on an endless loop inside my head.

Still overwhelmed, I headed through the lobby doors and walked outside. Ce was in the backseat of a large Checker, and waved through the window.

"Roooose, hop in!" she yelled.

I opened the cab door and climbed inside. She threw her arms around me. "Oh Rose, I've missed you!"

"Me too." I slid in beside her and slammed the cab door shut. "Where are we going?" I asked as the cab sped off.

"Dangerfield's." She put her hand in mine and gave it a gentle squeeze.

"Oh." I slouched down into the backseat and managed a weak smile. My eyes rested on her left hand that was cupped on top of mine and I spied the ring she'd had since kindergarten. Sometime between college and New York more elaborate ones had replaced that simple ring. But there it was again around her pinkie.

"It's the hottest comedy club ever!" Ce squeezed my hand and then took out her compact from her oversized purse.

"That's nice." I watched while she looked into the small hand mirror. How did that flower ring with the red stone still fit on her finger?

"We're gonna have some laughs tonight, Rosie." She smiled at her reflection while she swept a powder brush across her face.

"Whatever." I mumbled and noticed she wasn't wearing her cubic zirconium and matching wedding band. Was she still married? Having had enough drama for one day, I put my head into the sand and ignored the implication of her missing jewelry.

The bumper-to-bumper traffic sucked. After twenty minutes, Ce tapped on the glass partition that separated us from the driver in a frantic frenzy! "Oh sir. Mr. Cabbie. Can ya speed it up!"

The driver changed lanes, then wove in and out of traffic and scared the shit out of me.

"Can you believe this?" Ce wailed as I held on to her arm for dear life.

"Slow down!" I closed my eyes and prayed while the cabbie cut off three cars and a truck. A moment later, we experienced a miracle. We'd made it to the curbside alive. Ce paid him while I walked behind the cab, leaned over the curb and puked.

"Oh sweetie, are you OK? Here, let me wipe off your mouth." She pulled a tissue out of her coat pocket and then blotted away a piece of cheese that dangled off of my bottom lip. "There, all better." She grinned. Ce was there when I needed her, and I was grateful. She sprinted toward the club and I lagged behind.

Suddenly, Ethan popped into my head. "Rooooose, I loooooove you." His voice was so clear I turned around to look for him but no one was there.

Ce stopped short. "Oh Shiiiiit. The line is halfway down the block!" She screamed over her shoulder, "Rose, hurry up." Her shrill screech vaporized any further thoughts about Ethan.

"I'm coming," I answered in a low whisper.

"I'm not standing in that friggin line!" she screamed again, as she turned around, walked back and got me. "Let's go!" She slid my arm through hers, and then pulled me along, heading toward the front.

We passed about a hundred people who'd been waiting to get inside the club, and their nasty death glares made me nervous.

"Hey, Blondie, where do ya think you're going? The line's back there!" an unquestionably large man with a skull tattooed on his forehead screamed.

"I don't do lines," she told him, flipped him the bird as we forged ahead. Ce was on a mission, and her pace remained steady until we reached the bouncer who blocked the entrance to the club.

"Now what?" I whispered.

"Hey, Ce." The large beefcake body-builder guarding the door smiled. Ce and he exchanged a brief embrace. "Go right in." His smile broadened and we swept past several more irritated people who stood behind a red velvet rope.

"Thanks, Tony." Ce blew him a kiss over her shoulder and we walked inside the club like two celebrities.

"How do you know that guy?"

"Tony? Oh. From a commercial shoot."

"What commercial?"

"The nonprofit ad. Don't you remember, Rose?"

Vaguely. She'd picked up a guy during our "bee" gig that directed commercials. He'd later cast her in some public service campaign about venereal disease. Tony, yes that was his name. She'd drooled over him until the gynecologist said the muscle aches and swollen glands weren't caused by the flu. Neither were the painful blisters near her *not*-so-private-parts. "It's herpes," he had told her.

Life had imitated art, and not in a good way. Was this Tony that Tony?

"Same Tony." Ce said as if reading my mind. "Who needs Walter's contacts?" Ce's tone hardened, "I have my own!" She sounded indignant and took off her faux-fur then threw it at the coatroom attendant. "Here ya go, honey. Don't lose it." Ce's eyes darted around the packed club.

The coat-check clerk handed me Ce's claim check and a moment later I faced Ce and against all my better judgment asked, "How is Walter?"

Avoiding the question, she rummaged inside her handbag. "Got any cigs?"

Scrounging through my purse, I found a crumpled Marlboro pack. "Here." After handing her a cigarette, I dug around the bottom of my purse for a match.

"We're taking a break," Ce quipped. She took my cig out of my hand and put it in her mouth. Then with a single flick of her Bic, lit both. "Take my advice, don't get married." She sounded bitter and a tad hostile. She inhaled deeply on her smoke, then handed me mine. "Don't get married, Rose," she repeated. "Ever!"

"A break? What does that mean?"

She turned away and again didn't answer. "I'll be right back." She strutted off through the lobby.

My feet throbbed while my eyes scanned the room for somewhere to sit. After holing up in my apartment for four days, the crowd inside the small lobby felt like dangerous strangers as my claustrophobia kicked into high gear. I was certain that all bald men were Lucky and anyone dressed in a suit was with the FBI. My hands felt clammy and the back of my neck was drenched with sweat while the newscaster's voice echoed inside my head, "Dr. Berber was found dead. Dead. Dead." My body trembled as I closed my eyes and tried in vain to fight off a full-blown anxiety attack. "Ohm mm Ohm mm," I repeated, but my mantra wasn't working. I leaned against a wall, praying for Ce's return. My entire back was soaking wet and I wanted to run out the door and go home but my feet refused to budge.

And then, Ce reappeared. "C'mon, Rose. I got us a table up front." She smiled and wiped the sweat off my face with the sleeve of her dress. Placing her arm through mine, she maneuvered us through the crowded lobby to the door leading into the main room.

"Thanks, Ce." Zombie like, I followed her.

"Here we are," she said a minute later as she plopped me into a chair next to hers. "We're ringside!"

Ce grabbed the waiter as he walked by our table and then ordered two white wines. "We need them fast. It's an emergency."

I sighed with relief and felt my body return to a normal temperature and stopped shaking.

After a few moments of silence Ce's eyes met mine. "Rose. It'll be OK." She attempted a smile.

"Sure. Whatever."

"It will. It will all be OK." I think she was trying to convince herself as well as me.

"Right."

Ce grew quiet for several moments and then trumpeted, "EVERYTHING WILL BE FUCKING FINE!"

I had a sudden urge to laugh but shook my head instead. "My life pretty much sucks."

"Everyone's life sucks, sometimes." She closed her eyes and was quiet again. Then a few seconds later with her eyes still shut, she said with more quiet conviction than I'd ever heard from her, "Everything will be OK."

"Everything?"

She opened her eyes and laughed. "Yes, every fucking thing." She reached across the table and took my hands. "You worry too much,

Rose. You'll get another job. You'll get…"

"That's easy for you to say." I stared past her. "You're like Pirate, a cat with nine lives."

Ce squeezed my hand and I gripped hers tightly, as if she were the only thing solid in the room.

My voice cracked as my words started running together. "You've always managed to pick up the pieces and move on, Ce. But…" I looked down at the cigarette burn on the table. "I feel like I'm inside of a paper bag trying to punch my way out."

"Rose, I just roll with the punches and take life as it comes."

I wiped a tear off my cheek. "I wish I could."

"You can, Rose." She looked into my eyes again. "You just need to let go a little, learn to trust that things will work out. You can't make life happen. It just does." Now Ce sounded like she was quoting a passage from Walter's self-help books. "And besides, you always have your signs." She giggled.

"Oh yeah, my signs." I rolled my eyes "They haven't helped much lately."

Ce loosened the grip on my hands and slid the flower ring off her pinkie. "Wear this, Rose." She placed the ring in front of me. "It's always been my lucky charm."

"Ce! I can't take your ring. It's your special…"

"Rose, I want you to wear it for a while." She shoved the little flower ring with the ruby center closer to me. "Wear it until you get your lucky sign, good omen, or whatever else you need to be happy."

"Are you sure?"

"Abso-friggin-lutely!"

I put the ring on my pinkie finger and smiled for the first time in days.

"It's always brought me luck. Now it's your turn." She smiled back.

The waiter arrived with our drinks and when he placed them on the table, Ce said, "We're gonna need another round right away." She put a glass of wine in my hand, and then lifted up hers. "Cheers. To best friends… forever."

"Cheers."

The MC's voice boomed through the microphone, filling the room. "Ladies and Gentleman, welcome to Dangerfield's."

"Thank you, Ce." We clinked our glasses together, then chugged the wine. When I looked at her ring on my finger, a tear of gratitude rolled down my cheek. It seemed like ages since Ce had come through and been there for me, and although I never lost hope and knew in my heart that our friendship was timeless, I had felt abandoned. But now, here she was when I needed her most, and that confirmed what I'd suspected since kindergarten. We'd be best friends forever.

"The ring will bring you great luck." She winked.

I winked back and felt calm. Despite it all, when the rest of the world let us down, we'd always have each other, no matter what.

Chapter 32
Star Struck

A week later, the phone startled me out of a coma. The clock on my nightstand read 4:00! Who the hell was calling at this hour? "Hello?" My voice trembled.

The caller hesitated. "Rose, did I wake you?"

"Mitch? Oh my God, Mitch, are you OK?" Always assume the worst; that's what I'd learned from Dad. "Who died?"

"What? No one, Oh God, no one died, Rose." He laughed.

"Why are you calling at four in the morning?"

"Four in the morning? Rose, it's almost four-thirty in the afternoon! Are you OK?" Mitch panicked. "Rose, you didn't do anything stupid, did you? I'm coming right over there."

"No, Mitch, I'm fine. I was just sleeping."

"How many of those sleeping pills did you take, Rose?"

"I didn't take any pills! I was just taking a nap."

"Sorry to wake you," Mitch said softly. Then he shouted "Time to get up!" It was pitch dark outside, but as I heard the rain hit against my window, I realized I must've dozed off while watching Walter on 'One Life to Give.' "Rose, wake up!"

"OK. I'm up." Reaching over to my nightstand, I grabbed a cigarette. "So?"

"Are you sitting down?" I felt Mitch's grin through the phone line.

"I'm lying down." My curiosity piqued.

"'Cause this is exciting news, Rose."

"What's up?"

"I SAW AND HEARD YOU IN THAT MOVIE!" he screamed.

I held the phone away from my ear. "What are you talking about? What movie?" No longer groggy from my nap, now I was deaf.

"Rose, wake up! How many movies have ya been in where you had lines?" Mitch's voice dripped with sarcasm. "The movie where you play a secretary and you were replaced. I saw you in that purple jacket."

I shot upright, jolted awake, then jumped to my feet. "For real? If this is a joke, I'm gonna kill…"

"I'm not joking. I saw you up on the big screen. They got your good side! And I heard your line. You were brilliant!"

"How? They replaced me."

"I know."

How could he not? He'd heard all the details of that day at least twenty times. "So, tell me already!" I dragged on my cigarette and listened.

"You said they did a rehearsal and then shot it once before that sleaze director replaced you with some slut who was probably giving him blow jobs. When the film got sent to the editing department, the editor looked at all the frames and decided who's in and who's out. The editor had good taste and picked your take."

How did he know all this stuff?

"NYU film class, second semester." Mitch said as if reading my mind.

"Oh."

Mitch continued talking but I didn't understand half of his wordy explanation. "But when they tossed me, didn't they toss the reel too?" I asked.

"Rose, they never throw away any film before seeing everything they've shot. NYU editing 101."

"Wow."

"They might've replaced you, but your take was the one that got on the big screen. Trust me, Rose, I know your face." A half-hour later, we were still on the phone when Mitch said, "There's a 6:45 showing at the Lowes on Thirty-fourth Street. I'll meet you in front of the theater."

"I'm in the movies!" I told Pirate after we hung up.

"Meow," he yawned then stretched before curling into a ball ready for a catnap.

Not exactly the reaction I wanted, so I called Ce.

She picked up on the fourth ring. "Hello?"

"Ce, guess what?"

"Rose?" She sounded sleepy.

"I'm in that movie!"

Or stoned.

"Whaaat movie?"

"You know. The one where they replaced me?"

"Huh?"

Or both. How could she not remember? True, I'd never given her full disclosure about that day. Sure, I'd mentioned it, but I'd left out the important, painful details. Mitch was the one on the receiving end of all my devastation and angst from that film experience. Ce had just returned from Japan and her misery had taken precedence; commiserating wasn't an option.

"What movie?" Ce was alert and curious now.

"It's a surprise."

"Give me a hint."

"Ce, I'm in a hurry." I looked at my lucky watch and realized there wasn't time to play this game and so I cut to the chase. "Just meet me at the Lowes on Thirty-fourth Street. The movie starts in half an hour."

"But I just finished blow drying my hair."

"So?"

"It's raining out."

"Use an umbrella." I hung up the phone and put on my lucky jeans. Five minutes later I was racing up Second Avenue in the pouring rain. The strong wind stole my umbrella but I didn't care. I was in a movie! I smiled seeing Mitch standing in front of the box-office waving two tickets in the air.

"Are you ready for your 'close-up,' Miss Gardner?" He extended his arm.

"I am more than ready but we have to wait for Ce. She's on her way, too."

"OK." He looked at his watch. "It starts soon. I'll grab her a ticket."

Twenty minutes and forty-seven Ce-less cabs later, Mitch was antsy and so was I.

"Rose, the movie starts in five minutes. We should go in."

I stepped off of the curb and peered up and down Thirty-fourth Street. "One more minute."

"Are you sure she's coming?" Mitch looked at his watch again and shook his head.

"Yes, she's just on 'Ce time'."

Just then a large Checker Cab pulled up in front of the theater and Ce tumbled out. "I'm soooo excited. I loooove surprises. But what is it?"

"You'll see."

"Ready, girls?" Mitch slid his arm through mine, and for a moment

I was transported onto a red carpet, and being escorted into the Academy Awards.

I slid my other arm through Ce's. "So exciting!" She giggled.

"Here you go." Mitch placed the damp tickets in the usher's hand while we walked arm-in-arm through the lobby and into the theater. The movie started and forty-five minutes into the film, I saw my close-up and heard my line.

"Oh my God, Rose! That's you. Oh My God! There you are! There you are!" Ce bounced around in her seat and pointed at the screen.

All my feelings of rejection, failure and uncertainty vanished and for the first time since moving to Manhattan, I felt validated and like a real actress.

"That's Rose Gardner! That's my best friend!" Ce shouted to the theater rows in front of us.

A few people clapped while Mitch whistled and for a brief second I was a celebrity. But more important than the fleeting moment of fame, it was a sign. Not just an ordinary sign, it was *the* sign.

Chapter 33
Onward and upward

Two weeks after my screen debut, Ce left Walter and New York. "I got a gig as a magician's assistant!" She sounded euphoric on the phone.

"That's great. Where? What theater? "

"No, Rose, not here. On a cruise ship!"

I was silent as I realized that she'd be leaving me. Again.

Ce babbled on about her 'really sexy' stage outfits while I felt the familiar fear of abandonment creep into my bones. No. Not this time. I took a deep breath.

"Rose? Are you there?"

"Yeah. Wow! That's great, Ce. When do you ship off?"

"In two days. We're flying to Puerto Rico. That's where the port is."

I forced myself to be happy for her and made my voice cheerful. "Puerto Rico. I'll bet it's warm there. I'm jealous. But what about Walter?"

"What about him?" Ce laughed. "He's in L.A. for two months and besides the magician is *really hot*."

"Oh."

Ce continued talking and by the end of the conversation it was obvious she'd moved on from her marriage and that getting a divorce was now just a technicality.

"Gotta go, Rose. Love you."

"Love you, too." I hung up the phone and smiled. Once again Ce was gone, but this time I wasn't as frightened or sad. History would repeat itself and I knew she'd be back soon enough. Besides, I had my own magic acts to tend to.

I stared at her ring on my pinkie and traced the edges of the petals with my index finger. "It will bring you great luck," she'd said.

A moment later, I turned the gold band with the flower and tiny gemstone center 'round and 'round on my little finger and felt comforted. It wasn't long before the ring evolved into much more than just jewelry or another lucky charm. It became my totem and helped ground and connect me, not just to Ce but to myself and as important, to reality.

The Sunday phone call with my parents was in session and nearing the half hour mark. I kept my mouth shut about my new lucky charm. "It's a piece of garbage. I hope it doesn't turn your finger green," Mom would've said if I'd mentioned the ring. And Dad would've proclaimed that Ce was my lesbian lover. Instead, I closed my eyes and ignored the knot in my stomach, half-listening to Mom's litany of complaints.

"Your father's snoring keeps me up all night and I'm so tired all the time." She blabbed on while I waited to get a word in edgewise. All of a sudden, Mom stopped talking and I heard her take a long drag off her cigarette.

"Mom, I saw myself in that movie!"

"Wait. What are you talking about? What movie?"

"'A Whisper of Opportunity.'"

"What kind of opportunity?"

I took a deep breath, and felt frustrated and knew now I had to spell out my humiliation. "The movie where I was replaced. The one where I was a secretary and…"

"Oh yes, now I remember." She took another puff from her Pall Mall. "The purple jacket." A dramatic sigh followed. "Schmucks. If you were a lawyer you could sue the bastards!"

I ignored her and continued with my news. "Even though they replaced me, my scene still got in the film."

"Wait. You're in the movie?"

"Yes, Mom, they…"

"On the screen?"

"Yes. They used my edit. Not the other girl's."

"Edit, scmedit! What do I know from show business? Or films. Are you sure it's you, Rose?"

"Yes, Mom. Positive."

She took a long drag off her cigarette, and a moment later she sounded almost joyful. "Oh, Roseala, that's wonderful. My daughter is in a movie!"

"Thanks, Mom!"

"I am so proud of you," she continued.

Proud of me? Now *that* was a friggin miracle, and I smiled.

"Rose is in a movie!" I heard her announce to my dad and sister. Then, "I hope the camera didn't make you look too fat."

I turned Ce's ring around on my finger and cringed.

"It's about time," Dad chimed in.

"Is it a porn film?" Heather cackled in the background.

Five minutes later, I hung up the phone and felt depressed. It didn't matter what the news was, my family always put a negative spin on whatever I told them. "That's it! No more sharing." I turned Ce's ring around on my finger three times, and that confirmed my decision. No more sharing about anything. Ever!

"You're not five years old," Ce's voice played inside my head.

She was right. I wasn't a child anymore and didn't have to tell my mother a damn thing! Contrary to what I'd been taught, I didn't need Mom's approval, not for breathing or anything else. (Did I?)

Although this insight helped make the subsequent weekly calls more tolerable, they were still painful. "You're not wearing torn underwear, are you, Rose?" Mom asked. Then the next week she said, "Will you just think about law school?"

My face grew hot, and I wanted to lash out and tell her to back off. But instead of engaging in futile conversation, I'd turn Ce's ring around on my finger, take deep, cleansing breaths and maneuver around the minefields of her questions. "Yes," I'd say. I counted my words while telling her what I knew she wanted to hear. Although my new phone strategy felt dishonest, after a couple of months not sharing with my family soon became second nature. Why hadn't I thought of this sooner?

By the end of January, I resumed schlepping food at Mikos. It felt good to be out of hiatus and back in the struggling actress game. I was excited to be slinging hash and auditioning. My grim financial state left little room for thoughtless spending but I felt calmer and more hopeful. After my venture into the world of medicine, waiting tables at Mikos seemed normal. Yes, Mikos was a safe place to work, far away from that "regular job" where the FBI lurked around every corner and my boss dressed in drag.

When I returned to acting class on the first Tuesday in February, it felt like coming home. I smelled cigarette smoke as I opened the studio doors and walked over to the last row of seats. "Hi, Mitch."

"I saved your place," he teased and patted the chair beside him.

"Oh, Mitch, you're the best." I bent over and hugged him before sitting down. I didn't mind the uncomfortable hard wooden chair beneath my butt, or the stench of stale cigarettes. It was good to be back.

"Hello, Miss Gardner. We've missed you," Stephan said as he waltzed by. The familiarity of my acting guru's blue and white shirt was reassuring and even the arrogance and condescending lilt in his voice warmed my heart.

"Glad to be here," I said to Stephan's back. Yep, nothing had changed, and I took comfort in that. I looped Mitch's arm through mine and smiled. "Nothing's changed," I said and smiled at Mitch. Not a damn thing here was different, I thought. Except (perhaps) for me.

By the middle of the month, I'd gotten up the nerve to showcase a scene.

"Rose, I can't believe this is your first time up!" Mitch lit my cigarette as we took a break from our rehearsal. "Why'd you wait so long, girl?"

"Just nerves, I guess." I took a long drag off my Marlboro Light 100 and watched a stream of smoke billow out of my mouth. Just nerves? Yeah, right. I was terrified.

"Well, darling, there's nothing to worry about with *this*." He held up his copy of "It Had To Be You" and waved it in front of me. "You're so good. And so friggin funny; It takes every ounce of control to keep a straight face."

I was funny? "Really?" I got off the couch and walked into my kitchen. "Really?" I repeated and grabbed two diet sodas from the fridge.

"Oh my God! You were born to play Theda!"

I walked back into the living room and handed him a can. "Thanks, Mitch." I smoothed out the green sheet that covered the DNA couch, and then sat down beside him. Although the stains and cigarette burns were hidden, their memories would remain forever. "Mitch, don't lie to me. Tell me the truth, before Stephan does."

"I swear, Rose. You're hysterical." He took a swig of his soda, and then placed the can on the floor. "Why are you so nervous? It's not like you've never been in front of an audience before... jeeze Louise, you've been on off- Broadway."

"Off-*off* Broadway."

"OK, that still counts. This scene should be a cakewalk for you after 'Doom'."

We both laughed and even though Mitch hadn't witnessed my

forty-five-minute New York theatrical debut, he'd heard about it. Repeatedly.

"You're right, Mitch. Maybe I shouldn't be so nervous, but I am." Embarrassed, I averted my eyes from his.

"You're telling me that you're more nervous to do this scene in class than you were to act in that play?"

I nodded, took a sip from my soda and looked at him.

"That makes no sense, Rose." He shook his head, and then stared at me. "Why?"

"Stephan will be there," I said.

"Forget about Stephan!" Mitch was emphatic.

"He can be so mean, so critical. So…"

"Who cares? He may think he's a theater God, but he isn't." Mitch shook his head again. "Stephan needs to get over himself."

"Thanks, Mitch." Maybe Mitch was right, but I'd placed our acting teacher on such a high pedestal that I couldn't fathom him as a mere mortal. "Thanks," I repeated.

"For *what*, Rose? Telling you the truth?" He smiled, and the warmth from his grin reassured me.

I hugged him then leaned against the back of the couch, opened my script and was ready to resume our rehearsal.

"Don't worry, Rose. He's gonna love this scene." Mitch opened his script. "Love! It!" He repeated and winked.

Two weeks later, we showcased "It Had To Be You" in front of our packed class. Roaring laughter filled the room as we frolicked through our performance. Our scene ended to thunderous applause.

After the clapping stopped, God Stephan spoke a single word. "Brilliant."

Dumbfounded, I looked at Mitch and he mouthed, "I told you so," then wrapped his arm around my sweat-drenched blouse and guided us back to our seats.

After class, I raced home, and before I'd even shed my coat, picked up the phone to call Mom. Old habits were so damn hard to break, but how could she dampen my spirits about this? I dialed the familiar area code while the words 'Don't dial pain,' (a phrase I'd read in one of Walter's self-help books) raced through my mind. 'Don't dial pain' repeated over and over inside my mind until I stopped dialing and hung up the phone. 'Don't dial pain,' I thought and fought the intense urge of wanting to share my wonderful news.

"Anything you mention could be grist for her mill," I heard Ce's voice echo inside my head. "Anything." Her voice trailed off while I turned her ring around on my pinkie. Ce was right. Why risk listening to Mom, the judge and juror, when I felt so euphoric?

"I hope the camera didn't make you look too fat," she'd commented when I told her about the movie. The truth was that any bit of sharing was a terrible, idea. Although I knew that, I reached for the phone again anyway. Then a sudden, sharp, stabbing pain radiated from my elbow to my fingertips, physically forced me to stop dialing. I hung up, this time for good. I rubbed my forearm and walked into the bathroom for two aspirins. "Not setting myself up again." A moment later I was inside my small kitchen reaching for the one clean glass inside my cabinet. "Not this time." I watched the tap water pour out from the faucet with absolute resolve and realized the pain traveling down my arm had mysteriously vanished. "It's a sign!" I said out loud, an absolute sign from the universe! I patted myself on the back and smiled, I'd stuck to my guns and broken the cycle. (Momentarily.)

"I'm proud of you!" Ce's voice reminded me.

"Me too!" I deserved to bask in my joy for at least one night. Didn't I?

The unusual positive feelings lingered during the weeks that followed. It was a Wednesday afternoon in late March, (after a hectic lunch shift) when I sat on my apartment floor and perused the casting notices in *Backstage*. *"Wanted: Actors and actresses of all ages for Underdogs Inc. 'One Flew Over the Cuckoo's Nest.' Tri-state, nine-month tour starting on June 15. Auditions Monday April 1."* My heart raced. Had I missed the date? I ran into the kitchen where a calendar from Hunan Wok Chinese restaurant haphazardly hung off of the "Viva Las Vegas" refrigerator magnet. April 1 was the next day! I raced back to the couch and read the rest of the fine print underneath the notice: *"For further information and to schedule an audition time, contact the director: Osvaldo Oslo."*

Osvaldo? Could it be the same Osvaldo? How many directors could there be in New York City with that name?

Apparently two.

"I'm Osvaldo's cousin," he said with a substantial Spanish accent.

"Oh. I was in the play your cousin directed last year. At the Thirteenth Street Theater, 'Doom.'" The silence on the other end of the phone wasn't encouraging.

But a minute later he said, "Yes, I see that play, but I no understand it."

That made two of us. "It was pretty complex."

"What's you name honey… Which part jou play in Doom?"

His foreign accent combined with a poor phone connection made understanding Osvaldo de Cuckoo almost impossible.

"Rose Gardner. I was 'Doom Present'." My voice shook and I felt a thin layer of sweat form on my forehead.

"The China girl?"

"No. I was the girl with dark blond hair…" I wiped beads of sweat off of my forehead with the back of my hand.

"Oh jes, NOW I remember jou. I loved you in 'Doom!'

He did? "Thank you."

"That was some fire."

"Yes."

"I sprain my ankle jumping over the seats."

"Oh, I'm so sorry."

"Is no you fault honey." Another awkward silence followed, and I wondered whether Osvaldo was recapping my performance inside his head. Maybe he was changing his mind and no longer loved me. Sweat reappeared on my forehead as I closed my eyes and waited with dreaded anticipation for him to hang up the phone. But, instead of the sound of the dial tone in my ear, I heard Osvaldo's voice. "Can you come to the studio today and weeee talk?"

"Today?" I turned Ce's ring around on my finger, avoiding a full-blown panic attack. "Today? But, the auditions are tomorrow."

"Oh hoonee, you no need a audition. I see you in Doom, and you are wonderful actress."

I almost fainted.

Two hours and six cups of coffee later, I bolted off the subway car and raced up the dark stairwell inside the West Seventy-second street train station.

"The studio is on 81 Street," Osvaldo had said on the phone. "Next to Rico's Nail Salon."

I counted the blocks and found Rico's Nail Salon, then saw a storefront (without signage) next to it. Osvaldo hadn't mentioned the actual address. I looked at the dilapidated building and a wave of nausea washed over me as memories of Thirteenth Street Theater flashed through my mind. Just as I thought about bolting, the front door of the should've-been-condemned-years-ago building opened, and a girl dressed in black walked out.

"Is this… ummm? Is this…?"

"Studio 81?" The stranger in the mortician's get-up finished my question.

"Yes." I guess that was the name.

"Are you looking for 'Cuckoo's Nest?" She bent over and tied her left black high-top sneaker.

"Yes." Was she psychic?

"It's in there." She tilted her butt toward the door of the storefront.

"Thanks." The wave of nausea persisted but I powered though my gut feeling to flee.

The girl remained intent on tying her other shoe, never looking up. "It's confusing. There should be a sign."

Oh, there was a sign. More than just one. Not the usual unlucky numbers or dead animals, but the familiar panicked feelings, profuse sweating and the recurrence of the sharp elbow pain were all warning signs that danger was eminent. I took a deep breath and like a true trooper, I ignored them. "Onward and upward," I whispered, then walked up the two steps that led to the front door. I stuck my hand through the hole where the doorknob should've been and felt the unfinished wood scrape against my knuckles. "Fuck!" I yanked my hand out and cringed, seeing two large splinters embedded in my index finger. A second later, I jarred the door open with my other hand. While stepping inside the narrow, drafty hallway visions of "Doom" danced through my head. "Good job, Rose," I whispered to myself, and then heard a door creak at the end of the corridor.

"Rose? Come in." Osvaldo de Cuckoo peered out into the hallway, then ushered me inside an 11-by-15 dingy room and invited me to sit down. The resemblance was unnerving. He looked almost identical to his cousin. I wanted to run out the door and head home but sat frozen on the edge of a folding chair instead.

"So nice to meets you." He said and extended his hand.

"Uh, thank you for considering me."

"It's my pleasure." We exchanged a gentle handshake and even though I was still wary, I remained seated while Osvaldo de Cuckoo talked about the play. After fifteen minutes he was in wind-up mode.

"It very important we work together as a group. It's no one-people play. No one is a star. We are ensemble." He smiled at me and I relaxed a bit. Just because the two Osvaldos were cousins, didn't mean they were alike. Guilty by association wasn't a fair assumption. But deep inside I couldn't help worrying if I were headed for another 'bee' experience. Osvaldo de Cuckoo seemed different from his cousin, well maybe not that different, but at least he didn't wear a cape.

"Thank you again for coming in today," Osvaldo said, then handed me a copy of the play. "Here ju go, honey. Welcome to 'Crazy Town'."

Welcome? Hell, I'd lived there for years.

Our meeting was over. I left the tiny room feeling elated. Once outside "Studio 81," I breathed an enormous sigh of satisfaction and patted myself on the back. "Good job. Good job," I said to myself. "Great job!" I shouted at a passing cab then practically skipped all the way back to the subway station while the voices inside my head sang, "You got a part! You got a part! You're in a play! A real play!" I giggled and, from some of the glances I got from strangers on the street, I must have looked like I belonged in "Cuckoo's Nest."

"It's not Broadway but at least it's a play I've heard of." Even the voice of my mother, who always found fault with everything, sounded pleased.

Chapter 34
The Phoenix Rises

Rehearsals began a week later in a room diagonally across the hall from where I'd first met Osvaldo de Cuckoo. Although the space wasn't *as* tiny, with 23 of us gathered there, I felt like a sardine trapped inside a can. My claustrophobia kicked into high gear, so I sat cross-legged on the floor next to the door, just in case there was a fire or some other disaster and I needed to bolt. Feeling isolated, I watched my fellow cast-mates mill around the room. Some were laughing, several were smoking, and everyone was drinking coffee. Was I at rehearsal or waiting for an AA meeting to start?

"Rose?" A skinny kid clad in white stood in front of me.

"Yes?" I looked up while the stranger handed me a piece of paper. "What's this?" I asked.

"The production schedule," he answered.

"Oh, yeah, that's right." I'd almost forgotten that the play would be touring and in six weeks I'd need to pack a suitcase and take my act on the road. "Thanks." My stomach acid bubbled as I held the schedule in my sweaty hand and glanced at the list of unfamiliar cities. "Where's 'Intercourse'?"

"Somewhere in Pennsylvania," the boy answered with absolute certainty.

"Intercourse" was a *legit* city? For real? The area above my lips was moist and a droplet of sweat landed on my chin. What the hell had I had gotten into?

"So many actors in that crowded rehearsal space!" I heard my mother's voice loud and clear inside my head. "I hope you don't catch a disease." And then, "You're going on tour? Traveling by bus? You could get a brain aneurism from sitting so long. You could die, Rose. You could *die*." A moment later, her voice disappeared and I shook my head.

"Thanks." I wiped the sweat off my chin.

"You're welcome, Rose."

I looked up at the small oval face and got a feeling of déjà vu. Then I realized why. "Felix?" Although I wasn't completely sure it was he, I jumped to my feet and on a fleeting impulse hugged him anyway.

"How've ya been?" he asked, and then pulled away and stared at the ground. His meek demeanor confirmed his identity and I flashbacked to our days of "Doom."

"I've been great! I am so happy to see you." I was startled but seeing a familiar face was comforting, even if it were only Felix's. "What are you doing here?"

"I'm the stage manager." His lips pursed together and he sounded indignant.

Duh, of course he was.

"It's a sign!" I heard Ce's voice sail across the ocean. "It's a sign." The words rolled around inside my brain and landed on the back of my mind.

Although I still believed in omens and still wore my lucky watch, I didn't completely trust my life to signs anymore. Sometime after my screen debut, I realized that supernatural symbols didn't control my life. And finding a penny turned heads-up didn't always guarantee good luck, either. Sure, I'd gotten D's in science class but I didn't need to be Einstein to figure out that it was the choices I made that determined the quality of my life. I felt proud of my fresh insight but even with this newfound awareness, I couldn't help but wonder whether my reunion with Felix was a good omen or a bad one.

"Gotta get back to work," he said after a few minutes of polite chitchat. As I watched Felix walk away and circle around the small room interacting with the others, I thought that something about him seemed different. He pulled his shoulders back, held his head high, and he wasn't wearing that ridiculous beret. Thank God! Felix seemed less nervous, almost relaxed, compared to our days at the Thirteenth Street Theater. Had he experienced a Divine intervention? Or had life's hard knocks just made him a little more confident like someone else I knew?

After the first day of rehearsal, I was on cloud nine when I opened my apartment door and floated inside. Although my character, ("Katherine," a catatonic mental patient) had just one line, I was ecstatic and felt confident enough to call Mom. How could I not tell her about my triumphant return to showbiz! How the hell could I keep that a secret?

After five short rings I heard Heather's deadpan, joyless voice on the other end of the phone. "Hello?"

"Uh, wrong number." I hung up on my little sister. This time she wasn't going to rain on my parade. Telling Mom my news could wait. Forever. Perhaps.

The adrenalin rush that had sustained me through the day subsided and now I was crashing. Fast. Script in hand, I walked into the living room and plopped down on the couch. A minute later I stretched out and rested my copy of "Cuckoo's Nest" on my stomach. Thirty seconds later, my eyelids closed and within moments, I was sound asleep and lost in dreamland.

"No! I won't go see Rose in 'Peter Pan,' and you can't make me!" a 6-year-old Heather raged at our mom.

"Please, Heather, I'm pleading with you," Mom begged.

"No!" Her shrill voice vibrated against the walls as the house rattled. Next, a loud bang as Heather slammed her bedroom door in Mom's face.

"You're grounded! For a month." Shaking her head, Mom stood in front of Heather's closed bedroom door.

"Fine, I'd rather go nowhere for a year than be tortured by watching Rose make a fool of herself." Heather's words echoed while Mom put her head in her hands and wept.

The sound of my script hitting the hardwood floor woke me. I leaned over and retrieved it, clutching it for dear life as if it contained magical powers capable of warding off evil spirits and bad childhood memories.

I thought about calling Mom again but as the sudden pain shot down my arm from my elbow to my fingertips, I froze. "Don't dial pain!" I said, and the pain vanished. Although the play was wonderful news, I knew that sharing anything at all was too risky. There were explosives hidden within my family's kudos and it wasn't worth putting my joy in jeopardy. Not this time. They weren't a safe haven of unconditional support or joyfulness and although my old instincts told me to include them, my need for sanity said no. "Why couldn't they be more like The Waltons instead of The Addams Family?" I thought as I turned Ce's ring around on my pinkie.

Pirate jumped onto the couch then curled up into a tight ball on my lap.

"I'll tell them about the play. When it's over." I stroked Pirate's soft fur and my whole world brightened as if a giant spotlight had been turned on. Calmness and contentment washed over me. It wasn't Dr.

Berber's death that had been haunting me, it was my own life. Everyone was controlling it except for me and I'd had enough. A faint, unrecognizable voice spoke from deep within. It wasn't Mom's judgmental hocking or Dad's voice of gloom and doom. Or Heather's "You suck," either. It wasn't Ethan's, "I can't love you," or Ce's, "I told you so." As the voice grew louder, it became more and more familiar until I recognized it. It was my own. Finally, my own voice was strong, clear and unafraid while resonating from within and radiating from the tip of my head down to my toes, drowning out the others.

That moment of clarity became blurred as rehearsals continued for six more weeks. Do I really want to do this on a daily basis? Cramped inside the small rehearsal space that smelled like a locker room and felt like a sauna, I had serious doubts.

"I'm sorry the air conditioner no work," Osvaldo apologized.

Deja - fucking - Doom. Seated on the makeshift stage, I tried convincing myself that playing a catatonic mental patient didn't require much movement and kept my sweating down to a minimum. However, the other inmates were anxious to get out of this hotbox and onto a real stage.

I heard the actress playing Nurse Ratchet complain she couldn't take the heat anymore.

"Why is it so fucking hot in here?" the Jack Nicholson wannabe, cast as McMurphy, raged.

The tall guy who played the Indian chief remained silent, but I wondered whether a riot or breakout was eminent.

Osvaldo apologized all the time and I realized that guilt was not exclusive to Jews.

"Once we get to Pennsylvania we block ebryting on a nice big stage," Osvaldo reassured us. He smiled, and the warmth from his expression confirmed my initial gut feeling. Osvaldo de Cuckoo wasn't a bit like his cousin Osvaldo de Doom. Nothing. Nada. Zippo.

"No worry." He'd say with quiet understanding and a calming eloquence. "No worry," he'd repeat while he tried to keep order in the asylum.

Day after day, I heard Osvaldo's catchphrase and it wasn't long before I'd adopted it as my own and replaced my old mantra of "Ohm Ohm" with "No worry." The knot in my stomach remained but felt smaller and on most days it was easier to ignore. Before being cast, just the thought of traveling to unknown places was out of my comfort zone and the mere idea of a nine-month tour would've driven me into a real mental institution. But that fear dissipated, and I started looking forward to the road trip. And even though my weekly paycheck was modest, I felt content. "I am a working actress," I repeated and by some miracle, just like Osvaldo de Cuckoo, I "no worry." (Well, not as much.)

A few Sundays before the tour started, my family phone call was much more challenging than usual. Yes, I had perfected my phone technique and yes, my new mantra served me well, but nonetheless I was struggling.

"What's new, Rose? Have you met anyone? You've been so quiet lately. Are you feeling alright?" Mom fired off her questions in rapid succession.

I was tempted to spill the beans but held my tongue. "I'm fine. Not much is new," I answered and felt my voice quiver while I changed the subject. "How's Dad's snoring?" Then, "Have you finished redecorating the den yet?" In addition to not sharing, I'd implemented "re-direction" to my stress-management arsenal.

"How's your weight, Rose? I hope you're watching yourself," Mom asked a few moments later.

"How's the new leader at your Weight Watchers meeting?" I fired back. Answering a question with a question and refocusing the conversation onto Mom was a stroke of genius, and I patted myself on the back while her interrogation continued.

"How's the restaurant?" she asked. "Are you still working full time?" She'd caught me off-guard.

"Yes," I lied.

"Is she still schlepping food at that Greek joint?" I heard Dad bark in the background.

"Rose went to college to be a stupid waitress?" I heard Heather's condescending laugh and I almost lost it.

Oh, how I wanted to scream. *"I'm not a waitress anymore, ya little shit! I'm an actress, with a touring company!"* I wanted to put my spoiled, pain-in-the-ass sister in her place but I didn't. The price to pay for that justice was too high, so I breathed as deeply as my lungs allowed and ended the call three minutes later. "I escaped!" I shouted into thin air after I'd hung up the phone. "Hallelujah!" I sang out despite being drained and shaken after my Houdini act. "No worries," I whispered. I'd blocked Mom's magnetic pull. I ignored the bait she'd thrown out. I didn't allow her to drag me through hell. "No worry," I told Pirate. I felt relieved.

"Meow! Meow!" he cheered, trailing behind me into the kitchen.

Talking to Mom was exhausting, but I'd stuck to my plan and avoided being sucked into the abyss. "I'm a survivor!" I nodded my head, and grabbed a Tab off of the kitchen counter. "No worry!" I smiled, wiping off the top of the can with my shirtsleeve.

"Meow." Pirate stared at me and looked bemused.

"Oh meow, yourself," I giggled. My angst was negligible and I felt happy about being relatively unscathed from that family forum. But my anxieties were far from over. I looked at Pirate Kitty and realized I had a more urgent problem. "Who's gonna take care of you while I'm gone?"

Pirate Kitty blinked at me with what looked like a bored expression on his furry face, as if saying, "Duh."

I flipped open the can and sipped the warm soda as I stared back at him. He sat down without breaking his gaze. *What are you going to do?* he seemed to ask.

"Don't worry. I'll find someone perfect to take care of you and pay the rent. You'll see."

Pirate Kitty stood and left the room, tail twitching like a warning. "You'd better."

"Rose, I know you'll find someone for your apartment," Mitch assured me on the phone two weeks later. "There has to be someone out there who needs a place in Manhattan."

"Yeah? Well where the hell are they?" I snapped.

"Did you put up the fliers?" Mitch ignored the edginess in my voice.

"Yes," I said, and felt guilty about dumping my bad mood onto my understanding friend. Yep, I'd put up the friggin fliers all over the friggin city: "Must Love Cats," handwritten in giant black letters on neon-green paper.

"Where?" Mitch's tone was soft and compassionate.

"In D'agastino's, at bus stops, down in the subway stations, and inside coffee shops." The response from the flier was instantaneous, filling me with hope. But two weeks and 14 whack-a-doos later, my hope had faded, and I felt panicked.

"When?" Mitch prodded with an even voice filled with genuine concern.

"When?" What was this? Twenty questions?

"When did you put up the fliers?"

"A few weeks ago."

"So, any bites?" he persisted.

I recalled the last two applicants and felt nauseous. They were a guitar player from Boston who didn't have a steady gig and wanted to half me on the rent and a girl from Iowa who didn't like cats.

"She didn't like cats? Couldn't she read?" Mitch laughed. A moment later, his voice sounded serious. "Any others?"

"I interviewed twelve losers before those two." I could not hide my desperation.

"Well, I bet the fifteenth person will be the charm," Mitch encouraged.

"I feel like just giving up this apartment!" I blurted out. "It's like an albatross around my neck and I…"

"Oh no, Rose, you can't do that! You can't." Mitch's voice jumped two octaves, and he sounded alarmed.

"I'll deal with finding another apartment when I get back from the tour."

"No, Rose. No!" Mitch knew how difficult it was to find a decent living space in New York City and offered up some more advice. "Take it from a seasoned New Yorker. You don't want to give up your wonderful apartment. Listen, the worst-case scenario is you could cover the rent on your apartment, and I'll take care of Pirate."

"You mean, shell out money for my apartment while I'm on tour? Not even LIVING in NY?" Mitch's offer was sincere but unrealistic.

"I'll keep searching for a tenant for your place. I promise I'll have someone in there in no time." He reassured me.

"Thanks, Mitch." I was exhausted and had to go to bed. "I gotta get some sleep." My head was spinning, and I felt frustrated as I hung up the phone. Mitch had tried to be helpful during the 45-minute conversation, and I was grateful, but paying even one month's rent on an apartment I wouldn't be living in wasn't a financial possibility, and not an option.

"Meow." Pirate rubbed his back up against my bare legs. "Meow," he said a little louder and looked like he was aching to be held. I bent over and picked him up, then buried my head in his fur.

"No worry," I purred. "No worry," I told my feline companion. If only I could believe it.

Five days before we were ready to go on tour, Osvaldo made an announcement: "Keep your valuables at home. Specially jewelry."

"But... Why?" I'd asked him, panicked by the thought of removing my lucky totem.

"Mental patients no wear jewelry inside the asylum, honey."

He had a point.

I fixated on Ce's ring while riding the subway home after rehearsal. Once inside my apartment, I knew the ring had to be put away. I felt sick to my stomach. "Thank you," I whispered to the tiny flowered ring that had gotten me through the past months. I fought the urge to puke. A few moments later, I slid the tiny ring off my pinkie and placed it inside a small black velvet pouch. I stored the pouch inside my top dresser drawer under some old bras and prayed that I wouldn't need it.

The last few days of rehearsal zipped by, and when the eleventh hour arrived, I still didn't have anyone for my apartment. Thank God, Mitch agreed to stop by and feed Pirate and continue to interview potential tenants to sublet my place.

"I'll find someone for you, Rose," he'd promised. "Go on the tour, and relish being a working actress. Enjoy yourself and leave finding a renter to me." Mitch was on a mission (and also trying to get his real-estate license) and so I put my head in the sand and trusted him.

I sat on the couch and felt dazed while staring at my brown plastic suitcase. *What am I doing here?* I bit off all the nails on my left hand and felt my head pound. I was approaching melt down mode when the doorbell rang. Jumping up, I forced the panic attack away. Certain it was just another lost cause, I schlepped to the door. I finished biting the nail on my pinkie finger, then pulled my too-long bangs out of my eyes, and rested one eyeball on the tiny circle that contained the peephole.

"Ethan?" Oh my God. Was that him standing out in the hallway?

"Hey." His smile was distorted through the lens, but his tetracycline-stained teeth were as identifiable as hair plugs.

It felt surreal looking at Ethan waiting outside in the hallway. I unlocked the locks and opened my door. Ethan took two steps forward and hugged me.

The surreal feeling morphed into an out-of-body experience.

"I got thrown out. Again," he said trying to be casual as if it were yesterday, instead of well over a year (and not under the best circumstances) since we'd seen each other. "May I?" He dragged the familiar duffle bags through the door into the foyer. Ethan's voice sounded the same but he looked completely different. His thin beige T-shirt didn't conceal the ample belly that hung over green scrubs. And the dark circles under his puffy eyes were not attractive. The past year hadn't been kind to him. All the telltale signs of too much tequila indulgence were blaringly apparent. Yep, he'd lost his charismatic swagger and like men I'd met before, Ethan needed a bra. Karma.

We stared at each other for a long, immensely awkward moment.

"I'm ready." Ethan mumbled while he opened his arms wide, and half-expected me to run into them.

Ready? For what? Weight Watchers? A tummy tuck? AA? A Maidenform bra? "What?"

"I'm ready," he repeated, a little louder. He stared at the floor. "The truth is I've really missed Pirate." He laughed nervously. "And you." He looked up, and his eyes met mine. He pulled out the neon-green flier from inside the waistband of his scrubs. "You need a roommate? I'm in!"

"What do you mean, 'you're in?'"

"Completely and totally in. Relationship and all."

Was this a sick joke? "But, I'm out. It's a nine-month sublet." I pointed to the print at the top of the page. "See?"

Ethan looked down at the paper, and smirked. "You don't have to go."

"I've got a tour. I'm leaving for nine months. Did you not read the not-so-small print on the flier? "

"You don't really want to do that, do you, Rose?" He tossed the flyer into the air. "Not if we give us a try?" His dismissive tone infuriated me.

"Yes, I really have to. I want to do the tour!" Wait. What? Us? "Are you fucking kidding me?"

"It's always been you, Rose." He continued. "I was just too blind to see it." Ethan's words were so cornball, so cliché, but sounded astonishingly heartfelt.

I stared my former rejecter in the face and didn't flinch. If this had happened last year, I would've jumped at his offer. However, I'd changed and didn't need a life raft anymore. "No thanks."

"But, Rose, you can find another acting job right here. In New York. You don't wanna go on a silly tour and be alone. I'm here now, Rose." He puffed up like a peacock.

"And your point is?" The audacity and with that stomach to boot. "I won't be alone. I assure you."

"Rooose! I'm READY! For the 'R' word." Was Ethan begging? So many times while playing "Mystery Phone Caller," I'd imagined this moment, and now that it was here I didn't care. I looked at the New Ethan, the one in desperate need of a bath and a good support bra and felt nothing. Could looks and personal hygiene have made such a difference in the affairs of my heart? Was I that shallow? Yes, I guess I was.

"If you want to rent my apartment, fine," I told him, matter-of-factly. Hey, cash was cash, time was fleeting, and I had a bus to catch.

Ethan and I engaged in a staring match, after which he walked over to the couch, pulling his duffle bags behind him.

If that couch could talk! I thought as I watched him plop down on the orange sheet that covered it. Sure, the sheet hid all the couch's wear and tear but you only had to lift up the linen to see that it had been through the ringer. Like me, it had seen its share of burns and scars, but miraculously we were both still standing.

"Do you have a pen?" Ethan asked while scrounging through his bag.

"Sure." I walked inside the kitchen and grabbed a ballpoint from the coffee can. "Sure," I whispered, then walked back into the living room. "Here you go." I forced a smile and handed him the pen.

"Thanks, Rose." Ethan took the pen and smiled back. Our eyes locked in that veritable familiar way and for an instant I was frozen, back in time. Was I being sucked in again? Despite his new man boobs and disheveled appearance, I now felt a tiny spark and a flutter of a butterfly's wing. Feeling terrified, my heart began to race, and I fought an insane impulse to sit down beside him and explore where that might lead.

"You're asking for trouble, Rose!" Mom's voice screeched along with all the cast members inside my head. "Run, Rose. Run!"

Suddenly, those voices vanished, and I heard my *own* voice instead. "Haven't you learned anything, Rose? Haven't you had enough?"

"Enough!" it rapidly repeated. "E-frigging-nough." I listened to its urgent pleas with razor-sharp attention and I knew with certain clarity exactly what to do.

"Yes. I've had a lifetime of enough," I whispered.

"What?" Ethan looked up at me. "What did you say, Rose?"

"Nothing important," I lied, knowing it was time to be an actress instead of a doormat.

Ethan shrugged his shoulders and retrieved a checkbook from inside a zippered panel on the side of his duffle bag. I watched him from the corner of my eye while he tore out a check, and began writing. "That should cover it," he said a few moments after he'd scribbled an illegible signature at the bottom of a generic check. Ethan held the check out in midair and looked up at me. "Rose, I wish you'd stay."

"No can do." I took his check, and ignored that teeny tiny spark and I knew without almost any doubt that staying would be a terrible idea. (Wouldn't it?) "Thanks." I glanced at the check and noticed he'd covered the entire nine months' rent and then some. I dug into the left pocket of my jeans and felt for my house key. "Here you go." I handed over the key while Ethan grabbed on to my fingers.

I pulled my hand free from his grip, then bent down and picked up Pirate, who'd been hovering by my feet. "I'll be back soon." I nuzzled my cat in my arms.

"Meow." He leapt to the floor and retreated under the couch. I lifted my solitary suitcase off the living room floor, grabbed my purse off the dining room table and headed for the door.

Ethan leapt off the couch, raced across the living room, and blocked the doorway with his Buddha belly. He squinted his puffy eyes and looked at me in disbelief. "You're really going?"

"It's for the best." I parroted the words that Ethan had written on that note. The note I'd found with his apartment key propped on top of it. "It's for the best," I said again, remembering that ice-cold message he'd left for me a lifetime ago and I laughed out loud.

Ethan cocked his head and rolled his eyes. A few minutes later he mumbled "Good luck. I mean break a leg," then slowly opened the door.

I walked out into the hallway and over to the elevator bank and heard the sound of my apartment door close. A momentary sadness fell over me as Pirate's loud mewing filled the corridor. But as I pushed the elevator button, the sadness vanished and for the first time ever, I didn't care which elevator arrived.

Follow Rose Gardner as she continues standing up and speaking out on her Facebook page - The Society for Recovering Doormats. And on her blog site www.thesocietyforrecoveringdoormats.com

Praise for the Society for Recovering Doormats

"Congratulations for connecting with over 37,000 individuals. To be a Doormat would imply feeling inferior, not worthy, to be passive, never express yourself, and to be a victim. To be a Recovering Doormat would imply feeling a sense of personal worth, that you have rights, that your voice is meant to share your core values, and that you connect with others. In this case 37,000. And growing! Congratulations for being the conduit, the portal, and the vehicle that so many relate to and identify with. Keep making a difference."

—Dr. Harold Shinitzky, practicing psychologist and author of *Your Mind.*

* * * * *

"The Society for Recovering Doormats is a wonderful Facebook page serving the very useful purpose of helping people stand in their own power. A super page that lives up to its amazing name!"

—Graham Dietrich, author of *Shiny People*

CPSIA information can be obtained
at www.ICGtesting.com
Printed in the USA
BVOW08s0918060417

480386BV00001B/195/P